THE LAST POPE

THE LAST POPE

Luís Miguel Rocha

Translated by Dolores M. Koch

G. P. Putnam's Sons   *New York*

Roc

PUTNAM

G. P. PUTNAM'S SONS
Publishers Since 1838
Published by the Penguin Group
Penguin Group (USA) Inc., 375 Hudson Street, New York, New York 10014, USA · Penguin Group
(Canada), 90 Eglinton Avenue East, Suite 700, Toronto, Ontario M4P 2Y3, Canada (a division of
Pearson Canada Inc.) · Penguin Books Ltd, 80 Strand, London WC2R 0RL, England ·
Penguin Ireland, 25 St Stephen's Green, Dublin 2, Ireland (a division of Penguin Books Ltd) ·
Penguin Group (Australia), 250 Camberwell Road, Camberwell, Victoria 3124, Australia (a division
of Pearson Australia Group Pty Ltd) · Penguin Books India Pvt Ltd, 11 Community Centre,
Panchsheel Park, New Delhi–110 017, India · Penguin Group (NZ), 67 Apollo Drive,
Rosedale, North Shore 0632, New Zealand (a division of Pearson New Zealand Ltd) ·
Penguin Books (South Africa) (Pty) Ltd, 24 Sturdee Avenue, Rosebank,
Johannesburg 2196, South Africa

Penguin Books Ltd, Registered Offices: 80 Strand, London WC2R 0RL, England

Library of Congress Cataloging-in-Publication Data

Rocha, Luís Miguel, date.
[O último papa. English]
The last pope / Luís Miguel Rocha ; translated by Dolores M. Koch.
p.   cm.
Originally published in Portuguese. English version translated from the Spanish ed.:
El muerte del papa.
ISBN 978-0-399-15489-8
1. John Paul I, Pope, 1912–1978—Assassination—Fiction.   I. Koch, Dolores.   II. Title.
PQ9318.O34U5813   2008   2008016576
869.3'5—dc22

Printed in the United States of America
10   9   8   7   6   5   4   3   2   1

BOOK DESIGN BY MEIGHAN CAVANAUGH

This is a work of fiction. Names, characters, places, and incidents either are the product of the author's
imagination or are used fictitiously, and any resemblance to actual persons, living or dead, businesses,
companies, events, or locales is entirely coincidental.

This book is dedicated to John Paul I (Albino Luciani),
October 17, 1912–September 29, 1978.

And, as for you, my dear Patriarch,
Christ's crown and Christ's days.

—Sister Lucía to Albino Luciani,
    Coimbra, Portugal, July 11, 1977

May God forgive you
for what you have done to me.

—Albino Luciani to the cardinals who
    elected him pope on August 26, 1978

THE LAST POPE

1

_____

Why does a man run? What makes him run? He puts one leg in front of the other, the right foot follows the left. Some people seek glory. Others want to win a race or just lose a few pounds. But they always run for the same reason: they run for their lives.

Or at least that was what drove this man, his black cassock dissolving into the darkness of the place, running as fast as he could down the long interior staircase in the Secret Archives of the Vatican, a not-so-secret housing for supposedly secret documents. Those three imposing Vatican halls, and the buildings behind the Apostolic Palace, held documents of critical importance to the history of this small state and of the entire world. Only His Holiness, the pope, could examine them and decide who else could have access. The staff always said that any researcher could consult the Archives, but in Rome, and everywhere else on the planet, it was well known that not everybody was admitted, and those who were could not look at everything. There were many hidden niches in the Secret Archives' fifty-three miles of shelves.

The clergyman dashed through a secret passageway, holding some papers yellowed with age. A sudden noise, distinct from his own steps, alarmed him. Had it come from upstairs? Downstairs? He froze, perspiration streaming down his face, but all he could hear was the accelerated rhythm of his own breathing. He ran toward his quarters in Vatican City—or Vatican country, rather—because that was what it really was, with its own rules, laws, beliefs, and political system.

Under his weak desk lamp, he scribbled his name—Monsignor Firenzi—on a large envelope into which he thrust the papers, then sealed it. The name of the addressee was illegible in the dim light. His hands, slippery with sweat, struggled to hold on to the envelope. Perspiration clouded his eyes so that he couldn't make out even his own handwriting. Apparently finished, Monsignor left the room.

The bell at Saint Peter's Basilica tolled—it was one o'clock in the morning—and then silence reigned again over the dark night. It was cold, but in his haste this servant of God did not even notice. Soon he was out on the walkways that led to Saint Peter's Square, Bernini's marvelous ellipse, with its Christian and pagan symbols. Another sound caught Monsignor's ears. He stopped. Panting and in a cold sweat, he tried to catch his breath. It was surely the sound of steps. Maybe a Swiss Guard on nightly patrol. Monsignor Firenzi quickened his pace, still clutching the envelope. On any other night, he would have been in bed much earlier. As he reached the middle of the plaza, he glanced back and noticed a shadow in the background: not a Swiss Guard, or at least not dressed like one. The dark figure moved closer, but at the same steady pace. Now Monsignor Firenzi was running. He glanced back again, but at this time of night there was no one else but him and the briskly moving shadow.

HIS EXCELLENCY crossed the plaza and continued on Via della Conciliazione. Rome slept the sleep of the just, of the unjust, of the poor and the rich, of sinners and saints. Monsignor slowed down to a fast walk, and glanced behind him—the man was getting closer. Something glimmered in his hands. Firenzi saw it and started to run again, as fast as his aging joints would allow. There was a dull burst of sound and he had to grab, staggering, the first thing he saw. It was over so fast. The sound, and then nothing.

Still distant, the shadow got closer but the noise turned into a sharp pain darting through his ribs. Monsignor brought his hand to where it hurt, near his shoulder. He heard steps again; the shadow was approaching. His pain increased.

"*Monsignor Firenzi, per favore.*"

"*Che cosa desiderano da me?*"

"*Io voglio a te.*" The mysterious assailant took out a cell phone and spoke in a foreign tongue, perhaps from some eastern country. Monsignor Firenzi noticed the tattoo near his wrist: a serpent. Seconds later, a black car stopped beside the two men. The dark windows prevented anyone inside but the driver from being seen. Without violence or apparent effort, the man dragged the limp prelate into the car.

"*Non si preoccupi. Non state andando a morire.*"

Before climbing into the car, the man wiped the surface of the mailbox against which the prelate had fallen after being shot with such precision in the shoulder. Firenzi stared at him while pain racked his body. This is how it feels to be shot, he thought. The man was still wiping off any remaining clues from a few moments before. How ironic, to be wiping away the clues. How ironic. His whole body hurt. Then memories of his home came to him and he blurted out something in Portuguese.

"*Que Deus me perdoe.*"

The man got quickly into the car, which cruised slowly so as not to arouse suspicion. They were professionals, they knew what to do and how to do it. The street was quiet again, everything in order. The erasing of the clues was successful, leaving no trace of blood on the mailbox the prelate had leaned on, and where, almost miraculously and unnoticed by his pursuer, he had managed to insert the envelope he was clutching.

2

Don Albino
September 29, a.m., 1978

None of us lives to himself,
and none of us dies to himself.

—Romans 14:7

For some people, routine crushed and ruined life. They hated the events and actions that constantly repeated themselves for seconds, minutes, days, weeks, and despised the repetitive scenario where they would line up again, as if on an assembly line.

For others, submission to fixed laws was a necessity not to be altered by chance elements. What was unthinkable or new should never change the order of their existence.

Still, life for both was wretched.

Sister Vincenza never complained about the lack of variety in her life. For most of the last twenty years the venerable old lady had been at the service of Don Albino Luciani. That was the will of God, and who would dare question the ways of the Lord? Moreover, it was now God's will that after so many years Don Albino and Sister Vincenza would have a change of address. His Venetian home and his present one were 370 miles apart, but despite this severe disturbance in their lives, hardworking Sister Vincenza didn't complain.

The nun was up early that morning. The sun had not yet unveiled the grandeur of the immense plaza, still in semidarkness, weakly lit by yellowish bulbs. At exactly four twenty-five, Sister Vincenza humbly started her daily chores, part of a routine that she was quickly replicating in her new home.

She carried a pot of coffee with a cup and saucer on a silver tray, depositing it on a table by the door to Don Albino Luciani's sleeping quarters. The newly elected pope had undergone a surgical procedure for his sinusitis that left his mouth with a bitter, metallic taste, which he tried to mitigate with the coffee that Sister Vincenza brought him every morning.

Sister Vincenza had been here for over a month already, but she had not yet gotten used to the long, dark corridors. During the night hours only a wan illumination made objects scarcely visible appear threatening in the shadows. "It's very uncomfortable, Don Albino, being unable to see even what one is carrying," she had once told him.

The passing of centuries was reflected in every stone, every statue, and in the paintings and richly ornate tapestries hanging on the imposing walls. All this darkened splendor frightened Sister Vincenza. She almost screamed while passing by an unruly cherub she mistook for a child crouching down, ready for mischief. How silly of me! she told herself. No child had ever set foot in those corridors. The magnificence and lavishness of the Apostolic Palace were capable of disturbing the souls of the most sensitive people, and Sister Vincenza felt overwhelmed by such a spectacle of power and proximity to God. If it weren't for Don Albino, she thought. If it weren't for Don Albino, she would never have set foot in these galleries herself. Sister Vincenza tried to calm down. At such an early hour, these corridors were a source of fearful discomfort, but soon the new day would break and they would become thrilling again, vitally throbbing with the busy coming and going of secretaries, assistants, priests, and cardinals.

John Paul I had no shortage of advisers concerning protocol, politics, and even theology. Sister Vincenza, on the other hand, simply took care of Don Albino Luciani: of his food, his health, and the little inconveniences of daily life. Don Albino Luciani had only two people in whom to confide his concerns about the swelling of his feet or any other minor discomfort. Even though he had been told that in the Vatican there were specialized physicians that could take care of any complaint, Don Albino preferred to complain to Sister Vincenza, and to his favorite doctor, Giuseppe de Rós. Don

Giuseppe came to Rome every two weeks, traveling almost four hundred miles to see his patient. "I don't know how you do it, Don Albino," the doctor said. "Are you sure you still have birthdays? Every year I find you healthier and hardier."

"I'm beginning to doubt you, Don Giuseppe. You're the only one who doesn't notice my ailments."

Vincenza carried out all her duties with humble pleasure. To her, Albino Luciani was a good man who treated her with gentleness and affection, more like a friend than a mere assistant. For that reason he had brought her with him upon moving into his new residence, considerably larger than the preceding one and much more sumptuous, of course. That magnificence and ostentation irritated Don Albino. He wasn't a man who appreciated a profusion of useless objects. He was interested in spiritual issues. However, like everyone else, he sometimes had to deal with practical matters, if only to make life more livable for those around him. Albino knew that in time he would have to organize his home either to his taste or to that of others.

A heart attack less than a year ago had left Vincenza lying in a hospital bed. She didn't heed her doctor's advice not to go back to work, but just to supervise the work of others, and preferably sitting down. Instead, she continued to personally take care of Don Albino.

In spite of her kind disposition, Sister Vincenza frowned at the suggestion that she abandon the common chores she enjoyed doing, like bringing him that tray of coffee through the half-lit galleries so early in the morning. Of course, in order to keep doing them and to be near Don Albino, Sister Vincenza had to join the congregation of Maria Bambina, in charge of the pope's residence. Elena, the mother superior, along with Sisters Margherita, Assunta Gabriella, and Clorinda, all had been very kind to her, but none of them wanted to be in charge of anything having to do with Don Albino's daily matters. Only Sister Vincenza, with her skilled hands and delicate touch, was willing to take care of him. Usually when the nun reached the door of Don Albino's private quarters, she set the tray on a small table placed there especially for this purpose, and gently knocked twice.

"Good morning, Don Albino," she almost whispered. And she waited. A similar greeting would come from the other side of the door; Don Albino usually woke up in a good mood. Sometimes he stuck his head out to Sister Vincenza for his first smile of the day. Other times, when important Vatican business dampened his spirits, Don Albino mumbled his "good morning" and, to avoid complaining about the treasurers' or politicians' lack of diplomacy, lamented the swelling of his ankles.

But that morning, that morning, Don Albino kept silent. With Sister Vincenza's fastidious penchant for precision, any departure from the daily routine annoyed her. She leaned her head on the door, straining to hear something on the other side. But she heard nothing. She considered knocking again, but finally decided against it. This is the first time Don Albino slept late, she thought as she was leaving. After all, it wouldn't be such a tragedy if he slept a few more minutes.

Sister Vincenza silently walked back to her room to say her morning prayers.

It was already four-thirty in the morning.

MUTTERING THAT he couldn't sleep, the man was tossing and turning in bed. This was so unusual. He had always been able to fall asleep anytime, anywhere, whatever the circumstances. Sergeant Hans Roggan was methodical, steady, reserved. His mother had come to Rome that day to visit him. He took her to dinner and it was probably the coffee he had with dessert, he thought, that was keeping him awake. At least that's what Sergeant Hans wanted to believe, but in fact it had been a tumultuous day, the afternoon in particular, with many prelates coming and going in and out of the private quarters of His Holiness.

He finally decided to get up. If sleep won't come, what can I do? I'm not going to lie here forever, waiting for it, he told himself. He opened his closet and put on his uniform, which had been designed in 1914 by Commandant Jules Repond. If Commander Repond had known then that decades later people would attribute his design to Michelangelo, who knows whether he would have enjoyed the honor or felt bitter about being ignored. On this cool night when Sergeant Hans Roggan couldn't sleep, he was the one in charge of the Swiss Guard.

The vivid colors of his uniform, based on those in Michelangelo's frescoes, contrasted with his mood on this day. He felt deeply uneasy, an inexplicable anxiety like a premonition. Such a concern, for the moment at least, seemed totally baseless.

Hans Roggan had his dream job, the one he had yearned for since his earliest years: to be serving the pope as part of the Swiss Guard. He had had to pass many tests and lead a very disciplined life, in strict adherence to the Lord's teachings. Most important, though, he was graced with the basic requirements: being Swiss, unmarried, having the appropriate moral and ethical values, measuring more than five feet, nine inches tall, and above all, being Catholic.

Hans would never dishonor the image of the valiant soldiers of Pope Julius II. If need be, he was willing to die protecting his pope, as did the 689 Helvetian founders of the Swiss Guard, who, on the sixth of May 1527, protected Clement VII against a thousand Spanish and German soldiers during the sack of Rome. Only forty-two of them survived, but under Commandant Göldi, they had led the pope to safety in Castel Sant'Angelo. They took him through a secret passageway, the *passetto*, that linked the Vatican with the fort. The others perished heroically, but not before claiming the lives of almost eight hundred enemy invaders. That was the heritage Hans carried on his shoulders every time he wore his uniform, a pride that filled his soul every day. But today, for no apparent reason, he felt disturbed.

He was responsible for the security of Vatican City. The protection system of the city consisted of only a few inner patrols and a few guards at the most relevant, emblematic posts. Pope John XXIII had abolished the practice of posting two soldiers nightly by the door to his private quarters. The closest guard now was at the top of the stairs of the *terza loggia*. This was just a symbolic post, since the third floor was little used even during the day. Anyone could see that someone with bad intentions could easily enter Vatican City, and he would be right.

Hans went into his office and sat at his desk. He opened a dossier and leafed through it. It was just a list of bills that he had to pass on to his superior in the morning. He closed it after a few seconds. It was useless. He couldn't concentrate.

"What the hell!" he grumbled, "I need to get some fresh air."

He left his office not bothering to close the door and walked out of the Swiss Guard building, wandering through the inner gardens and then to the plaza. He passed two soldiers sitting on the steps. Both had dozed off.

I seem to be the only one who can't sleep, he thought as he woke them with a tap on the shoulder. The startled guards jumped up.

"Sir, pardon me, sir, excuse us," they both said.

"Don't let it happen again," Hans warned. He knew his men had just been through a very intense period of work. A little more than a month earlier, on the sixth of August 1978, Giovanni Battista Montini, better known as Pope Paul VI, had died in Castel Gandolfo, the papal summer residence. The funeral rites of a pontiff lasted several days, and the Swiss Guard did not leave the body of the deceased pope unattended for an instant. Four men stood in stationary guard, one on each corner of the catafalque. Numerous world leaders and heads of state paraded by, paying their last respects to His Holiness.

Once the funeral ended, preparations began behind closed doors for the conclave. Days off were canceled and the amount of work doubled. The last conclave was held on August 25, exactly twenty days after the pope's death, close to the allowed limit of twenty-one days. Despite the brevity of the conclave, lasting only one day, the habitual frenzy around the new pope had begun. Only a few days before had things returned to normal.

Taking leave of the two sleepy guards, Hans continued his walk.

He couldn't avoid a feeling of ownership about everything around him. At a distance he saw Caligula's obelisk, in the middle of Saint Peter's Square. How ironic: a tribute to a psychopath right in the center of the most sacred place in Catholicism. He continued slowly, feeling the soft morning breeze on his face. Suddenly, something attracted his attention. To his left rose the Apostolic Palace, and on the third floor the lights in the pope's bedroom were on. He looked at his watch: 4:40 A.M.

"This pope wakes up early." When Hans was coming back with his mother after dinner, at about eleven, the lights were on then as well. Vigilant, like any proud Swiss Guard, he decided to go back to the soldiers he had caught dozing off. Now they were talking to each other. The sergeant had cured them of their sleepiness.

"Sir," they greeted him in unison.

"Tell me something, did His Holiness ever turn off his lights during the night?"

While one of them hesitated, the other answered with assurance.

"The lights have been on since I started my patrol."

Despite having caught them dozing, Hans knew they must have been inattentive for only a few minutes.

"How odd," he mumbled.

"His Holiness usually turns his lights on at about this time. But last night he didn't turn them off at all," the guard added. "He must have been working on those changes people are talking about."

"That's no concern of ours," Hans answered, and changed the subject. "Is everything in order?"

"Everything's in order, sir."

"Very well. I'll see you later. Keep your eyes peeled."

As he went back to the Swiss Guard building, he felt his eyelids finally getting heavy. He could still sleep for a couple of hours. He glanced again at the still-lighted pope's quarters. No doubt things are going to change around here, he thought, with a half grin. Now he could sleep in peace.

IT HAD BEEN fifteen minutes since Sister Vincenza had placed the silver tray on the small table by the door to Don Albino Luciani's private quarters. It was time to go back and make Don Albino get up and take his medication.

Again a chill went down her spine as she crossed the somber corridor. She would face Don Albino and stand respectfully but firmly until he had taken his blood pressure medication. It was too low, according to Don Giuseppe. The medication consisted of a few white, tasteless pills that the pontiff always took with a gesture of mock surprise. This was one of Vincenza's responsibilities, as was giving him an injection to stimulate his adrenal glands before he went to bed. Sometimes she also had to make sure he had taken his vitamins after meals.

Don Albino used to joke with Sister Vincenza and gently reproach her for being so punctual, coming "religiously" between four thirty and four forty-five every morning to administer the medication that kept his blood pressure at the appropriate level.

Then Don Albino took his bath. Between five and five thirty he tried to improve his English with a taped correspondence course, a routine he resisted changing. After that, the pontiff prayed in his private chapel until seven. That simple routine was a remnant of life in his former residence, and afforded him some relief from the enormous burden the cardinals had placed on him.

As the nun reached Don Albino's quarters, she couldn't help but show her distress. That morning the whole routine, maintained for years, was crumbling. The silver tray with the pot of coffee and cup and saucer was still in the same place she had left it a few minutes earlier. She lifted the lid of the coffeepot to see if it was still full. It was. In almost twenty years nothing like this had happened, and Don Albino Luciani had never failed to respond to her greeting with a kind "Good morning, Vincenza."

Actually, that wasn't exactly right; some of the details had been altered. Before moving here, Sister Vincenza used to knock at the door and come in with the coffee tray, personally handing it to Don Albino. This routine was vehemently rejected when the new papal assistants found out. According to them, this was in flagrant violation of protocol. So, to please everybody, they reached a compromise. The nun was to continue to bring the coffee every morning but would leave the tray by the door to Don Albino's private quarters.

Leaning her head against the door again, Sister Vincenza held her breath, trying to listen for any sound coming from inside the room. She didn't hear anything or sense any movement. *I don't know whether I should knock again,* she thought, and finally knocked timidly on the wooden door.

"Good morning, Don Albino," she whispered.

She stood back from the door and examined it, wondering what else to do. "In Venice I just walked right in without a fuss," she muttered.

From the bottom of the door, a fine line of light escaped. "Well, this means that Don Albino must be up already." She knocked decisively at the door.

"Don Albino?"

No response. She knocked again softly, but silence was the only answer. She had no alternative but to enter the room, despite the dictates of protocol. She placed her hand on the golden doorknob and turned it.

"If I were to please all those secretaries, I would never find out whether Don Albino is up or still sleeping."

She tiptoed in. The pope was still sitting in bed, propped up with pillows, his glasses on, some papers in his hand, his head turned a bit to the right. The happy expression and kind smile that used to charm everyone around him had turned to a grimace of agony. Vincenza quickly went to him with a tremulous heart. She paid no attention to her own weak condition. With red, teary eyes she held Don Albino's hand to take his pulse. One, two, three, four, five seconds—

Sister Vincenza closed her eyes, tears streaming down her face.

"Oh, my God!"

She violently yanked at the cord next to Don Albino's bed, and the sound of the bell ringing was heard through the nearby halls and rooms.

I have to call the sisters, she thought, trembling nervously. No, first I must call Father Magee. No, he's too far away. Better call Father Lorenzi.

The bell stopped ringing, but nobody answered Sister Vincenza's call. She rushed out to the corridor and, without thinking, overlooking all the rules imposed by the rigid defenders of protocol, opened the door to Father Lorenzi's room. He always slept near Don Albino's quarters. The secretary, Father John Magee, was staying in a room on another floor until the remodeling of his own room was finished.

"Father Lorenzi! Father Lorenzi, for God's sake!" Sister Vincenza screamed.

He woke up stunned, sleepy, and taken aback by such an unexpected visit.

"What's the matter, Sister Vincenza? What's happening?"

He could scarcely understand what was going on. The nun went up to him, pulling at his pajamas and crying profusely.

"What's wrong, Sister Vincenza? What's going on?"

"Father Lorenzi—Don Albino! It's Don Albino, Father Lorenzi! Don Albino is dead! The pope is dead!"

The stars in the sky never failed in their routine, and on that day, September 29, 1978, the sun kept its daily appointment, spilling its golden beams on Saint Peter's Square in Rome. It was a gorgeous day.

3

There was constant turmoil in the house on Via Veneto: on the stairs, the landings, in the entryway. An endless stream of relatives, friends, occupants, employees, and messengers were going up and down, again and again, in the busy daily routine. On the third floor, however, there was deathly silence. Three men had broken in at dawn. Two of them stayed about ten minutes. Nobody saw them come in or leave. Nothing at all was known about the third individual. He seemed to be the ideal silent guest. No one heard his steps, or the sound of turning on a faucet, or closing a drawer, or a cabinet. Perhaps he was drunk, his friends brought him in, and he was still nursing a hangover. Or maybe he worked nights and slept by day. There were many possibilities but only one certainty: no one had heard him, though for sure he was still inside.

An elderly gentleman was climbing the stairs with a lot of effort, leaning on a cane, accompanied by a man wearing his usual Armani suit. When they got to the closed door of the third floor, so silent one could hear a pin drop, the assistant put a key in the lock.

"Wait," the old man said, gasping. "Let me catch my breath."

The assistant waited. It took some time for the old man to recover. Once he did, he stood up straight, his cane becoming an accessory, not a support. He motioned for the assistant to open the door, which he did, turning the key twice. With a little push, the vestibule to the private rooms was revealed. They entered quietly, the old man leading the way and the assistant closing the door behind them without a sound.

"Where is he?" the old man demanded.

"In the room. They left him there."

The two went in and found a man tied to the bed. The sheet was stained with blood. He was covered in sweat and wearing only his drawers and a short-sleeved undershirt. He raised his head to take a look at the newcomers, but despite his humiliating position, he showed no sign of submissiveness. It was Monsignor Valdemar Firenzi.

"Monsignor," the old man greeted him, smiling cynically.

"You?" Firenzi stammered, flabbergasted.

"Yes," and going around the bed, he sat on a chair facing the monsignor. "Did you think you could possibly escape?"

"Escape from what?" the cardinal asked, still in shock.

"Don't play dumb, my dear friend. You have something that does not belong to you, but to me. And I am here to get it back."

Firenzi glanced at the assistant, who was hanging his coat on the back of a chair.

"I have no idea what you're talking about."

A heavy blow was the reaction, with blood trickling from Firenzi's split lip. As he tried to regain his composure, the assistant towered menacingly above him. The expression on the cardinal's face hardened.

"My dear monsignor, I would prefer not to have to resort to unpleasant methods to recover what is mine. But you have disappointed me so much that I don't know if I'll be able to refrain. After all, you have stolen something that belongs to me," the Master said, leaning over Firenzi. "I am sure you must understand the gravity of this. You have committed a felony. If I cannot trust a man of the cloth, then whom can I trust?" The old man stood up and started to pace the room, thinking. "Do you understand the dilemma you put me in? I cannot even trust the Church, my friend. The Lord sent his Son to redeem us from evil. So I ask you, my dear monsignor, now what?" And, looking intently into his eyes, he added, "Now, what are we going to do?"

"You know very well what you have done," Firenzi remarked.

"What have I done? What? Action is what moves the world. People must act. We all must take some action."

"You are the one who's playing dumb," Firenzi interrupted, and he got smacked again to make sure he understood clearly that he couldn't address the old man that way.

"I can't wait all day. I want those papers. Now. Tell me where they are."

The prelate was pummeled again for no apparent reason, since he hadn't said another word. His face was swelling, and the trickle of blood from his mouth was staining his undershirt.

"Sometimes the Lord gives us heavy burdens to carry, but He also grants us the strength to bear them," Monsignor said.

"Sure, and we'll soon find out how much strength the Lord has granted you," the old man said, motioning to his assistant.

The insistent ringing of a cell phone interrupted the questioning, which, despite its violence, had so far produced very little: a man's name and the address of a parish in Buenos Aires. The assistant took his time fishing the ringing phone out of his coat pocket.

While he took the call, the old man moved in closer to Valdemar Firenzi, who looked tired and too old for all this turmoil.

"Come on, Monsignor, tell me where those papers are and we'll get this over with right now, I guarantee it. You won't need to suffer anymore."

The prelate looked at his torturer, seeming to draw strength directly from his own faith. Blood was now streaming from his mouth down his chin, onto his chest. His voice sounded amazingly strong, though he couldn't mask his pain. "Jesus Christ forgave. As He forgave, so will I."

It took the old man with the cane a few moments to fully grasp the tortured man's comment. Then, with a resigned, hateful sigh, he admitted that he could get nothing more out of Firenzi.

"As you wish."

The assistant ended his phone call and then whispered a few words into his boss's ear. "They found an address in his room at the Vatican."

"Which address?"

"Of a Portuguese journalist, a woman who lives in London."

"Strange."

"She's been traced. Daughter of an old member of the organization."

The old man thought for a few moments.

"Call our man. Have him pay a visit to the parish priest in Buenos Aires. Maybe he can find something out. Then he's to wait in Gdansk for further instructions. Later you'll go to Argentina yourself."

"Very well, sir," the assistant said obsequiously. "And what about Monsignor?"

"Give him the last rites," the old man shot back in a sarcastic tone. "I'll wait for you in the car."

The old man gave his assistant a friendly pat on the shoulder and left without a word of farewell to Monsignor Firenzi, without even a last look. Nor did he hear the shot that ended the prelate's suffering. With the cell phone pressed to his ear, he went down the stairs, leaning on his cane. He no longer needed to preserve his command stance. The image of a decrepit old man was good enough for him now, and closer to the truth. Someone answered the number he had dialed.

"Geoffrey Barnes? Listen, we have a problem."

4

There was no city like London, thought Sarah Monteiro. She was on her flight back from Lisbon to her home on Belgrave Road. Her plane had been circling the airport for about half an hour, waiting for a runway. This was all part of her pleasurable anticipation after a monotonous two weeks' vacation at her parents' home—her father a retired captain in the Portuguese army; her mother an English professor (hence the addition of the *h* to her name, as well as her love for everything British). It wasn't that she didn't like Portugal. On the contrary, she thought her birth country was beautiful, but despite its long history, there had been too many revolutions and too few reforms. But Portugal was Sarah's usual destination two or three times a year. She loved to spend Christmas on a farm near Beja in Alentejo, where her parents had retired a few years ago. Its fresh country air, so different from that of the British capital, had become essential to her.

The plane seemed to land normally, just the usual rattles and jolts. In about twenty minutes they would be deplaning, but the passengers were already jostling to collect their belongings first and get out.

"We have just landed at Heathrow. The temperature in London is twenty degrees centigrade. Please remain seated with your seat belts fastened until the plane has come to a complete stop, and . . . we wish to thank you for choosing to travel with us," the flight attendant trailed off mechanically. No more than two or three people were listening, certainly not Sarah, so used to flying, not only on her trips to Portugal but also to other destinations, in her job as a London correspondent for one of the largest international news agencies. It was a convenient and interesting career for foreigners, getting paid for simply bringing news from their hometowns. She still had two days of vacation left before having to get back to the newsroom, to the daily flow of news and the never-ending search for sensational events.

The plane finally stopped, and as the passengers hurried to leave, she got her carry-on and handbag. Going down the aisle, she called her parents to let them know she'd arrived safely, and that she would call them later. She trekked through the long carpeted halls, decorated in green and black, and stood in line for customs. Citizens of the European Community, Switzerland, and the United States on one side, other nationalities on the other, all ready with their passports or equivalent documents. Sarah was waiting dutifully behind the yellow line so as not to disturb the spectacled man ahead of her, nor pressure the customs officer at the booth.

"Next, please." He didn't sound friendly at all. She could have chosen another window. The female officer in the next booth looked much nicer. Too late now.

Sarah held out her passport with her best smile, and he looked at it.

"It's nice to be back. How's the weather been?" she asked, hoping to smooth out the situation.

"You can't see the weather from in here," the officer grunted, sounding even surlier. He had probably gotten up on the wrong side of the bed, or maybe had had an argument with his wife, if he had one. "There seems to be something wrong with your passport."

"Something wrong? I can show you my ID, if you wish. I've never had a problem with my passport."

"Could be a system error."

The ill-tempered officer's name was Horatio, according to the tag on his uniform. The phone on the counter rang. "Yes, but there is something wrong with the passport." He listened for a few moments more and then hung up.

"Everything seems to be in order now. You can go."

"Thank you very much."

The unpleasant attitude of the man had put Sarah's nerves on edge. Now all she needed was to find a taxi driver just like him to top off her less than smooth arrival. But first she had to claim her baggage, so all in all it would be about an hour before she got home, assuming her luggage wasn't lost.

IN A SECURITY OFFICE elsewhere in the airport, while Sarah dealt with the customs officer, an alarm had flickered on a computer. A young officer in his twenties responded to the routine alarm. The stripes on the shoulders of his white uniform shirt indicated his rank as a security officer. He was trying to determine the source of the flickering red alarm. Probably it was a false or expired passport, or maybe just one in bad condition. He carefully observed the image on the security camera: a beautiful woman, thirtyish, facing window 11, the one manned by Horatio—a very meticulous, dull widower for whom everything had to be in perfect order. Still, he had to notify his superior.

"Sir."

A fiftyish man, graying at the temples, came in and leaned over the computer screen.

"Let me see." He glanced at the information, typed something in, and new details appeared. The name Sarah Monteiro and other data scrolled by very fast. "Don't worry, John. I'll take care of this." Picking up the phone, he called Horatio. "It's Steve. Let her go. Yes, don't worry, let her go. Everything is in order." Still holding the handset, he called another number. "She just came in."

WELL, THINGS WERE NOT going too badly, after all. In barely half an hour she was already in a taxi, leaving Terminal 2, on her way home.

"Belgrave Road, please," she told the driver. In another half hour, maybe forty-five minutes, depending on traffic, she would be soaking in a very welcome bubble bath, almost overflowing her tub. She was thinking of a soothing combination of strawberry and vanilla, an effervescent mix that would relax her muscles and bring peace to her spirit.

The taxi went around Victoria Station, overcrowded as usual, and continued on Belgrave. The street, lined with cheap hotels and busy sidewalks, was very London. A porch supported by two columns, some plain and others a Corinthian imitation, depending on the taste of the architect, or owner, fronted most of the houses. With exposed red bricks or a new coat of paint, these Victorian houses were at least a hundred years old but very well kept.

The taxi was approaching her home at the corner of her block when it had to brake suddenly. Sarah almost bumped her head against the glass separating driver from passengers. A black car with tinted windows had passed them, then abruptly cut in and stopped. The taxi driver honked hard, in a rage.

"Get the fuck out of the way!" he shouted. The driver in the car ahead of them lowered his window, stuck his head out, and hollered, "Sorry, mate," and sped away. Seconds later the taxi stopped in front of Sarah's house, and the driver graciously took care of her luggage. Inside she found a mountain of mail strewn on the floor. Postcards from colleagues, the inevitable bills to pay, junk mail of all kinds and sizes, and some mail she didn't feel like opening then. She took her suitcase to her bedroom on the second floor, went into the bathroom to fill her tub, and changed into something more comfortable. She was finally home. In two minutes she was enjoying her honey-scented bubble bath; she was out of vanilla, but the result was equally soothing—relaxing. She had already forgotten the surly customs officer at the airport, and the disturbing incident in the taxi. Downstairs by the entryway, in the midst of the scattered correspondence, was an envelope clearly displaying the sender's name: Valdemar Firenzi.

5

A lot could be said about the painting this man was contemplating. Infanta Margarita, a very young Spanish princess, was in the center, flanked in the right foreground by Isabel Velasco and Agustina Sarmiento, the two dwarfs, and María Bárbola and Nicolás Pertusato, with his foot on a dozing mastiff. In the dark background, Doña Marcela de Ulloa was with an unidentified man—something unusual, because the artists of that period didn't usually include anonymous faces in their canvases. Everything had its meaning, and since he wasn't a known figure, the artist, who had included his own self-portrait on the left, must have wanted it that way. This artist had held his post for life, painting the illustrious figures of Don Felipe IV and Doña Mariana, who were reflected in the mirror at the back. Only because of that mirror could one see the whole scene in the painting, since his canvas faced away from the viewer. The queen's chamberlain, Don José Nieto Velázquez, was standing by the back door. It was a magnificent painting, no doubt, but the man of advanced age looking at it was of greater interest at the moment. Though it was almost closing time at the Prado in Madrid, the man in gallery three seemed unaware of this and kept looking, almost without blinking, at one of the museum's jewels, *Las Meninas,* the famous masterpiece by Diego Velázquez.

"Sir, the museum is closing. Please walk toward the exit," a young guard advised. He was meticulous and needed to make sure that his polite suggestion was being followed. He had seen that man almost every day in the museum, in this same gallery, and always looking at the same painting, hour after hour, while tourists kept strolling by. It was almost like one picture looking into another.

"Have you ever looked carefully at this painting?" the man asked.

The guard glanced around and, seeing no one, said, "Are you talking to me?"

The man kept gazing intently at the painting. "Have you ever looked carefully at this painting?" he repeated.

"Of course. This painting is to this museum like the *Mona Lisa* is to the Louvre."

"Nonsense. Tell me what you see."

The guard felt intimidated. He had gone past this painting every day, aware of its importance but never knowing why. He was so used to it, like his own street, that he had taken it for granted and not really looked at it. Anyway, it was time to close the museum, and what counted now was getting this man out of there and making his last round so that he could go home. And after that he still had at least half an hour of travel.

"Sir, you cannot stay any longer, the museum is now closed," he said more firmly, but still politely. The man seemed hypnotized by the Velázquez painting, which was pretty enough, the guard thought, though he could add little to that. He studied the elderly man more intently, and noticed his left hand was trembling. A tear was running down the right side of his face. It might be best not to antagonize him and instead say something innocuous.

"It is a beautiful painting, *Las Meninas.*"

"Do you know who the *meninas* were?"

"Those girls in the painting."

"The *meninas* are the two women on either side of the Infanta Margarita.

Meninas is the Portuguese word the royal family used for the princess's nannies."

"Well, there is always something to be learned."

"The artist on the left is the same painter who did this—he expected the nannies to convince the child princess to pose for him. As you can see in the image in the mirror, King Don Felipe and Queen Doña Mariana had already done their part. They brought the dwarfs and the dog to try to convince the infanta, but the princess didn't feel like it, and the painting as planned was never done."

"Excuse me, sir, but it was. It's there in front of us."

"I'm referring to the intended painting, as the image in the mirror suggests."

"Maybe you're right, but the painting exists, and it's done."

"I mean that the painting inside the painting was never finished."

"Well, if you look at it that way, you might be right."

"Just notice how a simple child's tantrum changed the course of things by not allowing the completion of a family picture."

"It allowed another picture, a much better one, to be painted."

"Perhaps. The thing is that a decision at a particular time could affect a work, or a whole life, a whole personal behavior, a whole—"

The man began coughing, and would have fallen were it not for the quick reflexes of the guard, who caught him. As best he could, he helped the man sit on the floor.

"I'm thirsty," the man explained in a hoarse voice.

"I'll go get some water."

The guard of the Prado's gallery three left in a rush. The elderly man, still leaning against the wall, took a piece of paper out of his jacket pocket, a crumpled letter. He placed it on the floor beside him. Next to it he put a picture of Pope Benedict XVI.

The water fountain was some distance away and the guard couldn't return as quickly as expected. He had called another guard for help. When he finally got back, carefully carrying a glass of water, there was no one in the room but the sick man still on the floor, in the same position. The guard crouched down and saw that the man was not as he had left him. The elderly man sat motionless, eyes wide open. He was dead. The young man jumped up, startled, and called for help on his radio. Summoning all his strength, he took a closer look at the man—whose eyes were still fixed on the painting he had been looking at for hours.

6

The Plaza de Mayo in Buenos Aires was the center of historical protests for the Argentine people. Both the Casa Rosada, the president's house, and the Metropolitan Cathedral stood facing it. From its columns, a young man burst into the spacious nave, running as fast as he could.

He was panting and covered with sweat after his mad rush from the residence of the parish priest, Padre Pablo—a simple enough name for a priest who didn't particularly wish to be identified. At that moment, the cathedral was closed to the public, but the priest knelt at the foot of the altar, hands joined in prayer.

Then he noticed the young man, who usually stood back a few steps, waiting for the priest to finish his prayers. On this occasion there didn't seem to be enough time.

After crossing himself, the parish priest got up and turned to the youth.

"What's wrong, son? Were you looking for me? Did something happen?"

"No, *padre*. A man . . . knocked on your door . . . looking for you."

Padre Pablo noticed how flushed the young man was.

"Manuel, you're dripping with sweat. Did you run all the way here?"

"Yes, *padre.*"

The aging priest put his hand on his visitor's arm.

"Come sit with me. Calm down, and tell me what happened. Who was this man? What did he do to get you in such a state?"

"I don't know him. He seemed to be from Europe, Eastern Europe."

The priest became agitated, as if suddenly remembering something, and then he, too, started to perspire.

"What did he want from me?"

"To see you right away. I told him that was impossible. Then he said that everything was possible in the eyes of the Lord. But the worst thing was—"

"The worst—did he do anything to harm you?"

"No, *padre,* but I could tell he was bad." Then, lowering his voice, he added, "He had a gun."

Pablo wiped the perspiration off his brow with his handkerchief. He closed his eyes and remained quiet for a few moments, without saying a word. He opened them again, and in an exercise of self-control, slowed his breath. "What did you tell him?"

"That you'd gone to the hospital to visit a friend."

"Why did you lie, Manuel?"

"Forgive me, Padre Pablo, but I couldn't think of anything else. The man looked evil—he had a tattoo on his left arm, of a serpent."

"Did he try to get into my house?"

The boy, still upset, hesitated before answering. A gun was not something he saw every day, much less when talking to a complete stranger.

"No, *padre,*" he said finally.

"It's okay, Manuel. Go back and take care of your things."

Now calmer, the young man stood up, kissed the priest's hand, and walked to the center aisle, crossing himself.

"Manuel . . ."

"Yes, Padre Pablo?"

"Did you see that man again on your way here?"

"No, no. I was so upset that as soon as he left, I came to tell you. I didn't see anything and didn't look. I started running like crazy."

"Fine, Manuel. You may go. God bless you, and keep your faith in Him."

Father Pablo quietly knelt and started praying devoutly even before the boy had gone.

He heard footsteps, not the boy's, but someone else's, someone with a decisive stride. Padre Pablo felt something on his shoulder, but rather than a hand, it was cold metal.

"I was expecting you," the priest said.

"I'm not surprised. Some people have very strong instincts. Were you expecting something in particular?"

Padre Pablo crossed himself and got up, eyes fixed on the man. "My future is in God's hands, the same as yours and everybody else's. What is mine is well kept, don't you worry. You didn't come to give me anything that wasn't already rightfully mine."

"Maybe I came to take something away."

"That would depend on how each of us sees things."

"Where are they?"

"Buenos Aires, New York, Paris, Madrid, Warsaw, Geneva. There are so many places in the world."

There was a pop, and the priest tumbled over the pews. The man with the serpent tattoo was the same one seen in Rome, with a foreign accent, probably from Eastern Europe. He stood closer to Padre Pablo, who was bleeding profusely from his right side and trying to cover his wound with a bloody hand.

"God is not here to save you, my dear sir. You'd be better off telling me where they are."

"God has saved me already. You will never find them."

The man leaned over Padre Pablo and spoke in a confidential tone ."You know, *padre,* an assistant is good precisely because he helps do what one has to do, such as finding things. The most inexperienced and anxious are best. You can't imagine the amount of information they are able to gather. I didn't find them and I know you're not going to tell me where they are, but with a clue here and another there, a letter, a note, an e-mail, a photo . . ."

The dice were cast for a new game, one in which the priest would not take part, since he was about to abandon all games. Padre Pablo could only hope that the man with the serpent tattoo on his wrist knew a good deal less than he pretended to.

Showing the priest a photo, the man said, "I'm sure he'll be more willing to cooperate. I'll give him your regards." Then he fired a second shot, this time to the head. He calmly walked to the center aisle, crossed himself, and left by a side door.

7

It was always a joy to come back, even if only for a couple of days, and to breathe the Baltic Sea's salt air, which wafted over the city God had chosen for his birth. Coming to this part of the world was like an omen, an unmistakable sign of the importance of the mission entrusted to him. He walked around the familiar streets of Gdansk, Poland's economic center and the cradle of the famous Solidarity movement. He had always known a great mission awaited him, and he was right. When he was on Chmielna Street six years before, it had been confirmed by a phone call in the middle of the night. Now, going past the small apartment where he had grown up and spent his early adult life, he remembered his parents, who died when he was young. It was all a divine design, completing the circle of perfection he admired so much. The phone call didn't happen by chance—nothing ever did—but by specific providential design. This was the first time in six years that he had been back in Gdansk and seen the Wisła again. The Master had asked him to wait there for the next stage of the plan, and the Master always knew what he was doing. He was one of the Illuminati, a saint guarding the higher interests of the Holy Trinity on Earth.

It was almost noon now. He walked on Mieszczanska toward Chiebnicka, turned right and then left, on the way to Długie Pobrzeże. He was having dinner at the Gdanska Restaurant, as if it were a familiar place, though he had never patronized it. The sumptuous setting resembled a palace dining room more than a restaurant.

"*Na zdrowie*," the impeccably dressed waiter greeted him.

"*Dzień dobry*," he answered politely. It had been a long time since he had greeted anybody in his native tongue. He ordered the specialty of the house for two, and a bottle of red wine.

The food came quickly, efficiently, and the waiter departed with a friendly "*Smacznego.*"

"How are you?" a voice behind him asked.

"Very well, sir," the man answered, getting up obsequiously. Someone who had seen him a few moments before wouldn't think he was the same man. His self-assurance was transformed into subservience before this newcomer, who sat down across from him. He was wearing an elegant Armani suit, discreetly black, similar to that of the man who'd arrived first. There was no doubt he was the boss.

"You have done a good job."

"Thank you. It's an honor to serve you."

They were speaking Italian.

"The Great Master as usual will know how to reward your efforts. He will soon summon you to his presence."

"I'll be honored."

"You're right. It's an honor not many enjoy. And very few live to tell about it. Only those closest to him and those who serve him with dignity, like you."

The Polish man lowered his head in acknowledgment and, pulling out an envelope from an inside pocket, he placed it on the table.

"This is what I found in Buenos Aires. The photo I told you about. It's a simple trick. Under ultraviolet light, another image appears. Take a look."

The other man examined the photo. "Interesting what these people can come up with," he said, keeping his eyes fixed on the Pole. "It won't be long before we find a name for this face."

Now it was the boss's turn to hand over an envelope, which he did, placing it on the table without any attempt to disguise his action.

"Here are your orders to go ahead. Everything you need is inside," he said, returning the photo. "Take it with you. The plan is on. Beware of traitors, many people are after this. Don't arouse suspicions, and do not fail. So long."

He left without another word, without even touching his food. The one who stayed took the envelope and put it in the inside pocket of his jacket. He wolfed down the house specialty, enjoyed the wine, and, once satiated, paid the check, leaving a generous tip. A celebration was in order. He who served well, deserved to be well rewarded.

"*Dziękuję,*" the waiter said gratefully, happy to see the green American dollars that the well-dressed man deposited on the silver tray.

"See you tomorrow," the man said.

By the Wisła, he opened the envelope and examined its contents. A document with his photo and his new identity, a plane ticket from Frankfurt, and some papers. He added the photo he had brought from Buenos Aires.

"Now it's your turn," he said in a paternal tone, not so much addressing the personage in the photo as the task ahead, which he intended to carry out meticulously, as he had all the previous ones. He decided to go for a walk in the small Sunday market, perhaps to enjoy for the last time the flavor of a city he might not see again. He took off his jacket and his short-sleeved shirt revealed the tattoo of a serpent that extended down to his wrist. He put everything back in the envelope, after taking another look at the photo he had obtained in Buenos Aires from the home of the parish priest, Padre Pablo. The priest had another home now, a more permanent one, underground. The photo, if anyone was watching, showed only the face of Pope Benedict XVI.

8

CONCLAVE OF AUGUST 26, 1978

Let the peace of the Lord be with you,
because I did absolutely nothing to get where I am.

ALBINO LUCIANI TO HIS FAMILY AFTER HE WAS ELECTED POPE

A*nnuntio vobis gaudium magnum: habemus papam,"* Cardinal Pericle Felici proclaimed from the balcony of Saint Peter's Basilica on the twenty-sixth of August 1978.

But in order for the Holy Spirit to decide who would be the next pontiff, the 111 cardinals had to have numerous meetings disguised as luncheons and come to many agreements disguised as inconsequential, polite chats. No one in the Vatican would admit that immediately after the death of Pope Paul VI, an aggressive electoral campaign had been launched. Those humble promotional ventures were modestly disguised by a false lack of interest.

Some prelates remembered with a smile the evening Cardinal Pignedoli, surrounded by his peers in the College of Cardinals, declared himself unqualified for the role being proposed for him. He declared it was best to vote for Cardinal Gantin, a black prelate from Benin. In this manner, the necessary scrutiny could be carried out by elimination rather than by selection. Acts like this didn't single out any particular cardinal because many prelates did the same thing, declaring their humility and submission only to remind the others that actually they were the best option. Not all of the cardinals were aware of these electoral manipulations, posturing, and declarations of religious fervor. Albino Luciani, for example, in his disregard for these matters, took advantage of his stay in Rome to arrange repairs for his Lancia 2000, a vehicle that had served only to make his trips miserable. He told Diego Lorenzi, his assistant, that he wanted the car ready by the twenty-ninth, the day the conclave was supposed to be over, in order to return to Venice early that morning.

Though it was possible to guess the will of the cardinals, no one could be sure of the choice of the Holy Spirit. And this time an unexpected outcome seemed more likely, a decision arrived at in collaboration by the prelates and the Holy Spirit. Once more, the mysterious ways of the Lord demonstrated how unpredictable events could be.

After the morning vote was over, Albino Luciani was kneeling in prayer in cell number sixty. The results had not been conclusive, but there had been some unexpected results, such as the thirty votes Luciani received on the second scrutiny. As he prayed, he felt great uneasiness in the pit of his stomach, so instead of asking Divine Providence for courage and clarity of thought when voting for the best cardinal to occupy that position, he implored God to please take care of it and relieve him of a great burden. He prayed that the cardinals would cease voting for him, and for the Holy Spirit to inspire the prelates to write the name of Cardinal Siri on their cards. At last count, Cardinal Siri was only five points away from him. The third on the list of reluctant candidates was Cardinal Pignedoli, who, despite having lost prestige, received fifteen votes. He was followed by the Brazilian Cardinal Lorscheider, with twelve. Nineteen of the remaining votes were distributed among the Italian cardinals Bertoli and Felici, with a few for the Polish Karol Wojtyla, the Argentine Pironio, Monsignor Cordeiro (archbishop from Pakistan), and the Austrian Franz Koenig.

An unintended competition arose between Siri and Luciani. Cardinal Siri wanted to win, while the cardinal from Venice, Albino Luciani, wanted to flee, and might have done so had the doors to the Sistine Chapel not been closed.

Before entering the conclave, Don Albino told those present, as well as his relatives and friends, that if elected, he would utter the well-known

formula, "I decline, for which I ask for your forgiveness." But this was a possibility that he, like most others, considered very remote. However, His
Holiness Pope Paul VI, on a visit in Venice to the Adriatic Queen, had not
only granted Luciani a stole, but had personally placed it on his shoulders.
That public gesture in the presence of a large group was quite unusual for
Paul VI, and was his way of acknowledging the Venetian cardinal's loyalty
and his defense—due more to obligation than to devotion—of the encycli-
cal *Humanae vitae,* one of the most unfortunate in history. In July 1968,
Paul VI had issued that totally radical pastoral letter banning any device or
method of birth control, of course including abortion, sterilization, and
even the interruption of pregnancy when there was evident danger to the
mother's life. In *Humanae vitae* everything was up to a supposed divine order, to an improbable marital responsibility, and if need be, to chastity. As
the pope decreed, the divine plan could not be subject to social, political, or
psychological conditions.

These recollections of the past would have been irrelevant, were it not
that Paul VI was among those mainly responsible for Albino Luciani's dread
of being elected by his peers and by the Holy Spirit.

"Let them choose Siri," Luciani begged the Creator. "I have so much to
do in Venice!" Paul VI, consciously or not, had placed Albino Luciani in
that difficult situation. He had made him cardinal, made a public display of
his preference, and graced him in word and gesture. But that responsibility
could not be solely ascribed to him. Had John XXIII not made him bishop,
he'd never have come to this, and had his mother, Bartola, not given birth
to him (in Canale d'Agordo on October 17, 1912), he wouldn't find himself
in this position, either. He had to dismiss all these thoughts. God alone
would be the one to decide. Everything must be following some divine
plan. Otherwise, his hometown priest, Filippo Carli, wouldn't have encour-
aged him to enter the seminary in Feltre.

After the first vote, Cardinal Luciani understood he was being swept up
in the current of the conclave, and that it was not possible to ignore such an
unfortunate situation, though he had naively attempted to go unnoticed,
which had succeeded before, in different circumstances. On this occasion,
his natural reserve and shyness had provided no escape, and the process

was completely incomprehensible to him. How could he have expected twenty-three votes in the first scrutiny, two fewer than Siri and five more than Pignedoli? As required by regulation, after each scrutiny all the ballots were gathered and burned in the furnace.

Paul VI had foreseen every detail of the conclave, nothing had escaped him. The preceding pope was the one to make the regulations, and this pope, for the first time, had ruled that cardinals over eighty years old could not participate in the conclave. In the apostolic constitution *Romano pontifice eligendo,* Paul VI had set this limitation for religious reasons. The responsibilities of being elected the Church's shepherd would no longer be added to the physical woes of being eighty. There were no frivolous concerns. The governance of the Church of Christ could not be left to chance. Some ignorant people lamented the fact that some pontiffs devoted themselves to practical matters instead of spiritual ones. But the Church didn't depend solely on Hail Marys, as one American cardinal pointed out.

After finishing his prayers, Cardinal Luciani got up and left his cell. Joseph Malula, the cardinal from Zaire, congratulated him warmly, but Luciano nodded in sadness, continuing on his way to the Sistine Chapel for the third vote.

"I feel I'm at the center of a great whirlwind," he lamented. After the third scrutiny, Albino Luciani received sixty-eight votes, and Siri, fifteen. Albino was but eight votes away from being declared pontiff.

"No, please, no," Luciani again prayed, under his breath. A few cardinals seated nearby heard their friend's sigh. Prelate Willebrands tried to calm him with uplifting words.

"*Coraggio,* Cardinal Luciani. The Lord weighs us down, but He also gives us the strength to bear up."

Felici came up to the nervous cardinal and handed him an envelope.

"A message for the new pope," he said.

To Albino Luciani this was a surprising commentary, particularly from someone who had always voted for Siri.

The handwritten message mentioned the words *Via Crucis,* The Way of the Cross, symbol and reminder of Christ's Passion. All the cardinals felt the same trepidation and unrest in the presence of Michelangelo's imposing frescoes. The prelates knew that they were part of a transcendental ritual in the history of the Church and, given the circumstances, in the history of the world.

Everything had been according to tradition. The Holy Spirit had come to the participants in the conclave and had stopped over the figure of one of them, or at least that was what the majority thought.

It was God's will.

Luciani received ninety-nine votes, Cardinal Siri eleven, and Lorscheider one (Luciani had voted for him). Destiny had been fulfilled. The cardinals erupted in fervent applause. They had scarcely taken one day to elect their pope among 111 cardinals, and that success was attributed, of course, to divine inspiration. By five minutes past six, the whole thing was over, a little before dinnertime.

The doors to the Sistine Chapel opened, and the masters of ceremony came in, following the Cardinal Camerlengo, Jean-Marie Villot, secretary of state of the Vatican with the preceding pontiff and keeper of Saint Peter's keys until the conclave ended. All the prelates, according to the secular tradition, surrounded Albino Luciani.

"Do you accept your canonic election to become the Holy Roman Pontiff?" the French cardinal asked.

The eyes of all the cardinals were fixed on the timid man. Even Michelangelo's figures seemed to adopt a more severe expression, lacking joy manifesting an almost unbearable sense of heaviness. Cardinals Ribeiro and Willebrand offered looks of encouragement to the Venetian priest, and Villot repeated his question.

"May the Lord forgive you for what you have done to me," Luciani finally responded. "I accept."

Everything continued according to the protocol established centuries before. The grave, imposing ritual proceeded with overwhelming precision.

"By what name do you wish to be known?"

Luciani hesitated again, and after a few seconds, smiling for the first time, he spoke the name he had chosen for himself in the historical records.

"Ioannes Paulus the First."

In the Vatican it was presumed that the name chosen by a new pontiff partly indicated the religious and political direction he wished his papacy to follow. The most experienced understood that Albino Luciani had started in an unusual way and that his papacy would be an exceptional one.

"Nothing will be the same," they said. His papacy was to begin with an innovation. In almost two thousand years of history, no other pope had used a combined name. Luciani was the only one who dared to go against tradition and in this way render homage both to the man who named him bishop and to the one who designated him cardinal.

"Congratulations, Your Holiness," Cardinal Karol Wojtyla proclaimed.

There was a great bustle in the Sistine Chapel. Everything had been ready for days, but always some detail would come up that demanded attention—a fringe to be fixed, or an untimely visit to take care of. The cardinals distributed the chores among themselves, moving to and fro, with the urgency of those who know they are taking part in a historical decision.

Luciani was taken to the vestry to conclude the required rituals, and to finish his prayers according to tradition. Other prelates burned the ballots of the last scrutiny, adding to the fire the chemical products needed to whiten the *fumata*. But after a few white puffs, the faithful thousands waiting in Saint Peter's Square observed that the smoke was turning black again, perhaps because of accumulated dirt in the chimney. Or perhaps because there was no new pope.

The brothers Gammarelli, tailors to the Vatican, bickered while trying to find a white vestment appropriate for the occasion. For decades now, the most famous tailor shop in Rome made sure to have on hand three cassocks—small, medium, and large—before each conclave. On this occasion, however, they had added a fourth—extra large—just in case. There had been rumors about the possible election of a heavy monsignor. The one chosen, however, had very narrow shoulders, and his name didn't even appear on the list of the most prominent, as culled by newspaper and television analysts. After trying several garments on Albino Luciani and circling him again and again, the tailors were more or less satisfied. Luciani finally appeared wearing white vestments to present himself to the world as the new Holy Father of the Catholic Church.

Cardinal Suenens approached Luciani to congratulate him.

"Holy Father, thanks for having accepted."

Luciani smiled, "Perhaps it would have been better to refuse."

Why didn't he? his conscience wondered. He wanted to refuse but didn't have the courage. In fact, his own true humility had been overwhelmed by the speed at which everything had evolved, and by the forceful will of the majority. But ultimately he accepted because he felt capable of executing the difficult task ahead of him. If he truly had not, he told himself, he would have declined.

The cardinals began intoning the Te Deum.

In the plaza, the groups of the faithful had begun to disperse. For them, it seemed that the cardinals hadn't reached an agreement, or that the inspiration of the Holy Spirit had not yet come to them, since apparently there was no new pope. The *fumata* had been dark, no doubt about it, symbolizing the indecision of the conclave.

The Vatican radio commentators reported that the smoke was black and white, and so they couldn't tell.

The commander of the Swiss Guard, who had to receive the new pontiff with a loyal salute in the name of all his men, did not even have the escort ready to accompany him through the corridors leading to the balcony on Saint Peter's Square.

The brothers Gammarelli argued in the vestry, each blaming the other for their lack of readiness.

In the midst of this confusion, the enormous door to the balcony in Saint Peter's Basilica opened, and the voice of Cardinal Felici thundered from the loudspeakers.

"*Attenzione.*"

The faithful, already on their way home or to their hotels, came running to the plaza. Then there was complete silence.

"*Annuntio vobis gaudium magnum: Habemus Papam!*"

Diego Lorenzi, Luciani's secretary for the last couple of years, had accompanied him from Venice to Rome, and he was among the faithful thousands waiting in Saint Peter's Square for the results of the scrutiny. He had seen that the smoke coming out of the chimney since six twenty-five was neither black nor white. For about an hour it had been kind of ashen, and nobody could decide whether that dirty smoke was the white *fumata* so eagerly awaited by all. Next to him, also waiting for the conclave's resolution, were a couple with their two girls, arguing about the inconclusive smoke. The younger of the girls, overcome by the religious spirit dominating the plaza, asked him whether he'd said Mass in that immense church before them.

Lorenzi answered with an affectionate smile. No, he was in Rome only temporarily. He lived in Venice. He also talked with the girls' parents, and all were in agreement that a conclave, even being outside of it, was a stimulating experience. It was all about the choosing of the Shepherd, and they felt certain that the voting of the cardinals received God's benediction.

For Diego Lorenzi the thrilling experience was about to end. Early the next morning he would be driving the Lancia, with Don Albino Luciani, back to Venice—375 miles separating the two cities, a whole world apart. Just then, the voice of Cardinal Pericle Felici was heard loud and clear, and everybody turned to the balcony of Saint Peter's Basilica.

"Annuntio vobis gaudium magnum: Habemus Papam! Cardinalem Albinum Luciani."

Hearing Luciani's name, Lorenzi started to cry with joy. An irrepressible emotion took hold of his spirit, and he couldn't understand how the cardinals had decided on Don Albino, always so shy and evasive. The girl and her parents looked at him with pleased appreciation. He was a priest, moved like them by the emotion of this historical moment. It all made sense.

Lorenzi bent down, tears welling, to speak to his new little friend.

"I am the new pope's secretary," he said finally.

So the new pontiff was to be Albino Luciani? And who was Albino Luciani? In fact, it didn't matter much. The important thing was that the Church of Rome had a new pope.

Lorenzi and the thousands of faithful gathered at Saint Peter's Square saw the figure of Albino Luciani as he appeared in the balcony, smiling and dressed in all white. That smile reached the hearts of many and filled their souls with heartwarming joy. His smile conveyed humility, benevolence, and peace. After Giovanni Battista Montini, the somber Pope Paul VI, this man appeared in the balcony with the smile of a young person willing to devote himself passionately to his mission. After the benediction *urbi et orbi*, the sun sent its last beams into the Roman dusk.

9

No one had any inkling as to why this had happened. Most of the directors of the countless secret service agencies around the world would obey any instruction uttered by this wrinkled old man who walked with the help of a cane embellished with a golden lion's head.

Any theory was possible, though probably none could even remotely approach the truth. There was one unquestionable fact: the CIA sustained and covered up all of his decisions, and lent its men, even whole units, to the organization headed by this fragile old man with a harsh demeanor. It was a vicious cycle. If the all-powerful U.S. Central Intelligence Agency placed itself at the service of a man like this, making its agents available to him, there was no need to inquire any further.

For his own personal service he always had a man with him, usually impeccably dressed in a black Armani suit, whose name, like that of the old man, could not be revealed because provoking the anger of such powerful men was dangerous. They were always together, except on the rare occasions when it was imperative that the assistant execute some special assignment.

And as for the old man, he was often seen walking around the gardens of his city or his hometown (whose names could not be revealed, either). There was a time when the old man had to stay abroad longer than he would have liked, but that was over when finally he could afford not to travel anymore. New communication technology had made this possible, though he still couldn't do without reliable help where his interests lay. There was nothing comparable to the air of his homeland, his dear Italy, and his city and estate.

At this moment the old man was sitting on his terrace at home, his gaze split between the *Corriere della Sera* and the distant horizon. From there he enjoyed watching the sea of green extending far beyond his own lands, vanishing behind a hill, disappearing like the sun's burst of orange at the time of its setting, in its unequal battle against the darkness, which increased with every passing moment.

The garden lights, with photoelectric sensors, were coming on all around, programmed to activate slowly and progressively for a continuous transition in harmony with the prolonged sunset. The lamps warmed their filaments until there was no more natural light. Even dusk didn't prevent him from reading the paper as the sea of green lapsed into total darkness, lit only sporadically by a sprinkling of fireflies in midair. "No artificial light has the power to illuminate the world," the old man mused. "Perhaps only faith has the power to brighten it." Lately his mind was more likely to follow a spiritual tangent. He might begin with a purely physical theme, which after going around and around always ended up touching on the spiritual. Only Heaven knew why. At an age often deemed appropriate to beg forgiveness for the sins of a lifetime, he was still not one accustomed to pleading for mercy. Nor was he a compassionate man. It had been God's will that he had lived so many years, facing so many dangers, doubts, and frustrations. The sufferings he had had to go through, which he was still experiencing, were God's will. The main difference now was the detachment with which he now received the provocations that the Almighty never failed to send. Whether it was a small sign or a great revelation, this old man, sitting there alone, with his newspaper as his sole companion, understood it all very well.

Unlike most mortals, he had no fear of God. Many had perished at the hands of this old man with a cane, or following his orders. He made others believe he used them thoughtlessly, when in fact he couldn't take a step without their help. Time was inflexible to all, without exception.

His assistant was nowhere around. He was surely abroad, engaged in resolving some matter of interest for the old man. Rather than an assistant, he was in fact his personal secretary. All powerful men, the pope included, had one.

A few years ago the old man could indulge the pleasure of lighting a cigarette and enjoying it to the end, letting out big puffs of smoke while reading the paper. But now he had to resign himself to just reading the paper, as his lungs no longer tolerated the pleasure of smoking. Heavy coughing would interrupt the calmness of his nights. He felt quite capable of resisting the temptations of the flesh as well as those of the mind. Many other matters distressed him, but he wasn't a man to be annoyed by small things. His motto had always been that everything had a solution.

Lost in a flurry of thoughts, he didn't notice the invasive presence of a maid trying to hand him a phone.

"Sir?"

Since there was no answer, she had to repeat her words.

"Yes, Francesca," he said, as if awakened from a dream.

"A phone call for you."

After handing the phone to her boss, the maid left quickly, leaving him to resolve his own affairs, not wishing to meddle in his private life.

"*Pronto*," the old man said forcefully, with the formidable tone of someone used to being in charge.

He recognized the even-tempered voice of his assistant, reporting in. In contrast to the voice of his master, the assistant's monotone made his competent report sound like a litany. The ability to get to the backbone, to what really counted, was a virtue he had acquired by listening to the old man. He knew that his master wanted only precise, fast explanations.

"Fine, come back. We'll handle it all from here," he said after a few moments of silence, interrupted by some whistling chirps on the phone. "He'll do a good job. It should be easy to locate Marius Ferris, provided he did as I ordered behind the scene. I'll be expecting you."

Ending his international call, he put his cell phone on the table, only to pick it up again. More and more often, he forgot what he was going to do next. For a few seconds his mind went blank, and the cold clarity of his reasoning, so dear to him, clouded over. So far, this had caused no damage since it happened at home, and not too often. But he knew it was only a matter of time, that little by little the white cloud in his mind would expand, gradually consuming his faculties. How soon? He couldn't say. Months? Years? A mystery. It was life's revenge.

He made a new call and, without waiting to hear the sound of a voice, knew who would answer.

"Geoffrey Barnes. The neutralization of the target can be effected. I'll await confirmation." And he hung up, without another word. Leaving the phone on the table, he went back to his newspaper. One thought kept pressing him: That Monteiro girl's time has come.

10

Why is nobody answering? Sarah wondered. That's odd. She hung up and made another call. After a few seconds a female voice said that the person requested was not available, but that she would relay a message.

"Dad . . . It's me, Sarah." She knocked herself on the head, realizing how stupid this sounded. After saying "dad," of course it could be only her. "I called you at home," she continued, "and nobody answered. Please call me as soon as you can. It's urgent. We need to talk."

Returning to her computer, she saw that Messenger was connected, though the icon for her father was red and said OFFLINE. He's not there, either, she told herself. Where can he possibly have gone?

Sarah took one of the yellowish papers out of an envelope from a Valdemar Firenzi that she found in her mail. There were three pages, all in Italian. Two of them showed only a typewritten list of names, preceded by numbers and capital letters she couldn't understand, a page and a half long and in two columns. There were also some words in the margins, tightly scribbled in a firm hand. In the same sure hand, some of the names were underlined, no smudges, no hesitation. It all ended in an arrow with some words in Italian above. But why in Italian? Her first impulse was to toss the papers in the wastebasket. There was no return address, making it impossible to send them back. While she was checking the envelope, a small key fell out. Very small, perhaps from luggage or an attaché case, definitely not a door key. Then something caught her attention. At first she hadn't noticed it among the many names ending in *ov* or *enko,* and, equally numerous, those of Italian, English, or Spanish origin. But there it was, not underlined or with any notes in the margin, clearly circled in ink, and undoubtedly added more recently: Raul Brandão Monteiro, typed with the same machine as the dozens of other names on the list.

What is my father's name doing here? Sarah wondered.

Then she carefully looked at the next page. A lot of scribbling, apparently done in haste, similar to the notes she made during press conferences. Had one of her father's colleagues sent her that list? Maybe. The apparent sender was Valdemar Firenzi, though he provided no address. The name seemed Italian, it sounded a bit familiar, yet she couldn't place it. There must be a reason, but she had to wait for her father's call.

18, 15–34, H, 2, 23, V, 11
Dio bisogno e IO fare lo. Suo augurio Y mio comando
GCT(15)–9, 30–31, 15, 16, 2, 21, 6–14, 11, 16, 16, 2, 20

She looked at it again and again, unable to figure it out.

Then the phone rang.

"Finally," she sighed, relieved. It could only be her father, returning her call.

"Dad?"

Silence on the other end. But it wasn't a sepulchral, unsettling silence. In the background, she could hear street noises—cars going by, steps, fragments of conversation. The call was coming from a cell or a public phone.

"Dad?" Nothing. Maybe it was a wrong number, someone misdialed, or a cellular that got jostled inside a handbag. Perhaps an admirer? Negative. No ex-boyfriend or former lover was that maniacal. The only one capable of something like this was Greg, a colleague from the newsroom, always up for a prank. In her mail, though, there was a postcard he sent her from the

Congo with a photo of the Lulua River, explaining that it was a miracle he was able to mail it at all. How could he be phoning her?

"Greg? Is that you? Is this another one of your pranks?" she asked, just in case.

But the urban street noise was unmistakable.

Easy, Sarah, she told herself. Don't start getting paranoid. But she had plenty of reasons to worry—an envelope from an unknown sender in Italy, with an old list of names that included her father's, that surly customs officer telling her there was a problem with her passport . . . Everything was upsetting, especially that envelope.

The caller was still on the line, but there was still no hello, nothing. No breathing, either, only a loud siren, a normal sound for any modern city. She listened carefully, noticing that a police car had just gone by. An important detail. The connection was cut off, only a sudden click. She could still hear the strident noise of the police car out on Belgrave Road. The blue lights caused weird red reflections on the curtains drawn closed on her ground floor.

What a strange coincidence, two simultaneous police sirens, in different places . . . Maybe too much of a coincidence?

Sarah abruptly turned off all the house lights, plunging her apartment into darkness. She moved the sofa away from the window, taking a deep breath before opening the curtains just enough to see without being seen. It was a normal night on Belgrave Road. Dozens of people headed here and there in their own worlds, totally oblivious of Sarah Monteiro. The traffic was heavy, all kinds of cars and taxis. At the bus stop across the street, a 24 bus to Pimlico/Grosvenor Road was letting out passengers and taking on new ones.

Nothing seemed suspicious. If someone were spying on her, surely he wouldn't be all dressed in black, wearing a hat and upturned collar, pretending to read a newspaper. That happened only in old movies. Now, anybody could be a spy. Even the sanitation man on the street collecting bags of garbage. Or the woman talking on her cell phone on the second floor of the Holiday Express Hotel, across the street. Perhaps they really were as they seemed. But perhaps not.

You're delirious, Sarah told herself, and this idea quickly calmed her down. How silly. Who's going to be watching me?

Something caught her attention. As the 24 bus left, it revealed a parked car with tinted windows, probably belonging to someone staying at the hotel. Had it been parked there a long time? That black car with darkened windows didn't look innocent at all. Quite the contrary, and something gnawed at her. I've seen this car before, she realized. The image of that dark vehicle came to Sarah's mind, but she couldn't figure out where or when she'd seen it. Her photographic memory came to her aid. It was the same car that had suddenly stopped in front of her taxi. The driver had opened the window, shouted "Sorry, mate," at the taxi, and sped away. Which meant that it could have been there for more than three hours. It could mean everything, or nothing at all—an imminent danger, or simply a spy movie running in her head. And her second hypothesis seemed closer to the truth.

A ring from her cell phone startled her.

"Hello?"

"Hello, Sarah."

"Dad, finally! Where were you?"

At last he was calling her back. The relief of hearing Captain Raul Brandão Monteiro's calm, deep voice brought her down to earth. It was over now, her fears dissipated.

"I was taking your mother to—"

"Where?"

"Sarah . . ."

Her father's voice wasn't that calm. In fact, she'd never heard him so agitated. The sudden relief of a few seconds before changed to anxious doubt, intensified by the shift in his usually warm, affectionate voice.

"I received an envelope from a man named—"

"Don't mention names, Sarah. From now on, do not mention names. Don't say where you are, either. To anyone, you hear me? Unless you're talking to someone who can be entirely trusted."

"Dad, you're scaring me. Do you know anything about those papers?"

Silence.

"Dad, please don't hide things from me. Your name appears on a list—"

"I beg you, Sarah. Don't say another word about this. I know what you received," he said, sounding constrained, like someone who had lost his grip on something he had somehow once controlled. "I know what you received," he repeated, making an effort to sound more at ease. "But they don't know it, and I'm completely sure they're listening to us now."

"They—who are they, Dad?" she asked, panic in her voice.

"This is no time to talk, but to act, my dear. Do you remember Grandma's home?"

"What—why are you bringing that up now?"

"Do you remember it, or don't you?"

"The house? Of course. How could I ever forget it?"

"Great."

Suddenly she saw a pair of eyes at the window. A chill ran down her spine.

"Sarah," her father's voice called out. He repeated her name again and again, but she didn't answer. She was petrified, staring at the window, where those eyes had been watching her without her noticing. "Sarah," her father insisted anxiously.

Then she heard unhurried, heavy steps. The sound paralyzed her. They were getting close to her door.

"Sarah." Her father's voice broke her stupor.

"Yes, I'm listening."

Ding-dong.

"Someone's at the door. I've got to get it."

"Don't!" her father warned, alarmed.

"Dad, I'm your daughter, not one of your soldiers."

"Guard those papers at all times, always keep them with you. Understand? And remember what your grandma told you when you were afraid to go out, to get too close to the cattle."

"I'll try."

Sarah thought about what her father had said. As a child in Escariz, where they spent some time every year, she had been afraid of the cows. She remembered how she hated to get close to those enormous animals. Her grandmother had to move the always threatening cows aside for her to go out. At some point her grandmother stopped clearing her way.

"You make them move aside," she'd say. "It's about time you stopped being scared of them."

"There's always a solution." Her grandma's words of wisdom.

Sarah kept the papers sent to her by that man, Valdemar Firenzi. She looked for her handbag and found it next to her computer. She took out her wallet and credit cards, and walked to the stairs, glancing anxiously back at the door. Whoever was outside was now twisting the doorknob violently after repeatedly pounding on the door with his fists. Her heart was racing. Slippers in hand, she crept to the second floor, while the stair planks creaked, giving her position away.

When she reached the second floor, she heard the front door screeching, being forced open. Going to her room, all her senses alert, she was overcome by fear.

The intruder was ambling around the first floor, not even trying to hide his presence. Sarah felt totally helpless, panic-stricken. A red curtain, identical to the ones downstairs, filtered the light, giving the room a surreal feeling. She opened it noiselessly. The black car was still down there. Its sinister stillness contrasted sharply with her agitated state. Don't let fear take over, she told herself. "Come on, use your head."

What could she do? "There's always a solution. If you can't go out one way, try another," her grandma used to say, "Try another way. . . ." In her grandma's house she could get out through a window on the second floor because of the short hop to the hillside in back, but in this house, in the absolutely flat capital of the UK, it wasn't the same, the jump was too high. There's always a solution, she kept thinking, and recalled a standard British regulation, the mandatory emergency exit. Since the great fire of 1666, when everything was made out of wood. There had to be an emergency exit. But where? This floor had no doors to the outside. The windows did not open enough and were too high. Maybe . . . from the bathroom, that's it. She knew that the bathroom window opened wide, and had next to it, anchored to the wall, a wrought-iron ladder—the emergency exit!

"Thanks, Grandma," she muttered.

Taking a deep breath, Sarah looked toward the bathroom, right there in front of her. All she had to do was get across the hallway and in, past the door. Just moments away from salvation.

One, two, three, she counted mentally, and started running. The intruder was climbing the stairs fast. She went in and tried to open the window. Not easy. It hadn't been open for years and there was no way she could unlock it. Applying all her strength, making a superhuman effort was of no use. Or so it seemed, while she kept desperately trying. The footsteps were getting closer. The intruder was now walking slowly. In the hallway, the man in a black overcoat put the silencer on his gun.

Sarah stood against the bathroom wall. Perhaps there was still time for something. If she could break the glass . . .

One more step, then another. The floor planks creaked, her teeth chattered, she was about to lose control. Fear was tearing her apart. The bathtub seemed safer. She thought she heard the would-be murderer breathing. He's used to this kind of thing. He's a professional, she thought.

"There's always a solution . . . for everything." Sarah felt she could hear her grandma repeating. "For everything. Except death."

With a sudden inspiration, Sarah quietly slipped out of the bathtub. Her eyes had fully adapted to the dim light. She searched about for something. The dryer? No. The shower spray? No good. Towels, perfumes, creams. No, no, no. Helpless, she leaned against the wall by the basin. Next to her, at eye level, she saw the extinguisher. That was it. If you think there won't be a struggle, you're dead wrong, she told herself. He had to be about three yards away from her. One step, two yards . . . another step, only one yard . . .

She quickly shot a cloud of foam. The intruder did not seem to react instantly, perhaps waiting for the haze to dissolve. But Sarah again squeezed the extinguisher lever. And waited for the intruder to show himself, to let himself be heard.

"Where are you?" he whimpered.

It all ended very quickly. Through the vanishing vapors, Sarah saw a black-gloved hand holding a gun. She threw the fire extinguisher directly at the man's head. But he ducked.

Sarah heard two shots. She let out a muffled cry. *Is this what being shot twice feels like? No pain?* The man's body hit the floor facedown with a heavy thud. She couldn't believe it, and had to refocus. It was a miracle. Not until moments later, however, could Sarah begin to understand what had just happened. She saw two small holes in the windowpane. The shots had come from outside. Somebody had been her guardian angel. But who?

"Dad, you've got a lot of explaining to do."

It was time to flee.

11

Times Square was one of the nerve centers of the first world, a lot like Trafalgar Square, the Champs-Élysées, Alexanderplatz, Saint Peter's Square, and a few others. In these places nighttime and daytime activity didn't differ much. Particularly Times Square in Manhattan, which was as mythical a place for Americans as for many Europeans. The neon lights and the frenzied traffic enthralled visitors, fascinated by the excitement of the labyrinth of streets, avenues, tunnels, and bridges.

Thousands of people traversed the neighborhood surrounding Times Square. One man was walking at a brisk, steady pace, his overcoat open to the wind like a cape. Where he'd come from didn't matter, only where he was going, following a plan devised by a mind brighter than his own. He reached the TKTS booth on Forty-seventh Street between Broadway and Seventh Avenue, got in line, and tuned in to the voices around him.

"One ticket for *Chitty Chitty Bang Bang,* please, the seven o'clock show," an elderly man, two people ahead of him, asked at the window.

Chitty Chitty Bang Bang. The man in the overcoat smiled. How fitting, he thought. When he reached the ticket booth, he bought a ticket for the same play, same performance.

He wandered around, looking at the store windows for a while, then stopped for an espresso at Charley's Co. One might have thought he was killing time until the theater opened, but on closer examination his behavior wasn't just whimsical. He was following the other guy, the old man who was buying his ticket at the TKTS booth a few minutes before.

They both headed south on Seventh Avenue, the man in the overcoat following, always maintaining a prudent distance from the old man. He knew how to do these things, not distracted by the people or the noise. Nothing seemed to interfere with his pursuit. In fact, he didn't need to follow the old man to know his destination, he knew very well.

His cell phone vibrated.

"Yes," he answered firmly, as he crossed Seventh Avenue at Forty-second Street. "Did everything go all right?" he asked, gesticulating impatiently. "What? Then make sure all the traces are cleaned up."

He turned right on Forty-third, visibly annoyed.

"If things don't go according to plan, I don't need to tell you what will happen to you. I want that woman erased today. I'll expect your call confirming it."

Right after hanging up abruptly, he called another number, still keeping an eye on the man he was following. The old man, seemingly over seventy, walked spiritedly, almost like an excited teenager on his way to a promising party, and evidently unaware of being followed.

"Hello. We're headed for the theater. Everything's fine here." He paused a few seconds, closed his eyes, and caught his breath. "But sir, things aren't going well in London. The target escaped and we took a loss. . . . Yes, I know . . . that's minor . . . I've already ordered the site cleaned up." He listened attentively to the instructions. "I don't know if they'll be able to finish the job. It could be better, Master, to activate the reserves."

He stopped at the Hilton, formerly Ford Theater for the Performing Arts. In fact, the Hilton Theater, with entrances on both Forty-second and Forty-third, was until 1997 not one theater but two, the Lyric and the Apollo. After the renovation it became one of the largest theaters on Broadway, while keeping all its centennial charm.

The man in the overcoat, cell phone still pressed to his ear, entered the lobby and handed his ticket to the usher, who indicated the location of his seat.

"You can check your overcoat, if you wish, sir."

"Thanks very much. Can you tell me where the bathroom is?"

"Of course. First door on your left, sir."

The man kept talking on his cell phone on his way to the restroom.

"Please confirm, once the reserve has neutralized the London target. . . . Yes, I know I can consider it done, but . . . of course, sir. . . . For now, things will continue as they are. . . . Fine. Good-bye."

He took the stairs to the mezzanine. It seemed totally full, but after a careful search, he located an empty seat in the first row right. Excellent spot. Not that he was interested in watching this children's musical, though it was based on a book by Ian Fleming, creator of the famous James Bond. He smiled at the irony. Secret agents, undercover plots—just like his own—Ian Fleming, James Bond . . . though in *Chitty Chitty Bang Bang,* there was nothing secret or undercover. It was two and a half hours of pure musical comedy. But this man hadn't come looking for entertainment. He had a job to do.

The lights came down slowly. The musicians began the overture. The man pulled a small pair of binoculars out of his pocket to see what was going on in the boxes and orchestra seats. It seemed innocuous, but this accessory was actually equipped for night vision, allowing him to scan the rows of seats in the dark. In less than a minute he focused on the person he was looking for. The old man was sitting halfway back, near the center.

Leaning back comfortably in his seat, he smiled. With his thumb and index finger, he pointed at the old man down below.

"Bang, bang."

12

The first thing is to get away from Belgrave Road, Sarah thought. And with that in mind she turned left, without thinking, toward Charlwood Street. She had the feeling she wasn't completely alone. Feverishly, she looked everywhere—corners, doors, windows—searching for someone who might be spying on her. It felt as if everybody, with just their look, was telling her, "You're doomed" or "They're right behind you."

She tried to regain her composure. If someone's following me, she thought, he's not going to let himself be seen, and I won't be able to find him.

She took another left, onto Tachbrook Street, looking for a public phone to call her father. Better in a crowded place. And the only place she could think of was Victoria Station. Taking Belgrave Road would have been shorter, but she opted for a roundabout route, choosing less crowded streets. Again she turned left on Warwick Way, followed by a right on Wilton Road. She darted across Neathouse Place and then Bridge Place, finally ending up at Victoria Station.

As soon as she got there she felt relieved. Despite the fact that the big clock on the main facade showed it was a bit before midnight, there was constant movement, hundreds of people wandering through the enormous station, with its many stores announcing countless sales. Going by a McDonald's, she realized she hadn't eaten for hours. A double hamburger and a Coke were just right.

Looking for a phone, Sarah mixed in with the people bumping against one another trying to read the enormous panel of train schedules. The PA system warned people to mind their luggage.

There was a special ticket booth for the Orient Express, with stops in Istanbul, Bucharest, Budapest, Prague, Vienna, Innsbruck, Venice, Verona, Florence, Rome, Paris. Cities full of mystery, intrigue, secret plots. But for Sarah Monteiro there were more important mysteries.

"Sarah, is that you?" her father inquired, answering her call.

"Yes. But the morgue was about to call to inform you that your daughter was shot dead," she answered, still enraged. "What the heck is going on? A guy breaks into my home, points his gun at me, and the only reason he doesn't kill me is because somebody else kills him first."

"Is that what happened?" Her father's voice sounded even stranger than the first time she had spoken with him.

"That's exactly what happened. Who are these people?"

"My child, I can't tell you anything over the phone. Someone's surely listening to this conversation and I can't go into anything that could compromise me—or you. You can't imagine how bad I feel about getting you into this mess."

"What the fuck are you talking about? What am I supposed do? I can't go home. Can't say anything, can't do anything. Shit. Son of a bitch!"

"Calm down, child."

"I'm not referring to you, Dad. I mean the people listening to us talk. I'm sorry." Taking a deep breath, she added, "Bastards! But who are we talking about? The MI6? The CIA, the FBI? The Mossad? Who?"

"All I can say is all those people are angels compared to who's behind this."

"Seriously?

"Yes, unfortunately."

"What have you gotten into, Dad?"

"Nothing you need to know right now. Past mistakes that I'm regretting every day of my life, you can be sure."

"So what do I do?"

"First, don't call me again, no matter what. And don't try to get me at home. No one's going to be there. In the meantime, don't worry about your mother and me, we'll be fine."

"Is Mother in this, too?"

"No. She didn't know anything. It's taken her by surprise, and it's been tough to calm her down. She's just as scared as you are. Please, you've got to trust me. It's crucial. Now I need to solve this. . . . Later we'll see, when all the dust has settled."

"Only if it's settled down for me, too."

After Sarah's sarcastic comment, there was silence.

"It will settle for you, too. A lot of people's lives depend on it."

"Good to know! I feel better already."

"What counts is to think about the here and now," her father said. "Do you hear me, Sarah?"

"Yes," she answered, her eyes closed.

"Someone's waiting to help you," her father added. "You can completely trust him. He's waiting for you at King William IV Square."

"Oh, that's better. How can I recognize him?"

"Don't worry about that. He'll recognize you. And another thing—"

"What's his name?"

"Rafael. His name is Rafael. One other thing, don't use your name anywhere, and never say where you are. . . . And pay cash for everything."

"Why?"

"Don't use your credit card."

"Oh, I just paid at McDonald's with the same card I'm using for this call," she responded, her eyes gleaming with anxiety. She glanced around, not feeling safe at all.

"Hang up immediately and go where I've told you."

"Didn't you say your phone could be tapped? How can you now be sending me to such a specific place?"

"I'm sure you've never heard of King William IV Square." With that, he hung up.

13

Staughton was an analyst of confidential data. That meant he was a professional who collected important private data for an operation and then transferred it to the agents in charge of the case. In fact, his position was known as a "real-time analyst," meaning the data he collected referred only to the immediate present. For example, phone calls, bank transactions, or if necessary even satellite images. The degree of confidentiality varied according to the particular operation, and it was divided into four levels. Level four, the most confidential, was available only to the president of the United States. Staughton worked for the Central Intelligence Agency, the CIA.

There were many sophisticated devices in Staughton's room. It looked more like an airplane cockpit than an office. He pressed a few buttons and then, with the ease of an expert, waited for the results.

What mess am I in now? he thought. Oh, come on, give me a sign, one simple sign.

"So, nothing yet? Nothing?" a man thundered, barging into the room.

A novice would have been petrified by the sudden appearance of the man in charge of the CIA London office. But Staughton was unruffled. Such outbursts were not unusual for Geoffrey Barnes, a man of great bulk who managed to walk incredibly lightly and noiselessly. His question came in a booming voice, and then he leaned expectantly over Staughton.

"Zero, zilch, *nada*."

"It's a matter of time. Let's hope it'll be soon."

Geoffrey Barnes headed back to his office, on the same floor. A glass-and-metal panel separated him from the rest of the staff, a symbol clearly indicating who commanded and who obeyed. There were people above Geoffrey Barnes, namely the CIA director at Langley, and the president who, as a rule knew very little about most of the agency's doings. But the president had no idea whatsoever about the present operation, and if it were up to Geoffrey Barnes, he never would.

A phone rang on a mahogany desk that seemed totally out of place in Staughton's futuristic setting. Of the three phones on the desk, the most important was the red one. It had a direct connection to the Oval Office in the White House, and with the president's plane, *Air Force One.* The second most important was the one ringing now. Geoffrey was upset.

"Shit," he said while it kept ringing. "I'm coming. The boss is out. I'll go look for him."

The worst thing that could happen to any intelligence service was not to have timely information when someone asked for it. How else to justify the agency's existence, if not to supply needed information? As his predecessor used to say, "When the phone rings, you better have what they want to hear. If not, you'd better have a fertile imagination."

But in this case, his imagination would be of no help. Eliminating a target couldn't be invented. It happened or it didn't. Whether it was about to happen wouldn't be of any help.

"I'm coming," he yelled at the phone, and lifted the receiver. His greeting was in Italian because the man calling him spoke the language of Dante, in addition to being fluent in a handful of dead languages that for Barnes didn't count.

A tense conversation ensued, in which Barnes attributed his lack of information to various external elements that caused the loss of one of his agents right when his operation was nearly completed. This had resulted in temporary confusion, allowing the target to escape. Barnes was fuming.

"We've got some movement!" Staughton announced at the door.

"Just in time," the big bulk of a man thought. "What is it?"

"A credit card in Victoria Station, used at McDonald's."

"Did you tell the staff?"

"They're on location right now."

"Good," he said, and relayed this to the person at the other end. After a while, he hung up, visibly upset. "Staughton, tell our people to stay in the background. Their people are going to act."

"What do you mean?" Staughton asked, failing to see the implications. "Are you sure, sir?"

Barnes glowered at him, in a more than eloquent reply.

"I'll give the order right away, sir."

"And by the way, Staughton, tell them to bring me a hamburger."

14

The old man hung up, annoyed. "How stupid. Damned Americans!" he said to himself, getting up from the sofa with the help of his cane, and hobbling over to the small bar cabinet. He dropped two ice cubes in a glass and poured himself a drink. The death of an American agent about to complete his job brought to mind all sorts of questions, besides problems of logistics. Who knew about the previously and secretly planned proceedings? How did he know to arrive in time to save the victim? An unexpected participant had joined the game. From this, a second scenario arose. Who's trying to interfere with our business? How did they get advance information on our plans? The two questions might have a single answer: an infiltrator. A traitor belonging to the CIA, the agency now responsible for the business of old Albion.

No doubt the best way to resolve this situation was to call in the Guard, his organization's group with a well-earned reputation for never failing. Given the present circumstances, he should activate this select cadre and have Geoffrey Barnes stand by, pending new instructions from general headquarters, his Italian villa.

The old man had always favored direct action and quick decisions, but lately he preferred to consult with his assistant, though informally, at critical moments. All his life he'd chosen his collaborators well, but this assistant was a real find. The man was diligent, competent, persistent, and willing to be at his service 24/7, year-round. The old man, having no children and no relatives, felt reassured to know he could count on this man, down the line. When his own time came to abandon this world, there would be someone to shepherd his organization. His right-hand man was his natural successor, sharing his vision of the organization's future.

His assistant would be coming to the villa within an hour by private plane. Although both of them had access to satellite phones, even in flight, there was no need to consult him about the present case. There was no doubt the assistant would agree with his decision. Besides, a call now from the old man might be interpreted as a sign of weakness, like begging for advice. If they were both already at the villa, things would be different. He would start a casual conversation and easily find out what his assistant thought about the situation.

Old age is a curse, he mused. For many years, he alone had made all the important decisions, but now the simple objective of doing away with one woman disconcerted him. Under normal conditions, he had to admit, she would have been dead by now. But a mole presented a serious problem. The Guard would resolve this problem in less than an hour. As for the infiltrator, he would take this up with Barnes once the target was neutralized.

His glass was now practically empty. He put it on the table and picked up the phone. It was time to start moving the pieces.

"Jack, the Yankees dropped the ball. We'll have to solve the situation ourselves." He brought the whiskey to wet his lips. "Rub her out!"

15

There were three different underground lines at Victoria Station. The District and Circle lines followed the same route from Tower Hill— the zone of the famous Tower of London, the Tower Bridge, and the financial center—up to Edgware Road, where they separated toward different destinations; and the Victoria Line, which joined Brixton and Walthamstow Central. For someone wanting to flee, the District and Victoria lines would be best, particularly because the Circle Line, as its name implied, was continuously returning to its original point of departure.

But Sarah Monteiro wasn't thinking clearly. The best escape was the first one she could find, even if its destination was the gates of hell. Anything was better than getting caught by an unknown organization apparently worse than the worst of those she knew about.

Sarah bought a one-day travel card at a self-serve machine. This would allow her to move freely the whole day within the 274 stations in the 250 miles of underground trains. Whoever wanted to follow her would have a tough job and need a lot of luck.

Even so, she couldn't relax. Ultimately they would be able to determine her point of departure. And in due time, they could also pinpoint her destination. Her father had scared her with his description of the organization dogging her. Was he exaggerating? How long would it take them to find and capture her?

While trying to figure out what kind of dangerous documents had fallen into her hands, she decided to run the risk. There was no other choice.

Sarah slid her transit card into the turnstile, which opened, then closed behind her. There was no turning back. She had selected the District and Circle lines, and fate would decide the rest. She went down the stairs to the tracks. In two minutes there would be a Circle Line train to Tower Hill. And another, to Upminster, would reach the station in three; that one was on the District Line, one of the city's longest and oldest, open to the public since the nineteenth century.

At that point, the trains on either side arrived and departed parallel to each other, which allowed passengers on both sides to see the other platform across the tracks. A train going to Wimbledon had just arrived on the other side.

There were only a handful of people on Sarah's platform. An older man was reading the *Times,* and two young women chatted excitedly, constantly interrupting each other.

The train on the opposite track pulled out. Sarah noticed the red lights as the train entered the dark tunnel on its way to Wimbledon. Looking at the train schedule, she saw that in one minute a train that could save her would open its doors. A cold gust of wind, out of nowhere, chilled her bones, making her situation even more uncomfortable. She was tired and sleepy, but her intense dread overwhelmed everything else. Being used to eight hours' sleep every day, she would have to pay for this when it was all over. Lack of sleep made her cranky, as her colleagues in the pressroom knew well. But escaping was her only thought now. She was unaware that her pursuers had at their disposal technology so sophisticated that any of her movements, such as paying for a hamburger, making a call from public phone, or buying a transit card would immediately be identified, sounding an alarm.

A rumble in the back of Sarah's mind brought her back to reality. At the far end of the tunnel where she had seen the lights turn red for a departing train, she now saw yellow lights, growing bigger and bigger. Her train was coming.

The doors opened to let passengers out. Only a few people were in the car. One young kid was sprawled out, sleeping.

Two men had just arrived on the platform on the other side, apparently executives. Something about their attitude, however, made them seem suspicious. They were nervously looking all around. Watching them, Sarah, motionless in her car, sank down in her seat, trying to disappear from view. The executives were consulting a piece of paper, perhaps the photo of someone they were after. By sheer luck, they were on the other side and didn't see her.

"Shut the damned doors and let's go," Sarah mumbled, mentally addressing the conductor.

Repeated chimes warned that the doors were about to close. A few seconds later, the train was picking up speed toward Tower Hill. Sarah sighed, relieved, and once her long train was inside the tunnel, she straightened up in her seat. She had never imagined that she could enjoy the monotonous clatter of a train so much.

Through the glass doors, Sarah observed the people in other cars. In the one just behind her, she saw two men and a woman. A teenager was watching a movie on a portable DVD player.

And then she saw him. He was wearing a dark suit, similar to the other two in Victoria Station. He was standing, comparing Sarah's face with a photo he was holding. It was obvious he had just recognized her.

Putting his index finger to his lips, he motioned her to be silent, and started moving toward her. Sarah also moved, but in the opposite direction, running toward the front of the train. She hastily opened the door between the two cars. The other passengers noticed her opening and closing doors, but took no interest.

The train started to brake as it entered Saint James's Park Station. The man was looking for anything that could tell him the whereabouts of the woman he was after, who had disappeared into the first cars.

For Sarah it all took an instant, her fright provoking a tremendous burst of adrenaline. Her strength seemed to multiply, following her instinct to escape. She curled up on the floor, wedged against seats that faced the door, waiting. In a second, she hurtled out of the car onto the platform and started running as fast as she could.

The man resembling the two other executive types quickly jumped out of the train and saw Sarah getting away, three cars ahead. Trying to run after her wasn't worth the effort. So he pulled out his gun and aimed with professional skill. A smile of recognition crossed his face: what an easy target.

The man pulled the trigger. At the same moment, Sarah jumped into one of the cars, and the bullet was swallowed by the darkness of the tunnel.

He had to get back on the train immediately, but the doors had already closed and the train was in motion. When the train finally left the Saint James's Park Station, the man grimaced. Seconds later he mumbled something, his hand near his mouth.

Still in shock and with tears streaming down her cheeks, Sarah didn't dare look at the other passengers. The train stopped again. As soon as the doors opened, she bolted out.

16

B ehind the green wooden doors and the beautiful carvings on the stone
facade, there were secrets, and great amounts of devotion.

The Convent of Santa Teresa for Carmelite nuns in Coimbra, Portugal,
the work of Frei Pedro da Encarnação, opened its doors long ago, on
June 23, 1744, perhaps under the same intense heat as on that July day in
1977, when two men were patiently waiting for the doors to open once more.

When the hinges of the heavy door turned, a Teresinha, a Carmelite nun,
appeared and welcomed them warmly. It was such a pleasure to welcome
these two important men, finally paying the convent a visit. Her white habit
and the dark wimple hiding her hair gave the nun the benevolent, maternal
air befitting the saintly women devoted to the service of God since a most
tender age.

"Your Eminence, what a joy to have you here!"

"Thank you very much, Sister. The pleasure is mine. This is my assistant,
Father Diego Lorenzi."

"How are you, Father Lorenzi? Please come in. Follow me."

The Venetian patriarch had come to say Mass in the church of the

Carmelite nuns. It was a standing commitment of his, which he had already performed several times.

The kind abbess welcomed the two visitors.

"Your Eminence, you can't imagine what an honor it is to have you here," the old nun said, walking slowly and with difficulty. "Sister Lucía is waiting for you. She has expressed her desire to talk with you and to ask for your blessing after Mass."

"Of course. It will be my honor, Sister."

After Mass, Albino Luciani and Diego Lorenzi walked through the convent corridors, guided by the same nun who had welcomed them. They crossed through the enormous iron grate that reached to the ceiling and enclosed the cloister. In that jail-like atmosphere, the Carmelites received visits from relatives and friends. The prelate from Venice and his assistant, however, weren't going to meet Sister Lucía through those annoying bars, which made obscured faces and caused more bitterness and pity than religious piety in a meeting between Christians. Don Albino Luciani and Father Lorenzi entered the Carmelite cloister under the arches that helped mitigate the summer heat outside.

"Very baroque, Don Albino," Lorenzi said, trying to relieve the heavy silence of those corridors.

"Yes," Luciani agreed, smiling. "No architects were involved in building this place. It was the work of a discalced Carmelite priest, more than two centuries ago."

"That's right," the sister confirmed. "We are so pleased to have Your Eminence honoring us with your erudition about our modest convent."

"Please don't exaggerate, Sister."

"Oh, Your Eminence. Your great humility is well known even here," the sister protested, her hands raised in a sincere gesture.

"Please don't make me blush, Sister."

"Nothing could be further from my intention, Your Eminence. But it's true that this convent is more than two hundred years old. Unfortunately, it hasn't had an easy existence, and only recently has had active, future projects."

"The republic," Don Albino reminded his assistant, by way of explanation.

"How was that?" Lorenzi asked, feeling he had missed something.

"His Eminence is referring to the establishment of the Portuguese republic in 1910. That same year, on October 10, the convent was violently invaded and all the nuns were thrown out."

"Incredible!" Lorenzi exclaimed.

"Actually, Father Lorenzi, the republicans were only continuing a brutal tradition," the sister added. "The dissolution of religious orders had already started during the monarchy with the rise of liberal politics. This convent was kept open under a special license granted by Queen Mary II, valid until 1910. I didn't really mean to get into a political discussion, Father Lorenzi, but this is my understanding.

"In the face of those calamities, the nuns sought shelter with relatives and friends, later joining Carmelite convents in Spain. But by 1933 conditions in Portugal were more peaceful; certainly there was less animosity toward religious orders. Three of the nuns who had been thrown out came back to Coimbra and tried to restore the Carmelite community. Since the convent was occupied at that time by the military, the sisters had to rent a house and faced many hardships. In 1940 it was rumored that the military was going to abandon the convent, and the sisters did all they could to get it back. That finally happened in 1947. Of those who'd been expelled, only two were nuns still alive. One of them was our reverend mother, who in due course received the keys to the convent."

"It's a very moving story, Sister," Luciani remarked.

"I'm sure Your Eminence already knew it."

"I did, but this is the first time I've heard it directly from a Carmelite nun from Coimbra. And I appreciate it very much, Sister."

Beyond the cloister, the three of them continued their tour through the interior corridors of the convent, behind the high walls that helped preserve a sort of somber freshness against the implacable sun outside.

They reached a smallish room with a pious, austere décor—just a simple oak table and a bookcase with a few books, some old chairs, and several pieces of furniture that had seen better days, probably going back to the founding of the community. They stopped to look at the large, stark crucifix that dominated one of the walls—just two crossed pieces of rough wood, with no figure of Jesus—infusing the room with a holy air.

"Sister Lucía will be joining you soon. Would you like something to drink? Perhaps a cup of coffee or a soda?"

"I'd like some coffee, Sister, if you'd be so kind," Don Albino said.

Father Lorenzi also accepted, and they both remained seated, waiting for Sister Lucía.

"We'll finally meet Sister Lucía, Don Albino! I've heard so much about her," Lorenzi said, with sincere admiration.

"So have I, Lorenzi. Fátima means a lot to the Church. It's very hard to know exactly how everything happened and why. But her visions were connected with decisive events. And she is still keeping a secret."

"The third secret."

"Yes, the third secret."

"Could it be the most important?"

"The others were very important. There was only one secret, but Sister Lucía divided it into three parts, and then revealed only the first two. That unknown part is what's being called 'the third secret.'"

"The first two parts of the secret of Fátima referred to the First World War—a hellish vision—and to Russia's adoption of Mary's Sacred Heart. Sister Lucía never wanted to reveal the third secret to anyone."

People were naturally curious. Who wouldn't want to know the third secret of Fátima? It was rumored that it had to do with terrible cataclysms, perhaps even the Apocalypse, the end of the world, the extinction of the human race. People fond of secrets and conspiracy theories rejoiced. The Church had to be prudent, and tried to avoid promoting unnecessary scandals.

"Sister Lucía has lived thirty years in this convent," the Venetian patriarch observed.

"A whole life devoted to Jesus Christ."

"Like ours. Like many. It's a despicable sign of vanity to think we're more deserving for devoting our lives to the Lord. No matter how much evil comes to us, all that counts is whatever good we can do for others."

"Wise words, Your Eminence," they heard a feminine voice say.

Sister Lucía, unannounced, dressed in the habit of *teresinha* nuns, had glided into the room without a sound.

"How are you, dear Sister?"

"Fine, Your Eminence, by the Lord's grace."

Lucía knelt to kiss the cardinal's hand.

"Please, Sister, we are the ones who should kneel before you," Don Albino said in perfect Portuguese, Sister Lucía's mother tongue. He could have chosen Italian, English, French, or Spanish, since they both spoke all of these.

Sister Lucía seemed vigorous for her age. She had enjoyed better health than the other two visionary young people, for whom Our Lady foretold short lives. Francisco and Jacinta, while still children, succumbed to a flu epidemic in 1919 and 1920, respectively. Only Lucía had survived.

It was long before that that the three little shepherds, as the press called them, had taken their flock as usual to a remote place known as Cova da Iria, in Portugal. The Basilica of Fátima and the Chapel of Hope and Aspirations stood in that same spot now. There, on May 13, 1917, the three children saw Our Lady, Christ's mother. Only one of them, Lucía, got to talk with Our Lady. Jacinta was able to see and hear her, but Francisco only saw her. The Virgin asked them to return there on the thirteenth day of every month, and to pray very often. And so they did. These events caused a great commotion in the region, and a great controversy arose around the three kids who claimed to have seen the Virgin Mary. That August there was another apparition nearby, on a different day, the nineteenth, because on the thirteenth the little shepherds were taken into custody by the skeptical mayor of Vila Nova in Ourém. In September, Our Lady promised a miracle that could prove to all—including the incredulous Church—that her apparition to the three little shepherds was real. A month later, on October 13, the last wonder occurred. The Virgin appeared as Our Lady of the Rosary and asked that a chapel be built there in her honor. But most important, the Virgin announced the end of the war—the First World War, of course—which was still raging at the time. The wonderful miracle promised to the thousands of devout believers who attended the weekly meetings afforded an incredible view of the sun gyrating and oscillating.

Those present said the sun seemed like a fiery star rushing down toward Earth. The 70,000 men and women gathered knelt before such a prodigy, driving away all doubts from their souls. That event seemed like a biblical passage, and became known as "the Miracle of the Sun." Christians saw it as irrefutable proof of the power of the Divinity.

In fact, the war ended a few months later, exactly as Lucía, the visionary of Fátima, had predicted.

As the miracles occurring in Fátima gained fame around the world, Lucía de Jesús became more and more cautious. After joining the school of the Sisters of Santa Dorotea in Oporto in 1921, she traveled to Spain, where she spent a few years to allow her religious vocation to ripen. In 1946 she joined the Carmelite religious order, finally becoming a nun in 1949 in the Convent of Santa Teresa.

The meeting of Sister Lucía with Albino Luciani was supposed to be just a few minutes of polite conversation, but it lasted about two hours. At no time was there any mention of the apparitions, the visions, or "the third secret." In Father Lorenzi's serene presence, Don Albino and Sister Lucía chose to talk about a variety of inconsequential matters. Perhaps it made little sense to bring up the serious religious, political, or national and international issues in which Sister Lucía had become involved. Facing Don Albino's benevolent smile, the nun lamented the prevalent lack of faith among the younger generations, as well as the older people's seeming lack of concern about it. Don Albino smiled beatifically, admitting that the world was going through complex times, but not blaming the young for their detachment and indifference.

While the two priests sipped their coffee during this enjoyable conversation, in such a peaceful room, time ceased to matter. Suddenly there was a silence, and a grave voice almost made the walls shake. A supernatural, luminous glow seemed to spread over everything for a fraction of a second, while the voice spoke.

"And as for you, my dear patriarch, Christ's crown and Christ's days."

Father Lorenzi, terrified and visibly shaken, looked at Sister Lucía. He could have sworn those words had come from her lips.

Don Albino, calm and collected, looked at his secretary and then back at the old servant of God. Right away he sensed that the cryptic message was directed at him, and yet he didn't seem disturbed at all. Quite to the contrary, he closed his eyes slowly, trying to understand what had happened.

"Don Albino," Father Lorenzi stammered, trying to catch his breath.

But the patriarch raised his hand, commanding silence, in order not to interrupt the visionary's trance. Don Albino wasn't sure what was going on. Was this a premonition? A warning? Or was it mere babble uttered by someone hypersensitive to strange energies?

At that moment, someone looking at the nun might have thought she had fallen asleep in her chair, with one hand resting on the table. But Sister Lucía was not asleep, and they knew it. It was Sister Lucía, but it was also the other world speaking through her. Lorenzi had never seen anyone in a trance, but Don Albino, apparently more acquainted with such phenomena, was unruffled. He kept his hand raised, still demanding silence.

"There is a secret not yet revealed concerning your death," the strange voice coming out of Lucía's lips continued, in a tone totally different from hers. "God will forgive, the Lord will forgive."

Lorenzi was aghast, caught between terror and religious fervor.

A moment later, Sister Lucía opened her eyes and recovered the sweet expression she had when she first appeared in the room.

"Would you like a bit more coffee, Your Eminence?" she asked.

"Yes, Sister, please," Luciani responded, looking directly into her eyes, without the least indication of any reaction to what he had just heard. "You already know how much I enjoy coffee."

As they walked toward the car that was to take them back to Fátima, Lorenzi was watching the patriarch, half astonished, half perplexed. Finally, gathering all his courage, he couldn't hold back his curiosity any longer.

"Don Albino, I don't know what to make of all this."

The Venetian patriarch stopped, and placed a hand on Lorenzi's shoulder.

For a few seconds he looked at him with the usual calmness he had come to expect since he became his assistant, almost a year before.

"Relax, Father Lorenzi. I'd say that Sister Lucía is a very interesting person. Wouldn't you agree?" The prelate continued walking, discreetly tucking in his pocket a little folded paper Sister Lucía had given him.

And they never mentioned the incident again.

17

London's darkness seemed ponderous, almost impenetrable to Sarah when she stepped out on Bridge Street, opposite Big Ben. The world's most famous clock told her it was almost midnight. Turning left, the young woman started running toward Westminster Bridge. There were a few, but not many, people on the bridge. This reassured her, a little, as did the knowledge that London was the city with the most video surveillance per square meter in the world. Sarah resisted the temptation to take a taxi. She needed to take care of something else first. Looming in the distance was the London Eye, the city's giant Ferris wheel.

Come on, think.

Across the bridge, and continuing on Westminster Bridge Road, Sarah turned left on Belvedere Road. Determined to enter the first phone booth she came across, she walked and walked, not letting up. In a business area near the Waterloo Bridge, she finally found one.

Picking up the handset, Sarah knew not to use her credit card this time.

"Good evening. I'd like to place a collect call. . . . My name? . . . Uh, Greg Saunders," she said, sounding more like a question than an answer. But the operator completely ignored the feminine voice giving a man's name, and asked her to wait.

Moments later Sarah could hear a phone ringing, and voices at the other end.

"Greg?"

"Natalie, it's not Greg. It's me, Sarah."

"Sarah?" was the quite surprised response. Natalie, in all the years as her boss, had never heard coolheaded Sarah sounding so distressed.

"Yes, it's me. I need to ask you a huge favor."

Sarah explained to her boss and friend, hastily but clearly, and with the succinctness to be expected from a news professional, everything that had happened to her since she'd come back to London.

"You need to go to the police," Natalie stammered, barely able to fully absorb the story she had just heard.

"No, Natalie, I can't. I don't trust anybody out here. I just need a favor. You don't even have to leave your house. I'm begging you, Natalie. I don't know who else to ask."

An uncomfortable silence ensued while Natalie thought this over. Yes, they had always helped each other and, except for the occasional early-morning flare-ups on her part, Sarah was her friend. And one of the best reporters in the world-renowned news service that she headed.

"Of course. What do you need?"

"Thanks, Natalie."

"Don't thank me. Tell me what you want before I change my mind."

"I just need you to tell me where King William IV Square is."

"That's all?"

"Yes."

"I'll get it for you right now. You want me to call you back, or can you stay on the line?"

"Whichever you prefer. You're paying for the call."

"Right. Then don't hang up." Sarah heard a chair being dragged. Natalie was now at the keyboard of her computer. "King William IV Square," she repeated, more to the keyboard than to Sarah.

"Yes."

"Wait a second." One . . . two . . . three . . . four . . . five seconds went by. "Do you really not know why these people are after you?"

"I don't have the slightest idea."

"Let's see, be ready for this." Her tone had changed from reporter's curiosity to information operator's signal. "Here it is. I mean, isn't. Under the name King William IV, there are only the gardens in the Crystal Palace district. Ahhh, wait a minute, there's also a street with that name. It's between the Strand and Charing Cross Road—that must be it. There's no King William IV Square."

"Are you sure?"

"Yes. You must be mistaken."

"No, absolutely not. The person who gave me the name did say it would be impossible for me to have heard of that plaza before. But I just assumed it was because it was someplace really out of the way, not because it didn't exist."

"But it doesn't exist. Let me do one more search."

"It has to be there."

"Well, if you want, you can ask a cop."

"No time for jokes, Natalie."

"Let me see. William IV. Born in 1765. King of the United Kingdom and of Hanover between 1830 and 1837. Son of George III, succeeded his older brother, George IV. Was the penultimate king of the House of Hanover. As king he was called 'the Navigator.' He reformed the electoral system, abolished slavery and child labor in the Empire. I'm starting to like this man."

"Natalie, I don't need a history lesson. Is there anything else?"

"No. Queen Victoria succeeded him. Let me look in Google." There was a soft clicking on the keyboard. "Wait a minute—"

"Did you find something?"

"Interesting."

"What?"

"King William IV Square. Here it is."

"Come on, tell me!" Sarah almost shouted, unable to contain her impatience.

"That was the original name of Trafalgar Square."

"Seriously?"

"Yes, without a doubt. Trafalgar Square was King William IV Square."

"Thanks a million, Natalie. You may have just saved my life."

"Or not."

"I'll be seeing you."

"Oh, Sarah—" Natalie said just in time.

"Yes?"

"If you get any big scoops, don't forget me."

18

Trafalgar Square was the busiest square in all of London. A place for meeting friends, commemoration, celebration, and national exaltation.

The immense size of the place, the two side fountains, and the enormous Corinthian granite column, 185 feet tall, crowned by the statue of Admiral Nelson, the hero killed in the battle, standing high above Westminster Palace, conferred on Trafalgar Square an enchantment that touched Londoners and tourists alike. Four huge bronze lions—reportedly made from the cannons of the ill-fated French fleet—flanked the column, creating an impression of absolute power. Four pedestals crowned with statues adorned the sides of the square. To the northeast, that of King George IV. To the southeast, the one of General Sir Charles James Napier, conqueror of Pakistan. To the southwest, General Havelock. The fourth pedestal accommodated temporary sculptures because there was never a consensus about whom it should honor. The original intent was for it to hold the statue of King William IV, but lack of public funds thwarted that, and as a result, the king who was supposed to be celebrated was instead completely excluded from the plans that he himself had set in motion.

At this hour of the night there were a lot of people in the square, particu-
larly groups of tourists and a few couples. Nobody looked suspicious to
Sarah, but everyone could be a suspect. Cars, limousines, taxis, ambulances,
buses, mopeds, and bicycles were in ceaseless movement around the square.
In the background rose the Admiralty Arch, built in honor of Queen Victoria, which marked the entrance to the grand avenue leading to Buckingham
Palace. To the east were the Saint Martin-in-the-Fields Church, the South
Africa House, and the Strand, which linked Westminster with the city. But
the street of particular interest here was Charing Cross Road in the Soho
district, the most bohemian section of the city of London, where a taxi had
just stopped at the corner of Great Newport Street.

Sarah Monteiro stepped out of the taxi. After her phone call, she had
gone to Waterloo Station and again put herself in jeopardy by withdrawing
300 pounds at an ATM in order to pay cash for whatever might be needed.
Having opted not to put herself directly in the lion's mouth, she asked the
taxi driver to drop her off half a mile from her final destination.

Sarah went around the square to the south, downhill toward Trafalgar
through Canada House, cautiously slowing her pace, and occasionally
sneaking a glance here and there along the way. She crossed in front of the
National Gallery and went a few steps farther, until she reached the central
stairway leading to the square. For a few moments she stood watching the
square, the fountains, Nelson's Column, and especially the people. Most
important were the people, since they were the danger. She surveyed the fa-
cades of the distant buildings in search of sinister eyes. A potential murderer could be anywhere, his gun silently ready to erase her life.

At last Sarah spotted him. A sweeper, one of many around the place with
their green-and-yellow fluorescent outfits. He reminded her of the man
she'd seen hours before from the window of her flat. There was probably
nothing to be afraid of, she thought. This guy wasn't going to put his hand
over his mouth to talk, like the agents in the underground, but he did have
a live walkie-talkie like everybody. A sweeper didn't need a radio transmitter to do his job. No, either that man was the Rafael her father had mentioned, or else . . . best not to think about it.

Sarah moved on, trying to blend in with the passersby. Then, sharply turning her head, she tried to locate her sweeper. She also observed the rest of the sweeping crew. Those in sight made no attempt to conceal their presence and, to be honest, showed no interest in Sarah Monteiro or anyone else. Each one indifferently confined himself to cleaning his assigned area.

Which one of those guys could be Rafael? she thought.

At any moment, Sarah could be dragged into a passing car. Or one good shot could end her erratic flight. So many movies, so many scenes, so many theories ran through her mind, she was overcome with vertigo, feeling faint. People, people, and more people everywhere.

"Sarah Monteiro?" She heard someone call her. It was the sweeper. "Come with me. Trust me."

Without waiting for her consent, the man took her by the arm, pushing her past people, heading out of the square.

"Where are we going?" There was no answer. "Are you Rafael?" Sarah insisted, still recovering from the daze that was overwhelming her.

There was a sharp buzzing coming from a pocket in the man's fluorescent uniform, and Sarah saw him pull out a radio transmitter and start talking in Italian.

"*La porto alla centrale . . . Sì, l'obiettivo è con me. . . . Negativo. Non posso rifinirla qui. . . . Benissimo.*"

Not really understanding what the man said, Sarah noted that the voice coming out of the transmitter was strong, hollow sounding—certainly that of the boss. Was this man Rafael, or one of the men trying to kill her?

Clearly her father had specifically mentioned Rafael, one man, only one person. Sarah tried to break free, but the sweeper firmly held her back.

"Don't be foolish. There's no need to force the inevitable. But if it's necessary—" A word to the wise.

Sarah had tried everything possible to avoid being caught, but at this point, what else could she do? Maybe her father should have chosen another place. What a terrible thing—to be killed without even knowing why. So be it, she thought. Once more she felt powerless, defeated.

But Sarah's fate was not yet sealed. A black car shot out from one of the square's adjacent streets, between the statue of Sir Henry Havelock and Nelson's Column, screeching to a stop.

"I'll take care of her," said the man who got out of the car.

Sarah had an alarming sensation of déjà vu. Her instinct put her on guard, and she instantly remembered. It was the man who had pursued her and shot at her in the underground.

"*Va bene,*" the sweeper said.

Without another word, the man in control pushed Sarah toward the car, shoved her into the backseat, and got in the front, next to the driver. The vehicle tore out at full speed.

With the car headed toward Parliament Street, Sarah Monteiro studied the man who apparently was in charge of her. He was middle aged and had a relaxed manner. She was troubled by a chaotic blend of sensations, doubts, and anxieties.

"Who are all of you?" she asked. Silence. Not even a glance in the rear-view mirror. "Who are you?"

There was no answer.

About a half hour later, according to Sarah's shaky calculations, the driver stopped the car, and the two men got out, disappearing from Sarah's view. Only one man came back to the car, the one who had taken her away from the sweeper. This time he sat at the wheel. A few minutes later, the car slowed down as it entered a very posh residential neighborhood. Sarah's heartbeat sped up with fear. Time was closing in. An automatic garage door opened, and their vehicle parked beside a shiny new Jaguar.

They both got out of the car.

"Come with me," the icy voice commanded. He opened the back door of the Jaguar and didn't need to say more. Sarah got in without delay.

"Where are we going?" He didn't answer. "I'm fed up. And I'm not going to keep putting up with this. What are you going to do with me?"

"Don't worry, I won't finish with you until I find out what treasures you're keeping." The man's voice was no longer cold, but warm. "Besides, what kind of help did you think your father sent you?"

"Who are you?"

"I am Rafael. And you will be my guest tonight."

19

PECORELLI
MARCH 20, 1979

It was already well into night, but Carmine "Mino" Pecorelli was still at work in his office on Via Orazio, resolving last-minute details for the forthcoming issue of *Osservatorio Politico*. Pecorelli knew that his weekly bulletin offended the taste of the most discriminating individuals, who not infrequently confronted him face-to-face for his tendency to delve into scandals and reveal sordid tales full of speculation and lies. But this didn't bother Pecorelli too much. His obligation was to his readers, and they were delighted by his work. The *Osservatorio* relayed accounts of celebrities linked with secret organizations, major diversions of government funds through illicit activities, unsolved murders, and a host of other scurrilous matters.

At fifty, Pecorelli bragged about his exclusives and inside scoops, access no other reporter was getting. His successes came from his presumed contacts in high places, and it was said that he frequented the powerful gatherings of newsmakers, cultivating relationships with important people. His paper received financing from one of those personages, a first-tier politician who managed a considerable portion of Italy's public business.

That day the lawyer-journalist was seated in his office, feet crossed on the coffee table, and leaning back in his executive chair. With his telephone anchored between ear and shoulder, he was conducting a serious conversation, replete with suggestions, invitations, interjections, and subtle taunts. His lips traced a slight smile as he rested in the chair, obviously comfortable or self-satisfied, or both.

That particular phone call, nevertheless, had no direct bearing on his weekly. It concerned a private matter. Pecorelli was attempting to augment his personal wealth by manipulating, or rather blackmailing, the individual on the other end of the line. For this he wielded certain detailed information in his possession that, if made public, could damage the person he was speaking to. This was no regular fellow, but the Grand Master of the Italian Masonic Propaganda Due lodge, or P2. His name was Licio Gelli. Pecorelli belonged to the same lodge.

"I'd like to meet personally to go over this," Gelli suggested.

"Fine."

"How about dinner tomorrow night, in Rome?"

"Sounds like a terrific idea," Pecorelli replied. "Don't forget to bring the money."

"Where's my assurance, Mino, that you won't use that information anyway? Don't you realize the trouble you'd be causing the organization by publishing that list?"

"It's journalism, Licio. Pure journalism."

"I know what 'journalism' means for you. Who's going to guarantee me that you won't be trying to make more 'journalism' in the future?"

"Fifteen million is a more than ample guarantee."

"Fifteen million!" he echoed, nearly screaming. Several moments of silence followed, but Gelli was in no position to argue. "We did not agree on that amount, Mino."

"Yes, I know. But I've concluded that this is what the information's worth."

"The list isn't worth fifteen million."

"Well, of course the P2 membership roster isn't worth that amount. But, you know, those on the ultrasecret P1 list, the one with certain compromis-ing details, *is* worth it. Also, as you know, the part of the world that supports you is going to crumble if I make it public." Mino tossed this in, making no attempt to keep his words from sounding like an implacable threat. "And the murder of Pope John Paul I, and the help that you and my boss offered Mario to put Moro in power are worth a lot more."

"We always use your bulletin for our purposes, Mino. Why this sudden change of attitude? Is the money we're contributing not sufficient?"

"Fifteen million would be a sufficient sum. I'll publish the P2 list. Actually, many already know it. When you see it in print, you'll know that the other one is waiting in the wings. Think about it. It'll be good for you, and for a lot of others."

Gelli reflected on this for a minute. At the other end, his silence indi-cated his gauging of Mino's obstinacy.

"Tomorrow we can review whatever's necessary, over dinner. You'll need to lower the price."

"I'm not going to do that. Bring the money and everything will be fine."

Fifteen million was the price, but he might consider the possibility of raising it at any moment, especially if Gelli took too long to pay.

"Yes. I'm sure. Everything will be fine. Good night," Gelli said in closing. "See you at eight, at the usual place." And he hung up.

Smiling, Mino Pecorelli turned off the lights in the office, closed the door behind him, and was on the way to his car. Everything was turning out favorably, just as he had imagined. He couldn't imagine that precisely at that moment, Gelli was making a phone call to an important member of the Italian government, to report the outcome of their conversation.

"There's no way to convince Mino. He's totally inflexible. Either we pay or he's going to publish everything," Gelli declared.

"I don't know what he has in mind. How did he get set on this idea?" the person at the other end complained.

"If we pay now, he'll do it again. And we can't trust him. He knows too much."

"Don't worry, Licio. It's already taken care of. He won't bother us anymore.

We've given him many opportunities, perhaps too many, and he hasn't listened. Finally, it was his own choice."

"*Ciao, Giulio.*"

"*Ciao, Licio.*"

SUCH WAS Carmine Mino Pecarelli's pleasure that he felt an irresistible urge to whistle as he sauntered down Via Orazi, now totally deserted, trying to recall exactly where he had parked his car.

Life was like that. Journalism offered such benefits. In this case it had offered him the possibility of making some easy money. It was stupid to waste time on remorse or burdens of conscience, especially when his bounty came to him from other people's surplus. Maybe he was unscrupulous, but as a man he still retained a detached sense of justice. It never would occur to him to exploit someone who was unable to pay. But a wheeler-dealer like Gelli, always involved in dark dealings and shady businesses, robbing one for another's benefit while enriching himself, and capable of anything to accomplish his ends, deserved to be humbled by a man like Carmine Pecorelli.

His car was near the end of the street, almost at the corner. He opened the door and as he settled into the seat, a hand shot out and prevented him from closing the door. The man who blocked the door grabbed him by the hair and yanked him backward. Letting go of the door, he pulled out a pistol, shoved the barrel into Pecorelli's mouth, and fired twice.

Licio Gelli's problem had been solved.

20

The man claiming to be Rafael drove at a moderate speed to avoid attracting attention. He seemed to know what he was doing. He picked up a package from the passenger seat, and offered it to Sarah in the backseat.

"What's that?" she asked.

"Food."

"I'm not hungry."

"If I were you, I'd eat something. A hamburger and a Coke aren't enough for a whole night."

"How did you know—" She interrupted herself midsentence, knowing the answer to her own question. "Forget it."

Sarah was confused. This man had pursued and shot at her in the underground, beyond the slightest doubt, and now he claimed to be Rafael, the one her father had said she could trust. Was he deceiving her in some way? Yes, that had to be it. She should be expecting some higher member of the organization to appear, interrogate her using atrocious methods, and end up killing her, whether he got what he wanted or not. She had in her possession a list that they knew more about than she did.

"I assume you have a lot of questions for me," Rafael said cordially.

"Huh?" Sarah was unsettled by his new attitude.

There was a silence, which didn't seem to bother the man, who kept driving calmly. He exuded a certain air of satisfaction, as if Sarah's torment amused him. But this could also be his natural way of being. The young woman's imagination was racing at full speed.

"I'm at your disposal," Rafael reassured her, apparently persisting in his attempt to make her feel more relaxed. Even so, and in perfect English, his tone sounded more like an order to Sarah.

"The first question that comes to me is, why did you try to kill me in the underground?"

"Did I try to kill you?"

"Yes. You know very well what I'm talking about."

"Hmm."

"Are you denying it?"

"I'm going to tell you, so you won't have any further confusion about this, that if I'd really shot at you with the intent to kill, we wouldn't be having this conversation now."

"And what the hell happened at my flat? Can you explain to me what's going on?"

"Yes, I can. The question is, would you be ready to hear it?" the man said in all earnestness.

"Ready or not, I need to know. No other choice."

"You're right," Rafael admitted, forcing a smile. Then he gave her a thoughtful look. "Have you ever heard of Albino Luciani?"

"Yes, of course." Sarah was offended by Rafael's condescending tone, as if she were an ignoramus.

"Albino Luciani was known as John Paul I, also popularly known as 'the Smiling Pope.'"

Sarah remembered the papacy of John Paul I. Although she had never been especially interested in religious matters, she knew that this pope had spent a very short time on Saint Peter's throne.

"He was only pope for a few months."

"No," Rafael corrected, "Albino Luciani held the post for thirty-three days, in August and September of 1978."

"Only thirty-three days?"

"Very little time for some, and too much for others. The death of John Paul I is shrouded in great mystery. There are some who think he was murdered."

"Well, there are always crazy people who subscribe to conspiracy theories."

"Try saying that to Pietro Saviotti, the prosecutor of the District of Rome. Apparently he's one of those 'crazies' who think there are still shadows that haven't been cleared up in that story."

"But who would want to kill the pope?"

"Instead of who, the more important question is, why. The motive for the crime counts more than the criminal's identity."

"All right. Why, then?"

"Let me answer you with another question. Have you ever heard of the P2?"

"Vaguely. Wasn't it a secret society or something like that?"

"Something like that. It's the initials of Propaganda Due, an Italian Masonic lodge whose objective is to conquer the political, military, religious, and economic power of all the communities it manages to penetrate."

Rafael gave Sarah a brief account of this organization, founded in 1877 as a branch of Italy's Grande Oriente, formed by people who had no possibility of creating their own lodge. In 1960 it had barely fourteen members, or that's what people said. When a certain man named Licio Gelli became its grand master, its membership increased to a thousand in one year. And later, at its peak, its body grew to 2,400 members, including generals, politicians, judges, television executives, bankers, professors, priests, bishops, cardinals, and many other people of different professions and levels of power. In 1976 Italy's Grande Oriente broke its ties with Licio Gelli and the P2. That was how the organization became a separate lodge, alien to Italian Masonry.

"Nevertheless," Rafael kept explaining, "Gelli didn't abandon his ambitions, and he continued to build networks for secretly gaining control of the Italian government. For this he devised the 'Plan for the Democratic Rebirth of the P2 Lodge.' Knowing Gelli's fondness for European fascism, it's easy to see that he meant to install a totalitarian system, not a democracy. He almost achieved his objectives in the late seventies, judging by the mass media news. Gelli's methods were not very different from those of other Mafia-type organizations around the world. Anybody who got in his way risked meeting his Maker ahead of time. A lot of the murders, attacks, and massacres of those times carried the seal of the P2 Lodge."

"So," Sarah concluded, "if I understood you correctly, you're suggesting that his organization was very interested in assassinating John Paul I. Fine, but where do I come in? Are the P2 men the ones running me down? Why?"

"Because God favored you with the possession of a very valuable list, containing the names of the members of the organization. An old list, more than twenty-five years old, that until now hasn't seen the light of day. Many on the list are already dead, but others aren't, and if their names were revealed, it could cause a lot of problems for a lot of people. It's worth the effort to kill anyone if that could prevent this from happening."

But Sarah had stopped paying attention. What this man was saying had already set her mind spinning. The list. The list she possessed contained the names of the members, dead and alive, of the Propaganda Due, the P2. And it included one name that weighed heavily on her heart, burying her in uncertainty and indecision—her father's, Raul Brandão Monteiro. How could it be?

Rafael was reading her thoughts but said nothing. This was a road she had to travel alone.

"Do you belong to the P2?"

Rafael reflected for a few moments before answering.

"I belong to a superior entity. I'm guided by a plan that happens to include the P2."

"I don't understand." The young lady sighed, aware that she was probing into some very complicated matters. But it was best to discover the truth directly, without detours.

"The P2 is after you," Rafael continued. "Now, as to my connection with the P2, I can say that it ended quite recently, when you got into this car, actually. In fact, I was an infiltrator."

"An infiltrator?"

"If you can't go after your enemies, join them. Destroy them from within. Obviously my work is now compromised. No longer is the P2 just chasing you. It's also after me. And, believe me, sooner or later they're going to find us."

"Then what's the point of this conversation, if we're going to die?"

"It all depends on what cards we get to play at that point," Rafael smiled faintly. "Do you have the list with you?"

Sarah pulled the papers out of her jacket pocket, took the two that made up the list, and handed them to Rafael. He examined them silently, without needing to slow down. After a few minutes, he gave them back to her.

"Do you know any of the names, besides your father's?"

"Well, from what you've told me, I'm sure we could Google all these names and probably find descriptions of important men."

"Maybe you're right. But give it a closer look."

Sarah looked down the columns, now studying them line by line, and no longer surprised by the predominance of Italian names. She noticed that the numbers before each name were unpredictable, not following any recognizable order. Each number was followed by a letter, and in some cases by two or three.

"The numbers aren't in order. And the letters don't seem to follow any logical pattern."

"Those are registration numbers within the organization for each person. And the letters refer to their place of origin. For example"—he reached again for the papers Sarah was holding—"let's take this one, which is right to the point, the Grand Master: '440ARZ Licio Gelli.' His registration number is 440, and he's from Arezzo. Get it?"

"Yes," Sarah answered, her eyes zipping down to the name that mattered most to her: 843PRT Raul Brandão Monteiro.

"PRT. Portugal."

"Sarah, you weren't even born yet."

"Neither were you."

Rafael smiled at the comment.

"I was probably five or six years old."

The girl continued perusing the papers, until she found another familiar name.

"This name, and this 'MIL,' is from . . . ?"

"Milan. But don't fool yourself. At that time he wasn't yet in politics. And he's no longer a member of the P2."

"Yes, but he was. A prime minister of Italy? The dimensions of this, I mean, I don't know what to think."

"Don't think."

Sarah buried herself in the list again. She was terrified by the magnitude of all this. But, besides, her father's name was on it. How far did he go? And how far could Captain Raul Brandão Monteiro perhaps still reach?

"What are these handwritten scribbled notes?" the girl asked, trying to push back her more painful thoughts.

"They are what give an incalculable value to this list. Handwritten annotations by John Paul I."

"Seriously?"

"Yes."

"And what do they say?"

"It's a classification. He underscored the names and the occupations of the ones he knew. For example, notice this one, Jean-Marie Villot: *cardinal segretario di stato*. That is, cardinal secretary of state of the Vatican."

"Was he a member of the P2?"

"Of course."

"And what's on this page? Are those also the pope's notes? And this key?" Sarah handed to Rafael the sheet with the hastily written scribblings. He read them closely.

18, 15–34, H, 2, 23, V, 11
Dio bisogno e IO fare lo. Suo augurio Y mio comando
GCT (15)–9, 30–31, 15, 16, 2, 21, 6–14, 11, 16, 16, 2, 20

"What does it say?"

" 'It is God's will and I will do His bidding. His wish is my command.' In not very correct Italian."

Seconds later, Rafael made a complete U-turn.

"What's wrong?" Sarah asked.

"We're going to see someone."

"Who?"

"Someone who knows."

"Knows what?" Rafael was driving very fast down a narrow street. He seemed to have no intention of answering her question. "Someone who knows what? Did you see something on that paper?"

The car entered a wider street and turned east. Rafael sped up, not caring if the police could see him in one of the patrol cars that passed by moments before.

"Yes," Rafael said finally, without going into detail, as if that one word were an adequate explanation. Then he took out his cell phone.

"What was it you saw?" Sarah insisted, alarmed.

"A code."

21

The Bentley was moving slowly on an unpaved narrow road, lined by trimmed hedges. The road connected somebody's private estate with the main highway.

Almost two miles from the highway, the car slowed in front of a pair of imposing automated gates, which immediately opened to receive the Bentley. Whoever was inside the car had to be very close to the lord of the manor. The driver didn't really have to stop fully or even announce the passenger in the backseat.

The car finally stopped by the three steps leading to the entry landing. The passenger didn't even wait for the driver to open the car door, as etiquette dictated, and just burst out of the vehicle. He didn't ring the doorbell, either, but pressed a six-digit code in a panel on the wall. Before going inside, he carefully dusted his elegant Armani suit and straightened his jacket.

The lord of the manor, or more precisely, the Grand Master, was waiting for him in a salon, not because this would be the usual or most convenient place, but because the operations to be carried out that night required space. The old man, his face livid, was listening to someone on the phone.

It didn't take a lot for the new arrival to see that things weren't going well. If the information he received about the success of the mission had been accurate, Geoffrey Barnes must have made a serious error. The assistant cleared his throat to make sure his presence was noticed. The old man lifted his eyes and greeted him with a nod. The newcomer sharpened his ears, trying to pick up some of the conversation as he prepared two vodka drinks. When the old man hung up, his assistant quietly handed him the drink and sat down.

"I understand there have been some changes since we talked," he said.

With a deep sigh, the old man sat down. It was unusual to see him sighing like this, though lately it happened more frequently. The assistant suddenly realized that for more than fifteen years he had been close to this man, and that during this time he had observed his progressive decline, a painful experience for someone who had witnessed the Master at his full physical and mental vigor.

"Things have changed in an incredible manner," the old man said after taking two sips of vodka. "What happened was quite unexpected, not at all part of the original plan I mapped out."

"I heard you mention an infiltrator." There were no secrets between them. "Geoffrey Barnes had a traitor in his ranks?"

The old man emptied his glass.

"That would have been better," he muttered.

"But how come?" Great anxiety and incredulity showed in the assistant's eyes. The answer was obvious.

"What's going on should never have happened."

"An infiltrator here, among us? I can't believe it."

"You'll have to."

"But where? Here in Italy? One of the new members?"

"No. In the Guard."

"In the Guard? Holy shit. Any idea who it could be?"

The old man nodded, "He has revealed his identity."

"Who is it?" the assistant asked anxiously. "I'll kill him with my bare hands. And first I'll make sure he knows why I'm sending him to hell."

"Jack," the old man answered coldly.

"Jack? Jack who?"

"Jack Payne," the Master added, and kept silent for a few moments, letting the assistant absorb the information.

"And who is he, really?"

"I've ordered an investigation, but it won't go anywhere. His true identity must be well covered up."

"It must be. Or else we'd already have discovered him."

The old man sighed again.

"This is unexpected, but we have to act fast."

The assistant got up, still recovering from the shocking news. He felt it was time to make coolheaded decisions.

"Anyway, we should first focus on eliminating the target, as planned. How's that going?"

"You don't really understand. She's with him. If we get one, we'll get the other one, too," the old man said, standing up.

"Do you think this calls for a trip to London?"

"I don't think that's necessary. Let's stay close to the plan but on maximum alert. An infiltrator might bring surprises. Sooner or later, the CIA will catch them."

"That may take some time."

"Anyway, a trip to London will only put more pressure on Barnes and make him nervous."

"What do you suggest, then?"

"Get the plane ready for the trip we planned. We're going to let Barnes do his job. Don't worry, they'll be caught. No one can live without leaving some clues."

"Especially in London. But let's not forget she's with someone who knows how to evade us."

"Yes, I know. But if you know Jack as well as I do, you'll know that even if he's switched sides, he's not the kind of man to avoid a fight. I don't think he'd want to become a fugitive for life."

"I'll give orders to the crew."

As his protégé was leaving the room, the sound of an incoming fax started. The machine swallowed a white sheet, spitting it out the other end, with a text and a photo. The old man took it and looked at the image of Jack Payne, the same man who called himself Rafael. At the bottom of the sheet, a phrase in all capitals appeared.

NO DATA AVAILABLE

Clenching his fist, the old man crumpled the paper, but after a moment his initial anger returned.

"You won't get away, Jack," he promised. Leaning on the cane that supported his bad leg, he got up and left the room. There were other things to take care of. He looked again at the crumpled piece of paper and, before throwing it away, muttered: "She'll bring you back to me."

22

The British Museum, custodian of great and important pieces of human history and world cultures, loomed imposingly in front of them. It housed more than seven million artifacts that witnessed the passing of the human race over the face of the earth.

The Jaguar quietly parked in front of the enormous building on Great Russell Street. Rafael and Sarah headed for the tall wrought-iron gate, crowned with golden arrows. The man went up to a small door next to the big gate. There was a guard and a sentry box.

"Good evening," Rafael greeted him.

"Good evening," the guard answered, chewing gum.

"I'd like to speak with Professor Joseph Margulies, please."

"Professor Joseph Margulies?" the guard repeated, curtly.

"Yes. He's expecting us."

"Just a moment." The man made a phone call from the sentry box. Sarah seemed to catch his attention.

Rafael had already phoned the professor from the car to tell him he needed to see him urgently. Though the scientist was somewhat reluctant at first, he finally agreed. Since he was working day and night at the British Museum on a temporary exhibit, they could see him there.

For Sarah, the silent wait brought up painful suspicions. There was a difficult but inescapable matter to bring up.

"Tell me, how does my father fit into all of this? What's his position in the organization?"

"He should tell you that, not I."

The dutiful guard confirmed the appointment and let them in.

"Professor Margulies will come for you presently."

"Much obliged."

"This isn't the first time you've come to see him, right?"

"No. But never at such an ungodly hour," Rafael answered, feigning a shy smile. The guard had changed his initial hostility, which he probably considered his duty, to a much more open attitude.

They all walked toward the center, to the main entrance. The sides jutted out, giving the building a squared U shape. Forty-five Corinthian columns adorned the facade, adding an imperial air. Several female figures supported the triangular pediment of the majestic entrance. Sarah stumbled on the steps leading to the ample landing.

"If this were a secret mission, our presence would already be revealed," Rafael said seriously, though he couldn't hide his amusement.

"If this were a secret mission, we wouldn't have approached the guard, or used the main entrance."

"You're right."

"And the pope, Albino Luciani, what part does he play in all this?"

"He's the catalyst."

"Catalyst? What do you mean?"

"That list you received was in his hands the night of his death. It was sent to him by an important member of the P2, a lawyer and journalist named Carmine Pecorelli.

"Pecorelli published a weekly bulletin, kind of a muckraker rag that exposed all sorts of scandals. The network of favors and allegiances was so complex," Rafael added, "that a publication of this kind, his *Osservatorio Politico,* was in fact financed by a former prime minister, a close friend of

Licio Gelli, the one who really promoted the P2 during the sixties and seventies.

"The Grand Master was a real chameleon, a manipulator who wasn't exactly known for his principles. He'd support the extreme Right or the extreme Left, whichever best served his interests. People said he had connections with all the political parties, according to his convenience and the situation of the moment. For example, in theory, the P2 Lodge was supposed to combat all the initiatives of the Left, and yet Gelli contributed to the founding of a terrorist group, called the Red Brigades."

"Okay. But then why did this Pecorelli send the list to the pope?" Sarah didn't quite understand all this juggling of names, time spans, and obscure interests.

"You're not going to believe this," Rafael replied, "but it was to make money. It was his way of blackmailing Gelli.

"It was all about ambition and greed. In principle, the *Osservatorio Politico* served Gelli's interests, but at some point Pecorelli realized that his own boss could be blackmailed. Gelli didn't realize that Pecorelli was a man who, if he could, would serve only his own interests. And he knew a lot of potentially harmful facts about Gelli, particularly involving financial scandals. Finally, Pecorelli published a partial list of the members of the P2, but he probably had another list, even more dangerous and compromising."

As far as Rafael knew, that ominous list was formerly in the hands of Paul VI and, if it didn't cause a huge problem then, it was only because the pontiff was very sick and surely lacked stamina to attack the disease that had thoroughly contaminated the very core of the Holy See.

When John Paul I came to occupy Saint Peter's throne, at some point he had the list of the P2 in his office. He made the appropriate inquiries to verify the information, and it seemed he was ready to make a clean sweep. It was a well-known fact that ecclesiastical offices were incompatible with membership in secret societies alien to the Church, and especially organizations connected with Masonry. When they found Albino Luciani, he was already dead and he had the list of the P2 in his hands.

"It's possible," Rafael concluded, "that John Paul I wanted to resolve this problem discreetly, as everything is done in the Vatican. Perhaps he just wanted to remove those deeply involved in the lodge from positions of ec-clesiastical power, without causing a major scandal. Perhaps he even made a copy for the Vatican Secret Archives, and that may be where Firenzi happened to find it. I'm not sure how all this business unfolded. If you still have questions, you'll have to ask your father."

"Ask my father? But what was his part in all this?"

The sound of steps in an adjoining corridor stopped the conversation. Sarah gave Rafael a quizzical look.

"Why did we come here?" she asked in a low voice.

"To decipher the code."

A fat man of about sixty in an overcoat came out and approached them. Rafael recognized his friend.

"Professor Margulies."

"How are you, old boy? Do you think this is a good time to inconvenience a man of God?"

"Any time is a good time for God."

"Who is this woman?"

Professor Joseph Margulies wasn't a man to beat around the bush.

"She's a friend, Sharon . . . uh . . . Stone, Sharon Stone."

"Sharon Stone?" Sarah repeated, astonished.

"Pleased to meet you, Miss Stone." He gave her a condescending look. "I'm sorry, but I haven't washed my hands."

"No problem."

Sarah observed the professor, trying to figure out what he did.

"We're involved in secret matters of national interest," Rafael said half jokingly. "We can't tell you what it's all about. But I have some kind of puzzle here and I'd like to know if you can help me." He pulled the paper out of his pocket and handed it to Margulies.

The big man just grunted and stared fixedly at the list. Five minutes later, he came out of his trance.

"I'll see what I can do. Follow me."

After going into the museum exhibits section, they went up a grand staircase and turned right and left several times. Then they entered a very long, dark corridor.

"Don't make any noise, you might wake up the mummies," Margulies joked. "Where did you meet this crazy nut?" he asked Sarah.

"He's not—" Sarah tried to explain.

"In Rio de Janeiro, in a convent," Rafael interrupted.

"A nun, eh?" The professor looked at him wryly.

"Not really," Sarah started to say, but Rafael squeezed her arm.

"Here we are," Margulies announced, opening a double door leading to a big hall full of shelves and books, and several tables placed in a row. This became visible only when Margulies lit two sad lamps, which lent a somber tone to the place. He left the paper on one of the tables and walked toward a bookshelf. "Let's see. Here it is: cryptography."

"Do you need any help?"

"No. Just have a seat with your girlfriend."

Rafael turned to Sarah, and their eyes met for a moment.

"Why did you tell him that load of crap?" she murmured.

"I told him what he wanted to hear."

"And what was that? That you're involved with a Brazilian nun named Sharon Stone?"

"Don't give it another thought. The end justifies the means. Or do you think he would rather know the truth?"

"Look, I don't even know my own name anymore."

Rafael grabbed Sarah's shoulders and exerted some pressure, making sure she paid attention.

"The truth can kill us all. You're the proof of it, even though you're still alive. Don't forget it."

Sarah shuddered. Rafael let her go and watched Margulies seated at a table, paper in hand, with three open books in front of him.

"How do you know him?" she asked him.

"Margulies? He was my professor aeons ago. I know he doesn't seem it, but he's a very serious scholar. He studied at the Vatican, and has a deep knowledge of cryptography. If this is actually a code, he'll decipher it."

"What class did you take with him?"

"Is this an interrogation?"

"No. I'm just trying to pass the time."

"A class in theology."

"Theology? Is he a theologian?"

"Among other things."

Margulies looked up from the paper.

"My dear old chap, this is going to take a few hours. I have to run a few tests to discover the kind of model used. I still don't know if it's a code or a cipher. Couldn't you find something to do in the meantime?"

Rafael thought for a moment.

"Yes. But can I copy it on a piece of paper?"

"Of course."

Intrigued, Sarah walked up to Rafael.

"Where are we going now?"

"Do you know how to get out?" Dr. Margulies asked.

"Yes, don't worry. As soon as you find something, call me at this number."

When he finished copying the mysterious words and digits, he handed Margulies a note with his phone number. Then he walked toward the exit, followed by Sarah.

"Where are we going?"

"To cut our hair."

"What? At this hour?"

They walked back along the long corridor leading to the door, and then to the front entrance. It was about fifty yards from there to the big gate and the sentry box, where the guard was watching a black-and-white monitor. Soon they were out on Great Russell Street.

"If we can visit a prestigious professor at the British Museum at two thirty in the morning, we can also wake up a hairdresser a little after three."

"But do we have to?"

"It's not my hair we're talking about, my dear. It's yours. It's definitely too long."

23

Some meetings were meant to occur sooner or later. Human beings aren't always masters of their fate.

A man of advanced age walked confidently amid a crowd of strangers, though he may not have been a total stranger to all of them. He hadn't realized yet that, among so many people, someone was following him. Of course, that man was very competent. They had both come out of the Hilton Theater, where they saw an excellent musical, *Chitty Chitty Bang Bang*, and then walked south, down Sixth Avenue. After turning on Thirty-eighth Street, the old man went into a residential building. A uniformed doorman greeted him.

The pursuer watched from a distance. He looked at the number above the door and compared it with his notes, confirming that it was the old man's address.

He made a call as soon as the old man disappeared into the building. A few moments later, a black van stopped beside him and he climbed in. The vehicle remained parked. One had to be patient.

"He lives here?" the driver of the van asked in some East European language, perhaps Polish, and then he whistled, admiring the luxury of the place.

The man in the black coat just nodded, his eyes fixed on the entrance of the posh residence.

"The London situation turned out negative?" the driver asked.

"Yeah, it did."

"Tell me something, then. Why can't we go in and rub that guy out, once and for all?"

The man took his time answering, as if considering several possibilities. "Because he is the key."

He kept watching a while longer. Finally, he asked the Polish man to keep an eye on the entrance, while he pulled a photo out of his pocket. It was the familiar picture of the present pope, Benedict XVI. Then he took out a small black-light lamp and aimed it at the photo. Thousands of filaments neatly depicted the image of the old man they were shadowing, while the photo of the pope seemed to fade out. When the ultraviolet light was turned off, the concealed image vanished, as with bank bills, and the original image came back, again showing the smiling pope, greeting the faithful with a wave of his hand.

"Yes, he is the key."

24

Aldo Moro
May 9, 1978

Aldo Moro was writing a letter to his family. It was one more among many he'd sent already, including those addressed to Pope Paul VI and to the main leaders of his party, during the fifty-five days he had been a prisoner of the Red Brigades.

By his looks, one would think he was a beggar, but this serene and peaceful man had been prime minister of Italy five times. The government, headed by Giulio Andreotti, would not negotiate with a terrorist organization such as the Red Brigades, which demanded that a number of prisoners be freed. Since that was not negotiable and the prime minister argued that the hostage himself opposed any engagement with these outlaws, it was difficult to anticipate what would happen to Aldo Moro, leader of the Christian Democracy at the moment of his kidnapping, on March 16 of that same year, 1978.

Since then, Moro hadn't seen or spoken with anyone except Mario, his keeper, guard, and kidnapper. At first, Mario treated him as if he wanted to make him endure harsh interrogation, and Aldo Moro thought that his guard was trying to get certain information, but soon their meetings became long face-to-face conversations. As Mario saw it, Moro proved to be an admirable man who, in spite of the situation, had gained his respect.

The position taken by the administration and by the militants of Moro's own party, however, deeply disappointed the prisoner. Nobody lifted a finger to help him, and in spite of the fact that in the letters he sent he had pointed out that the government had an obligation to put people's lives first, most of the members of the Christian Democracy, and those in government, including the prime minister, believed that Moro had been forced to write those letters and that they therefore didn't reflect his actual thinking. Nothing could have been further from the truth.

Mario, as leader of the Red Brigades, could abandon his claims and demands, but he also could make a show of force and kill Moro in order to ensure the success of any future kidnapping. Or perhaps this young man was only a pawn in a chess game, a pawn who would never have any power to do or decide anything. Perhaps he just followed orders. Regardless, Moro was totally convinced he wouldn't get out of there alive.

In another room of the same flat on Via Gradoli where Aldo Moro was writing his letter, Mario answered a phone call. Three other men were with him. Two were watching TV and the other was reading the newspaper.

"Hello."

"Today," said a male voice at the other end of the line. "Carry on as planned."

"Okay," Mario agreed.

"I'll call you again in an hour. The American wants this taken care of as soon as possible."

"Okay," Mario repeated, and hung up. "We're going to finish this," he announced to his comrades.

"Do you think this is the best thing to do?" the one reading the paper interjected with some hesitation.

"It's not for us to decide. We can't turn back."

"I still think it would be better to free him. We've gone too far already, further than we ever imagined. They've gotten our message and they've understood it. Now they know there is no safety for them," the terrorist said, folding his newspaper.

"It's not our battle, Mario. We didn't want this," one of the comrades watching TV confessed, seemingly with conviction.

"When we started, we knew this could happen. And we accepted," Mario pointed out.

"Don't count on me to pull the trigger."

"Don't count on me, either," the one sharing the sofa with him, still watching TV, warned. He'd been silent until then.

"We should free him. We don't have to answer to anybody."

"Don't even think about it. We have to finish this today. We are not going to back down," Mario asserted, trying to convince himself that it all was a political decision. He wasn't even willing to consider that Aldo Moro's life could depend on him. Moro's fate had already been decided on March 16. It was just a matter of time. And the time had come to do what they had to do.

Mario walked to the bedroom and turned the key in the lock. Aldo Moro was sitting, still writing a letter to his loved ones.

"Get up. We are leaving," the leader of the Red Brigades ordered, trying to hide his nervousness.

"Where to?" the abducted man asked as he tried to finish his letter in a hurry.

"We're taking you somewhere else," Mario answered, folding a blanket and avoiding his victim's eyes.

"Would you mind mailing this letter for me?"

"It'll be done," Mario said as he took the letter and the blanket under his arm.

The two men looked at each other for a few moments. Mario couldn't stand to meet Moro's frank gaze, and was the first to avert his eyes. No words were needed. The prisoner knew exactly what was going to happen next.

They went down to get the car in the garage. Moro, blindfolded, was walking ahead, guided by Mario. The three other men followed uncomfortably, repulsed by a decision that was not even in agreement with the political principles of the Red Brigades. When they got to the garage, they ordered Moro to get into the trunk of a red Renault 4.

"Cover yourself with this," his guardian ordered.

Aldo Moro covered himself with the blanket he was handed. Mario kept his eyes closed for a few moments that seemed to last an eternity. The terrorist was attempting to convince his conscience that this was inevitable. There was no other way. It was not up to him.

Mario pulled out his gun and shot into the blanket eleven times. None of the others pulled the trigger.

The plan had been carried out.

25

In a hotel room Rafael himself cut Sarah's hair. She looked like another woman, sitting at the edge of the bed and sighing. It showed her anxiety, her tiredness, her despair, her frustration. And all because an unknown and sinister organization had done away with any remnant of normalcy in her life, including the length of her hair.

"I think I'm more confused now than when I didn't know anything."

This made Rafael smile.

"That's natural."

There was a silence for a few moments. Rafael and Sarah respected their implicit agreement of not talking about personal matters. They had too many things to think about, particularly Sarah. Strange and familiar names, political and religious figures, stories badly told, horrible revelations, Masonic lodges, grand masters, assassinations. And at the center of everything, her father. What kind of world was this, where not even those who were supposed to protect our faith could be trusted? And they were mean liars who killed one another.

"It's obvious. That man Pecorelli sent the list to the pope, and that's why the pope was murdered."

"Don't let your journalistic inclinations dominate you. That spoils everything. I never said that he died because of the list."

"No?"

"No."

That was true. Rafael had never said that John Paul I was murdered because he was in possession of a list that, basically, was almost common knowledge. The only thing he had said was that the list had been in his hands when he died. It was the consequences of that list that took the pontiff to his death.

"Misleading assumptions are at the root of most problems," Rafael said cryptically.

The organizations connected with the P2, and the lodge itself, knew that Pecorelli had revealed the names on the list or that, at least, such actions had been attributed to him. There was no doubt that Pecorelli had tried to blackmail Gelli, and in fact, that was a very dangerous game to play with Gelli.

In March 1979, the body of the journalist was found, shot twice in the mouth. It was relatively easy to think of Gelli as his assassin, but that would be very difficult to prove. Besides, it would be very complicated to find the real capo behind that murder. Rafael could only suggest that behind the whole thing there was an ex–prime minister.

"A prime minister?" Sarah exclaimed in astonishment. "From what kind of country?"

"A country like any other," Rafael said. "If you knew just half of what happens in yours, or anywhere else in the world, you'd be horrified. The P2 listings are not dangerous in themselves," Rafael went on, "except for what they reveal or suggest, or what they prove, in connection with politics in Italy, in Europe, or the rest of the world during the past thirty years.

"Anyway, it seemed that Pecorelli knew too much. For instance, he knew that this obscure prime minister was involved in Operation Gladio, a paramilitary and terrorist organization created by the CIA and the MI6 after World War II, with the objective to prepare for the eventual invasion of Europe by the USSR. Later, during the sixties, the organization focused on preventing Communist and Socialist parties from taking power in Western

Europe and South America. For many years this network was sustained and financed by the CIA, NATO, the British secret services, and other Western institutions.

"In Italy, Gladio carried out a far-reaching operation, the so-called strategy of tension. Basically, it financed leftist terrorist groups so that democratic Communist and Socialist parties became the recipients of citizens' hate. In this strategy of tension, Gladio supported, financed, and carried out the attacks on Piazza Fontana in 1969 and on Peteano in 1972.

"And as far as its European structure was concerned, Gladio operated in Greece, Turkey, Spain, Argentina, France, and Germany, among many other places. The objective was always the same: to spread supposedly Communist-sponsored terror, and thus to create a favorable environment for conservatism and the extreme Right.

"Giulio Andreotti discovered this plot in 1990, when it was judged. It was revealed during the trials that the P2 was heavily involved in that plot. It made sense. The P2 and Gladio shared the same fascist roots.

"One of the dangerous details that Pecorelli knew was about the connection among Gladio, the P2, the Red Brigades, and the assassination of Aldo Moro, prime minister of Italy and a member of the Christian Democrats. According to Pecorelli, the Red Brigades were indeed a leftist terrorist group, but manipulated—even created—by Gladio and the P2. Some people thought it was heavily infiltrated by CIA agents. All these organizations, according to their strategic plans, promoted the kidnapping of Aldo Moro in 1978."

Sarah sat again at the edge of the bed, overwhelmed by the intricate network of conspiracy, corruption, and manipulation her roommate was describing for her. Nonplussed, she looked at Rafael, nervously wringing her hands.

"Could you bring me something to drink?"

"Of course."

Rafael got up and went to the minibar by the door. He returned with a bottle of water and a soda.

"If the P2 took part in Operation Gladio, in addition to the CIA and all the others"—Sarah was trying to make the right connections—"that means

that the world intelligence services not only knew about the existence of the
P2, but had some relations with it, right?"

"Exactly. Except that it's 'have,' and not 'had.' To give you an idea, the CIA
hands the P2 eleven million dollars every month. They still spend a lot of
dough on them."

"Even right now?"

"Yes, now. This whole network of lies and manipulations stemmed from
World War II. Right after the end of the war, a period of total mistrust developed. The old Soviet Union sealed itself off and became isolated, together with its satellite countries of the Warsaw Pact, always fearful of some
destabilizing action from the West. On the other side, the democratic countries were afraid of tricks by the KGB and other Soviet secret services.

"The Soviet Union and its own or closely related agencies used to spend
a lot of money to finance Communist parties and even terrorist groups in
the West. The secret services of the United States, Great Britain, and other
democratic countries maintained a similar campaign to prevent leftist parties from gaining power and, to do that, didn't hesitate to form alliances
with Masonic lodges, violent groups, fascist associations, whatever they
needed."

"Masonic lodges, the military, secret services . . . Who is actually govern-
ing us?"

"In theory, we are free citizens."

"Yes, but who's in charge? The governments we vote to elect are manipulated by secret organizations."

"That's a pretty good assessment."

"It was meant to be a question."

"A question, yes, but also an answer."

"This is terrifying."

"Then don't think about it."

"As if it were easy not to think about it."

"It is," Rafael asserted. "Try to think about less worrisome things."

Sarah put down the bottle of soda and wrung her hands impatiently.
"What an incredible amount of lies! This is terrifying," she said again.
"What're we going to do now?"

"We're going to see your father."

"Where? Is he in London?"

Rafael got up and pulled his cell from the pocket of his jacket. He dialed a number and waited. When someone answered, he spoke in fluent German. *"Hallo. Ich benötige einige Pässe. Ich bin dort in fünf Minuten."*

26

W ho were you just calling?" Sarah asked, back in the Jaguar, sitting beside the driver.

"A German guy who's going to make you a passport."

"Just me?"

"Yes. I've got several."

"Can he be trusted?"

"No."

"What do you mean?"

"Just that—he can't be trusted. These counterfeiters work for money. That's what keeps them in business. He'll do anything for money."

"But—"

"But he'll only talk for money, too. If you're worried he'll go running out to report us, that's not going to happen. You can relax."

"Oh, yes, I feel much more relaxed now," Sarah answered sarcastically.

"You should."

It was a short trip, less than five minutes, including the time it took to park in front of a crowded, noisy pub. Next to it, a door was ajar. They climbed to the third floor, where Rafael rang the bell. The door opened instantly.

"Hello, how are you?" the German greeted them effusively.

"Terrific. And you?"

"Wonderful. Come in."

"You're the best," Rafael said, stepping in and winking at the German.

Hans was a young man, barely in his twenties. His forgeries, besides being fast, were clean, and hadn't drawn attention at any border post so far.

"So, old chap, tell me what you need."

"I need you to make a passport for this lady."

"For this *lady*. I like your elegant words, my friend."

The young man took a camera and grabbed Sarah by the arm.

"Stand there."

It was a wall prepared for making ID photos, with a neutral blue background.

"Don't smile."

"What?"

"Don't smile. For passport photos you don't need to smile."

"Right."

Sarah turned serious, perhaps too serious, while Rafael inspected a wall covered with photographs.

"Who are all these people?"

"All the chaps who've passed through here."

"You've got quite a sizable clientele."

"No complaints." He connected the camera to a computer and began his work. "Do you have a particular country in mind, or a name that you especially like?"

Sarah was embarrassed. She hadn't thought about this.

"Sharon Stone," Rafael answered.

"I like that name, old chap. I think I might even know someone by that name."

"As for the country, anything in the Schöningen region."

"Okay, man. Do you have five thousand?"

Sarah went back to Rafael.

"Did you know this character?" she asked in a low voice.

"I didn't. I know somebody who knew him."

"Anyone would think you were friends for years."

"Well, we aren't."

Hans continued working on the passport on his computer, typing and retouching the photo he'd just taken. Then he stood up and opened a cabinet. Reflecting for a few moments, he picked out several blank passports of different countries.

"Are you only going to be traveling through Europe, sister?"

"Good question. We might need to go to the States," Rafael intervened thoughtfully.

Sarah looked at him, intrigued.

"The United States?"

"All right, old chap. Then I'm going to make one French and the other American. The French one to use in Europe, and the other for across the pond, okay?"

"Great."

Sarah watched while Hans took two blank passports from the cabinet, one American and the other French.

"Are those real?"

"Why do you think they're never detected?" Hans replied, as if offended by such an idiotic question.

"Coming here is almost like going to the embassy, with the advantage that you can choose your country and invent a name," Rafael said. "That, of course, costs more."

"Quality, my dear fellow," Hans emphasizd. "You have to pay for quality."

Rafael's cell phone rang.

"Hello? . . . All's going well . . . No problem . . . Where? . . . We've still got to go to one other place, and then we'll be over there."

"Who was that?" Sarah asked.

"Now, why is it I'm always explaining everything to you?"

"You're my hero, old chap," Hans broke in, admiring Rafael's response. He used this opportunity to bring the passports over to a special printer. Placing them in what looked to Sarah like a scanner, he closed the top. "Ten seconds, and they'll be ready, partners."

27

Geoffrey Barnes continued talking on the phone. This time, his commanding tone, in English, made it clear he was not talking to a superior. Not on the red phone, with the president of the United States, or on the one he used to talk to the Italian man, but rather on the one reserved for giving orders and controlling his operations. Twenty-seven years of service and a spotless record gained him certain privileges. His work was still his primary passion. Beyond a doubt, one of the great advantages of his position was not having to be out in the field, but to manipulate the pieces as he pleased from an air-conditioned location, without major risks.

He was talking with his chief of operations about the progress and setbacks of the ongoing operation.

"He disappeared?" Barnes couldn't reveal his jitters to his agents, but this entire operation now seemed like a useless endeavor. The woman vanished while his agents were pursuing her in one of the most frequented squares in London—very surprising. The old man had ordered him to hold back his men while the special cadre neutralized the target. Certainly the failure to do this would have its consequences, and even worse, cast doubt on the surefire reputation of his agents.

"An infiltrator? A double agent?" Holy shit, he thought. "Right, keep on searching. They couldn't have become invisible."

He hung up and leaned back in his chair, fingers interlaced behind his head. If they aren't found, we're screwed, he thought.

"Sir?" said Staughton, rushing into the office.

"Yes, Staughton."

"Sir, are we still on hold, or do we have authority to act?"

Barnes considered this briefly, just for a moment, not wanting to appear indecisive. Here, nothing escaped interpretation, even silence.

"At this point we both hold the rod. Let the first one to spot the fish do the fishing."

"Understood," Staughton answered. "We intercepted an interesting phone call from the British Museum to the local police."

28

With the Jaguar going at a good speed on the way back from the British Museum, Sarah was staring straight ahead, thinking, somewhat annoyed.

"I hope you're not waiting for me to apologize," Rafael said, perhaps regretting his offhand comment at Hans's place. If he was now attempting to soothe her spirits, he hadn't chosen the best way, since that wasn't what Sarah wanted to hear.

"You're wrong," the young woman responded, glaring at him so intensely that he turned his head back to the road.

"Wrong?"

"I'm not expecting any apology."

"You're not?"

"No. What I want is an explanation."

"I'm already aware of that."

"You are?"

"Yes. But a forger's den is not the place to be making plans or revelations."

"Then you'll tell me who called?"

"Your father."

"My father? What did he want?" Her need to know was so intense that it made her angry with herself.

"He wanted to know how things were going."

"And how are they going?"

"As well as can be expected," Rafael answered, not taking his eyes off the road.

Sarah, too, was staring silently at the ribbon of asphalt. How could a life get torn to shreds in a matter of hours, or seconds? Yesterday she had a normal existence, and today she didn't even know if she would live to see tomorrow.

"If the CIA is financing the P2, one could suppose it knew about the plan to kill the pope. Or is that just a reporter's intuition?"

"It's a good guess."

"And why would the CIA want to eliminate the pope?"

"That calls for a very complicated answer."

"I already see how complicated this is. Give it a try."

Rafael looked at her for a few seconds, sighed, and went back to focusing on his driving. After a while he spoke.

"If you analyzed the geopolitical map of the world over the past sixty years, you wouldn't be able to find a single major change that didn't involve the CIA, and therefore the United States. In all this time there hasn't been a revolution, a coup d'état, or a massacre in which the CIA didn't play a part."

"Give me an example."

"Take your pick. Salvador Allende in Chile. Killed in a coup d'état directed by Pinochet, who in turn was totally financed by the CIA. Sukarno in Indonesia, unseated because of his relationship with the Communists. The Americans helped the military bring him down, through Suharto. More than a million supposed Communists were killed in a mop-up operation financed by them. In Zaire they put Mobutu in power. In Iran, Operation Ajax brought down the democratically elected prime minister Mohammed Mossadegh, and returned the shah to the throne. In Saudi Arabia, they rearranged the map according to their whim."

"And there's Iraq," Sarah concluded.

"Yes, but that's too obvious. The CIA confirmed the existence of weapons of mass destruction. At least they could have put them there, and later pretended to find them. That's what I would have done."

"Now they're getting what they deserve."

"No. Now innocent people are paying for the colossal errors of organizations that act only for themselves, without the backing of the country's people. They represent only themselves."

"We're all potential victims of terrorism."

"Terrorism was invented by them. Now they are—and we are—victims of the weapons that they themselves created."

Sarah was fidgeting in her seat. "So the pope was one more victim."

"Yes. The P2 needed it and the CIA didn't care. The same thing happened with Aldo Moro."

"There's only one person in the world who the CIA has never managed to neutralize, despite numerous attempts."

Sarah pricked up her ears.

"His name is Fidel Castro."

29

It was well established that Geoffrey Barnes generally moved the pieces out in the field from his office on the third floor of a building in central London. But a telephone call from a certain house in Rome, more precisely on Via Veneto, made him get his butt out of his chair considerably faster than usual. Actually he climbed into one of the agency cars, accompanied by three other vehicles, in order to meet with the agents who were already posted around the critical area.

"I'm leaving now," the voice told him, "and I want this solved before I get there. See to it personally, or you won't sit in that chair again. Get moving."

Very few people could talk that way to him. Those who did had so much power that Barnes had no means to counter them. He confined himself to nodding, or to murmuring "Yes, sir," in order to clarify his compliance with whatever the order was.

"You have carte blanche," were the farewell words. He was authorized to do whatever seemed most effective, to move the pieces however he saw fit, in order to achieve checkmate posthaste.

That explained how Geoffrey Barnes found himself in the backseat of a powerful car, his service weapon in its holster, watching the lights outside. "How could an infiltrator reach such a high level?"

This is going to end badly, he thought. Then he attempted to banish the evil spirits. What needed to be done would be done. Neither a woman nor a double agent, no matter how dangerous the latter might be, would cause him to fail before his superiors. This certainly was going to end badly for the target, known as Sarah Monteiro, and just as badly for her savior. Damn you. How could you dare do something like this? he lamented in silence. Taking his radio transmitter, he leaned forward in the backseat. They were already approaching their destination, and this time it was necessary to manage the pieces correctly, including his own position.

"Stop the cars a good distance back. We mustn't reveal our presence. Over."

"Roger, over," came back through the device.

30

The subject was sitting in a black van, in the middle of Sixth Avenue in New York. He always answered when his cell phone rang, since it could be from the man who was calling now, and that caller could never be kept waiting. Once again the conversation unfolded in Italian, though it couldn't exactly be called a dialogue, since the man in the dark overcoat restricted himself to occasional interjections and assents, listening, acutely tuned to the message—its order, its information, and its news.

The capacity for synthesis was an intrinsic quality of the speaker, who in a matter of seconds parceled out all the information, making it perfectly comprehensible, leaving not even the slightest doubt on the listener's end. The one who listened considered him a lion, someone born to dominate men. Though he would like to see the man in person, just thinking about him made his hair stand on end. Not many other people could achieve that effect.

He hung up the phone, infused with a kind of ecstasy, as if he had just finished speaking with God. But he immediately pulled back to his usual bearing, not wanting his associates—in this case, the driver of the van—to catch him so awestruck.

"Any news?" The driver had tremendous respect for the Master, with whom he had never spoken. His respect escalated to fear when he observed, sitting beside him, the incredible reverence that his superior, a man of few feelings, showed toward him. "Any news?" he repeated.

"Things have gone badly again in London."

"Is it so difficult to kill that wretched woman? Even with the help of the CIA?"

"We had an infiltrator."

"Who? One of our own, in the Guard?"

The man in the overcoat didn't answer right away. He watched the moving traffic of the city that never sleeps, the neon lights flashing their advertisements, their invitations to consume. It was all for money. Also working for money were the doormen guarding the entrance of a building. Even the sack of Rome was paid for, as was the elimination of Father Pablo in Argentina. Ideals did not fill anyone's stomach. Nothing was done for free.

"Jack," he finally replied.

"Jack? Are you sure?"

"He fled with her. He didn't come back, and he killed Sevchenko."

"The driver?"

He just nodded.

"Goddamn bastard," the man at the wheel cursed.

"Jack. Who would have thought it? This complicates things a great deal."

"Indeed. So much so that the Master's coming over."

31

We'd like to speak with Professor Margulies," the man told the watchman at the guard station beside the giant doors of the British Museum.

"Professor Margulies is busy. Who would like to see him?"

"We're the police, and we received a call—"

"Oh, yes. I called you. Go on in." Proud, self-satisfied, he opened the entrance for the man with the tie and the five people who were with him. "You've come fast. I only called ten minutes ago. Why aren't you in uniform?"

"We're not uniformed police," the fattest one answered, showing his badge with a quick gesture, but sufficient to satisfy the gum-chewing watchman. "We know that two individuals we're seeking have been here, two suspects."

"That's why I called," said the watchman. "I mean, as for the man, I don't know if he's a criminal—it's not the first time he's been here. But the woman, definitely. I recognized her the minute I saw her, from the telly news on the local station. She's the Portuguese woman who killed that guy."

"When you called, you said they were looking for a Professor Margulies, right?"

"That's right. One of the main conservators of the museum."

"Do you know why they were looking for him?" It was the fat one asking all the questions.

"I don't have any idea."

"Fine. Can you take us to his office?"

"But of course. Follow me."

They went ahead, the six moving in single file, with the guard in front, the fat man behind him, and then the rest. They walked until they got to the spot where they would find Joseph Margulies, engrossed in his cryptographic pursuits. The guard's proud smile expressed his satisfaction. To have called the authorities, at the number listed at the bottom of his television monitor, was a good deed for him.

"The Metropolitan Police requests anyone who sees the person shown in the photo to call 0202 . . ." They were looking for a young female reporter as witness to a shooting. The woman had such an angelic face that the image had stayed with him. He couldn't have expected to actually see her a short time later. It totally astonished him. Nevertheless, he didn't rush things. At first he even feared for Dr. Margulies's safety. So he decided to keep an eye on them. A short while later he saw them leave. Damn it, he scolded himself. Missed my chance. Afterward he went to see the director, to find out what they were up to. The professor had a serious expression, amid his books, absorbed in his thoughts.

"Is everything all right, Professor Margulies?"

"Fine, Dobins."

"Do you need anything?"

"No, you can return to your station. I'm just looking at some things for a friend," Margulies answered, his eyes still on the books and a sheet of paper. "They'll be returning in a little while, so you can let them back in."

Music to his ears. The suspect was coming back. It was his chance. He was going to have his fifteen minutes of fame. He already pictured himself being interviewed by all the television networks. Maybe his superiors would reward him with a raise and all.

That was how he made the phone call to the Metropolitan Police that was intercepted by the men looking for Sarah.

Eagerly attending to his duties, the watchman stopped in front of the door to the room where they could meet Joseph Margulies.

"His office is right in here."

Without a moment's hesitation, the fat man pointed his gun with a silencer at the watchman and shot twice.

"Take him away," he ordered. Then he opened the door and entered the room. "Professor Margulies? I'm Geoffrey Barnes."

32

All was peaceful around the British Museum. Rafael parked in the same spot he had used the first time. They retraced their steps along Great Russell Street, up to the doors. There was no one at the guard station, so they rang the bell and waited.

Sarah was immersed in her thoughts. Rafael could easily sense she was still caught up in their recent conversation.

Finally a watchman appeared, a bald man who came running out of the building.

"Yes?"

"Professor Margulies is expecting us," Rafael confirmed.

The man looked at them for a few moments, his gaze icy.

"Please go in."

Sarah didn't like his manner. He had just dashed her theory that bald men were usually nice. One more myth crumbled, on a night when everything she had taken for granted had gone on to a better life. All of it because of that Firenzi, whose connection to the whole thing she still didn't understand.

Rafael walked quickly to the room where Margulies should still be working.

"Do you think the professor has deciphered the message?" Sarah asked softly, trying not to disturb the oppressive silence.

"No."

"If he'd deciphered it he would have called."

"Is it that complicated?"

"I don't know."

"It seemed like rapid scribblings, like our reporters' scrawls at press conferences. Whoever wrote it was in a hurry."

Upon opening the door to the room where they had last seen Margulies, they did not anticipate the scene awaiting them. Three men sat there, dressed in black like Rafael. Professor Margulies was with them, his face badly bruised and smeared with blood.

"Jack," the fat man said.

"Barnes," Rafael said calmly.

"Jack?" Sarah wondered, confused by the new name. She instantly forgot her confusion when two men pounced on Rafael, striking a blow to the back of his neck.

Rafael fell, but wasn't knocked out. He instinctively raised his hand to his neck.

"And the girl can only be the famous Sarah Monteiro," Barnes remarked from his comfortable perch.

Sarah was startled to find herself the center of attention.

"Geoffrey Barnes?"

Rafael's words resurfaced in her mind: "Believe me, sooner or later they're going to find us. It all depends on the cards we get to play at that point." Dread paralyzed her; she couldn't think.

"Isn't that Sharon Stone?" Professor Margulies asked, gasping with pain.

Geoffrey Barnes roared with laughter.

"Sharon Stone? I assure you she's not Sharon Stone. Give me the papers," he ordered.

"The papers?" Sarah looked at Rafael, who stood up with difficulty. Of the two men, the one who'd struck him took this opportunity to grab him by the collar of his coat while the other searched him. They removed two guns equipped with silencers and used one to cuff him on the head, sending him back to the floor.

Geoffrey Barnes looked at Sarah.

"The papers?"

Sarah saw a glimmer of light at the end of the tunnel.

"They're in a safe place." Her voice didn't quite carry the assurance she'd hoped to project. A slight quaver signaled the precarious value of the card she was playing.

"Don't make me laugh. And, above all, don't waste my time."

"Do you think I would come here holding that list so I could hand it to the first person who asked for it? Who do you take me for?"

"You didn't know we would be here. Don't make me lose my patience."

"Don't you make me lose mine."

I'm digging my own grave, Sarah thought anxiously, but I can't turn back now. She continued the argument.

"How dare you underestimate me like that? I knew"—and here her words started to fail her—"I knew that sooner or later you were going to find us. The only question was when."

Rafael looked up at her, out of the game for the time being. Barnes had a thoughtful expression, never taking his eyes off Sarah. For her part, she opted to gaze straight back, trying not to betray the fear threatening to consume her—fear of him, of them, of everything.

Barnes turned to face one of the men behind Rafael and Sarah.

"Search her."

It's over, Rafael thought, half leaning against the foot of one of the several tables around the room.

The man who had struck Rafael approached Sarah, who stood up and spread her arms, ready to be searched. The man used his hands liberally, patting down the young woman's body with no restraint. All that remained was to check inside her undergarments, which he promptly did.

"Nothing," the agent reported, stepping back with a professional air.

Rafael looked up at Sarah, intrigued.

Barnes opted for a change of tactics, He had to give the woman some breathing room, to let her relax for a few moments.

"We're going to forget about the papers for now."

Sarah tried to compose herself. She had spent the entire night on the verge of disaster, and now would be the worst moment to lose it.

"Here our friend Margulies was involved in a chore that you asked him to take care of. We know that he doesn't have the papers. But these books on cryptography provide us with some clues. Do you know what books on cryptography are used for?" The question was addressed to Sarah.

"To study crypts?"

Geoffrey Barnes got up, and with two swift paces he stood right in front of the young woman and backhanded her. The pain was instant, and seconds later her tongue tasted blood. A red trickle flowed from a corner of her mouth.

Bastard, she thought. Immediately her eyes welled, but she avoided shedding a single tear, not wanting to show any sign of weakness.

"To a crypt is where you'll be going, and very soon," Barnes said, looking at her with the same coldness as before. Then he returned to his seat and again made himself comfortable. "Now that we've clarified this point, let me explain to you what I think has happened. You received something besides the papers. A coded message that in my opinion your limited brain capacity wasn't capable of deciphering. Because of that, you resorted to Professor Margulies. Am I right?"

"Yes, you're right, he ought to have the message," Rafael said, trying to shift the focus of attention to himself.

"Correct," Barnes agreed. "But, unfortunately, your loyal friend swallowed it before we had a chance to read it. And, as you can see by his condition, we tried to get him to tell us what he had discovered. But it seems we haven't made any progress."

"Great, Margulies." Rafael's voice was sarcastic. "You did it. You swallowed the coded message. How remarkable."

"And, because of that, he's no longer of any use to us," Barnes announced, signaling to the agent behind Rafael. The man went up to Margulies, dragged him to the center of the room, and ordered him to kneel. The professor's hands were tied behind his back.

Sarah didn't even want to imagine what was about to happen, and turned her head in order not to look. She had never seen anyone die, even of natural causes. Sensing Margulies's presence a couple of steps away, kneeling before an inevitable fate, she was unable to hold back her tears.

"So, now Sarah doesn't want to watch the spectacle we've prepared for her," Barnes boomed, displeased. "We can't have that."

Again the man who had searched Sarah approached her. A strong hand gripped the back of her neck, forcing her to witness the scene.

"No," she protested.

"Yes," the man holding her head answered in her ear. "Enjoy the unique experience of watching a body abandon life. It's a most beautiful spectacle." A snide chortle reached her ears.

The professor, on his knees, mumbled a litany to himself. It was his farewell, the offering of his spirit to the Creator, so that He would receive him under the best conditions. The way in which one faced one's last breath gave humans greater or lesser dignity. And Margulies did it with integrity.

Rafael looked at the professor very soberly, showing no feelings. He seemed to be an impassive bystander, lacking sentiments, as the drama unfolded before him.

Margulies's head bent forward in submission, for the executioner to pull the trigger. The silencer was pressed against the nape of his neck. Margulies looked at Rafael for the last time.

"Count the letters," the cryptographer whispered.

Sarah did not hear what the professor said to Rafael. She was about to immerse herself in darkness. They could make her face Margulies, but not force her to keep her eyes open. Shut your eyes fast, shut them. Defend yourself against this violence, don't let them torture you.

A dull thud marked the end. The body dropped to the floor, inert, in the middle of a pool of blood that Sarah imagined but didn't see. The tears flowed uncontrollably down her face. Margulies had fallen forward, his head turned toward Rafael, a red hole at the base of his skull.

Bastards! Sarah thought, aware for the first time that, no matter what she did, she wouldn't get out of there alive.

"Now we return to the whereabouts of the papers," Barnes said. "I'm sure that you're readier to reveal it than a moment ago."

The agent who had killed Professor Joseph Margulies still stood, gun in hand, ready to kill his next victim, the man he knew as Jack and who had turned out to be a double agent, the highest treason, always punished by death. Once Jack was dead, the woman would say where the papers were, and then—

And then nothing. A tremendous kick broke the agent's knee and made him fall, screaming. Before he knew what was happening, he lay dead with a bullet from his own gun, which Rafael had snatched from him in the blink of an eye.

Rafael then shot at the head of the man to Barnes's right. The agent to his left and Barnes himself took cover behind the first thing they could find. Meanwhile, the agent holding Sarah tried to use her body as a shield, but she elbowed him powerfully in the chest, making him double over.

"Get out! Fast!" Rafael shouted at Sarah. "Run! They can't shoot at you!"

Sarah ran toward the door. Barnes and the other man aimed at Rafael, but he protected himself with the body of one of the fallen agents. He fired for cover and rushed out of the office.

"The woman has to be captured alive!" Barnes yelled. "Son of a bitch."

33

Rafael flew down the corridor with no idea where he was headed, opening doors at random. His priority was to find Sarah. They found each other quickly, at a nook in the hallway.

"I told you to run. If they'd caught you, you'd be completely fucked."

They ran blindly. The light was minimal, but their eyes eventually adjusted. The interior of the British Museum was an immense labyrinth.

At the end of the hallway was a door providing access to one of the stairways. They descended to the floor below.

When they got to the lower landing, Rafael opened a door and cautiously peeked through.

"Let's go. Stick close to me."

Barely visible signs pointed to the emergency exit.

They came to an enormous hall, the King's Library, and stopped in front of a huge door, leading to the museum's covered grand atrium. The large annex was a recent addition, with a rotunda in the center that housed the Reading Room, various shops on the ground floor, and a restaurant on the floor above. On the other side, facing the exit, were numerous tables and chairs anchored to the floor that belonged to the snack bars that offered fast food to the thousands of daily visitors.

Sarah and Rafael hugged the wall of the grand atrium, quickly moving toward the exit. The stretch that remained before them was like an open, barren field. The moonlight, now visible through the glass dome, gave the area a grayish white tinge.

A flash cut through the shadows and Rafael was hurled against the wall by an unknown force: he'd been hit. Sarah instinctively knelt and tried to lift him. He groaned, but the wound didn't appear to be too serious.

Two shadows darted out from the bar area, moving toward them.

"Take the pistol."

"Are you crazy?"

"Shoot two or three times, at random," Rafael insisted.

Sarah looked back. The shadows were gaining ground. Finally she took the gun Rafael was handing her, and fired three times without turning her head to aim. They were both barricaded behind the museum reception desk. Rafael took off his overcoat and ripped his clothes in the area where the bullet had grazed him, almost by his shoulder.

"I was lucky."

"Really? I thought you were going to die in my arms."

"That could still happen."

"Jack," boomed a voice from somewhere in the atrium. It was Barnes.

Rafael got up and roughly pulled Sarah to his side.

"What are you doing?" she asked in a low voice. Her heart seemed to be stuck in her throat.

"You can't kill her because you don't know what she's done with the papers. She's the only link you have to them. What's gonna happen if she dies now?" He raised his gun and pointed it at Sarah's temple.

"What are you doing?" Sarah thought she was about to faint.

The cards were stacking up against Barnes.

"C'mon, Jack, are you really capable of taking an innocent's life?"

"Barnes, you know me very well. I'm made of the same shit as you."

"What do you want?" he asked, already guessing the answer.

"Pay attention. I'm going to leave here with her, and you're going to tell your men to put away their guns and let us go. You're going to tell the guys with you and the ones you've got posted outside."

"Let's be reasonable, Jack."

"Even more reasonable?" Rafael tossed back sarcastically.

Barnes had no choice but to accept.

"Abort the operation. Lower your guns. Let them go," he said, turning his head to the tiny microphone on his lapel.

Rafael dragged Sarah out from the protection of the counter, backing toward the exit.

The cold night air wrapped around them. They went downstairs and to the giant doors bearing the Queen Elizabeth II coat of arms. The gun was still pressed against Sarah's temple. From there to the car was a very short stretch.

34

What were you thinking?" Sarah yelled at the top of her lungs, while the car turned toward Bloomsbury Street at top speed.

"I was trying to save us," Rafael answered, not looking at her.

"To save us?"

"Stop asking questions. They're following us and it's not going to be easy to shake them."

They turned right on New Oxford Street. Rafael grimaced as pain blazed through his shoulder. At the Tottenham Court Road intersection, the light turned red and he stopped the Jaguar.

"Let's trade places," Rafael asked.

"What?

"You drive. I'm not in any shape for it."

Sarah proceeded on Oxford Street, London's main business thoroughfare. She leaned over to the glove compartment and took out the list, which she threw in Rafael's lap.

"There you have it. I'd left it here and forgotten it when we got out of the car."

"Your forgetting it saved us this time."

They drove on in silence for several minutes.

"I don't know where I'm going," Sarah said finally.

"It doesn't matter, keep going. It's all right if you go by the same place several times."

"Were you really planning on shooting? If things had gone badly, would you have been able to kill me?"

"Yes," Rafael answered without hesitation. "And I would've killed myself next. Believe me, it would have been a favor for you if things had turned out badly. It's better to be dead than in their hands. Not having the list with you, whether you forgot it or not, was the best thing that could have happened. It was wonderful."

"So if we find ourselves in the same situation again, but with no cards to play, you wouldn't hesitate to pull the trigger, first on me and then on yourself?"

"Exactly," Rafael affirmed, without showing the slightest emotion.

"Did my father give you that order?"

Rafael looked at the girl, who looked back at him, both of them for a moment taking their eyes off the street traffic.

"No. But I'm sure that, given the situation, he'd approve."

"Of course." Sarah looked ahead again. "Of course, *Jack*." She pronounced the name with deliberate emphasis, as if it were the key to all the lies, doubts, and frustrations torturing her. "Is your real name Rafael?"

"Who knows?"

"Jack?"

"No."

"So?"

"It's better for you not to know. Look, Rafael is the name of your savior, who hasn't turned out bad, so far. A few ups and downs, of course, but also with a certain success. Jack is the alias of John Payne, member of the P2, who was unmasked as a double agent. So, technically because of that, John Payne is dead."

"And Geoffrey Barnes—who is he?"

"A director of the CIA. Immoral and corrupt. I did some operations under his orders, and I assure you, if he left his office to come looking for us in person, it's because we're giving him a devil of a time."

"Fine. Jack Payne or Archangel Rafael, I have to ask again, what is your real name?"

Rafael laughed for the first time since they'd met.

"Nice try."

"You can't lose by trying." Sarah took her eyes off the road for a few seconds. "Rafael Jack Payne, what do we do now?"

He looked at her closely before answering.

"Now? We're going to disappear."

35

To Caesar That Which Is Caesar's
September 1978

Reviewing his schedule, checking his audiences and meetings for that morning, the Holy Father frowned when he came across a commission from the New York Department of Justice. There was a note stating that this commission would arrive accompanied by representatives of the FBI and of the National Bank of Italy.

The petition had been sent months ago, when Paul VI was still alive. The pope's illness must have prevented that very strange meeting. In the notes for August, besides the indefinite postponement of the meeting, it was specified that the members of said commission would be received in a public audience, between a group of Belgian nuns from Liège and a group of orphans from Genoa.

The last note did not suspend the meeting, but wedged it between a representation of pious widows from Piedmont and of a religious school from Spain.

Pope John Paul I went into one of the auxiliary offices and observed at length the two priests acting as personal secretaries.

"These gentlemen will feel uncomfortable at the audience. Call them and tell them to come to my office now, as soon as possible. Oh! It's a courtesy visit, so it's not necessary for them to inform Cardinal Villot. Thank you."

A few minutes later, while Don Albino Luciani was preparing coffee for himself, one of the young secretaries came in to tell him there were six men waiting in the next room. The pope felt a bit intimidated by the imposing presence of those gentlemen. Nevertheless, they all humbly bowed their heads when they attempted to shake hands with the pope. Hours later he couldn't precisely remember all the names—there were the two Italian inspectors or auditors from the Bank of Italy and the four Americans representing the FBI and the Department of Justice—but they all were assigned to units dealing with financial crimes.

"Sir," said one of the Americans, obviously unacquainted with Vatican protocol, "we greatly appreciate your having permitted us—"

"Oh!" John Paul I interrupted, smiling, and speaking in respectable English. "You're missing out on the good hospitality of the Lord's House! Would you like some coffee? I'm afraid that I, at least, will need some."

They sat in comfortable chairs on one side of the office, around a low table with a silver crucifix in the center. John Paul I seemed ready to listen to these men, who were somewhat awed in the presence of a cleric who had millions of followers worldwide. One of the FBI agents, as if afraid the entire meeting would dissolve in their coffee, spoke too soon.

"Sir, we have brought you a report that provides evidence of criminal malfeasance in the financial institutions linked with the Holy See."

Albino Luciani gave the agent a deeply serious look.

"Tell me what the report shows. The Lord, as you say, is listening."

"The finances of the Vatican," the agent said, failing to catch the pontiff's joke, "are linked with the IOR, and this to the Banco Ambrosiano of Roberto Calvi, and this, in turn, to the businesses of Michele Sindona and his Banca Privada. We know that Sindona is the link between Roberto Calvi and Archbishop Marcinkus. I remind you that Sindona is known as 'the Mafia's banker,' and that a seek-and-capture order has been issued against him in the United States, for fraud, financial crimes, and racketeering. And, if you'll permit me, I would also remind you that Roberto Calvi belongs to the Masonic P2 Lodge, headed by the fascist Gelli, instigator of Operation Gladio. Surely you'll not have forgotten the bombing of the Piazza Fontana in 1969."

"Are you telling me that they're planting bombs in Milan, using the Vatican's money?"

"No. I'm telling you that they're planting bombs in Rome and in many other places around the world. From Poland to Nicaragua."

Don Albino Luciani didn't move a single muscle, though the burning in his throat could have incinerated the Apostolic Palace.

The FBI agent was not inclined to hold back.

"In 1971 Roberto Calvi and Paul Marcinkus founded the Cisalpine Overseas Bank in Nassau, Bahamas. And that bank is used to launder money from drug and arms trafficking; to conceal fraudulent real estate speculations; to launder money produced by prostitution, pornography, and other similar activities. From there, by means of a network described in the report, funds are diverted to distinct destinations. For example, the labor organizations in Poland, dictatorships like Somoza's, and revolutionary or terrorist organizations."

"Doesn't it seem strange that we would be financing fascists and revolutionaries at the same time?" Pope John Paul I inquired.

"They're not financing politics, they're financing crimes. In Italy they are bribing and blackmailing politicians of all stripes. Just from a close reading of the *Corriere della Sera,* you can see it clearly. It's the official paper of the Gellis, the Sindonas, the Calvis, and the Marcinkuses."

"Holy Father," one of the auditors from the Bank of Italy said, "the Banco Ambrosiano has a deficit of $1.4 billion. And, as you know, the Vatican Bank has twenty percent of Banco Ambrosiano's stock. You need to take measures, because the Bank of Italy cannot risk—"

"Sir," the Department of Justice official interrupted, "the president is going to take action anyway. It will be difficult to keep this scandal from splattering on the Holy See. I'm fulfilling my superiors' orders by providing you with this report. It may take a year or two for us to bring it to light, but we will. During that time, sir, you could intervene to distance the Vatican from this network."

"Yes, my son. But I don't know if I have that much time available."

"Your Holiness!" one of the Italian auditors exclaimed. "You must distance yourself from Marcinkus, from De Bonis, from Calvi."

Albino Luciani got up from his chair, visibly disturbed. He'd known since he presided over the Banca Católica del Veneto, many years ago, that Marcinkus and his cohorts, rather than directing the Church finances in keeping with the dictates of the Lord, were instead following the schemes of Wall Street.

The pope opened the door of the office and left without saying good-bye.

In one of the private rooms, in front of a mirror supported by a marble table covered with ebony boxes, small silver monstrances, crystal balls, and photographic frames, Don Albino Luciani gritted his teeth, enraged. He swept the table with his forearm, sending all the objects flying through the air, shattering to smithereens all over the room.

"I curse you! You've turned the house of the Lord into a den of thieves!"

36

How can a plan fall apart? It was going so well a short while ago."

"We still have time to head to London, sir," the assistant suggested to the old man nestled comfortably in the seat of his private plane. "Consider it a minor detour."

"Don't even think about it!" he adamantly refused. "We'll stick with the plan to the end."

"Aren't we running the risk that they'll make an irreparable change in the plan?"

"Have faith, my dear friend. It will all work out in the end."

"We usually leave faith to the believers," the assistant argued, convinced that this change of destination could make the difference between success and failure. "It's important to recover the documents."

"The documents are the reason for all this. We're making this trip for them. It isn't necessary to remind me. Besides, our presence in London won't be of any use. Things are going well."

"What? They are still free and we are wasting time."

"But they are within our grasp."

The assistant hadn't realized that the Master had a new, still-undisclosed plan.

"Would you like to share your plans?" he asked.

"You'll soon see. You've got access to more information than most men. And you can connect the dots quickly."

"As you wish," the assistant answered, somewhat irritated. The old man loved having secrets, controlling information until it had redeemed its value. When its uselessness became apparent, that meant he had already accomplished his objective. Privileged information was useful, but he hated the old man's keeping it from him. If he didn't know him well, he would think this was from lack of trust. Instead, it had a very simple explanation. The Master wanted to send a message to his own demons: "I'm still here, I'm still in command, deciding everybody's fate."

The old man picked up the satellite handset on the left arm of his seat, and pressed a few numbers. Moments later someone answered.

"*Ciao,* Francesco," he said, smiling coldly. "A short while ago I found out that you lost one of your associates." He allowed time for the message to sink in. "Consider this firsthand news. The body will appear in due time." Again he gave Francesco time to absorb his meaning. "But that isn't why I called. I might be in need of your services. . . . When? Yesterday . . . I want you to get on the next plane. They'll give you all the necessary information at the airport, and then you'll wait for my call." He cut off without another word. "Soon they will both be in front of me," he muttered aloud to himself, his eyes fixed on the small plane window. "And we'll see who's the smartest."

At this moment while he was thinking out loud, he was again approached by the assistant. At least it seemed that his irritation was gone.

"They've called from London," the assistant said in a low voice. "The worst has happened."

37

Geoffrey Barnes hadn't slept a wink the whole night. Despite the fact that the one giving the orders was an Italian, or at least spoke in Italian, Barnes was more worried than if it had actually been the president of the United States giving the orders. He could handle the president better than this character from the P2.

While the old man was in flight, Barnes had spoken with him twice. First, he explained what had led him to the decisions he was making. The man didn't react with any kind of feeling, but limited himself to a singular theme.

"What's essential is to recover those papers. Obviously we underestimated our adversaries, but that won't happen again. Use all necessary means. Once the papers are in your control, get rid of all witnesses. Understood?"

"Of course, sir," Barnes affirmed.

The second call was to remind him that he mustn't lose sight of the adversaries, not even for a moment. He needed to follow those orders, whatever the cost.

"Should there be collateral damage, put the blame on any Arab group.

The next day, have some protest marches, paying homage to the victims and condemning terrorism. Problem solved," the Italian said, with no tinge of irony whatsoever.

"That's what we'll do," the CIA agent agreed. Barnes knew that in the course of operations there could be a stray bullet, or several of them. A bomb might explode at the wrong moment. And targets could pick up reinforcements. That's how it was.

"One more thing. Wait for my instructions. Don't do anything without my authorization."

And the Master hung up in the abrupt manner to which Barnes had grown accustomed. It was five o'clock in the morning.

SARAH AND JACK were driving in circles around London, forcing the agents who trailed them to retrace a tourist's itinerary through the historic central city. Several times they had gone by Buckingham Palace, then followed the Mall to Trafalgar. Again they took Charing Cross Road or any other street. And finally, back to the beginning. All at a leisurely pace, as was required for an enjoyable visitor's tour. And that was the impression Barnes got every ten minutes from Staughton's methodical reports.

"It's strange that they haven't even attempted to flee," Barnes thought out loud, alone in his office. "They haven't stopped for gas. At some point they'll have to," his soliloquy continued while he awaited new information. "I need something decent to eat."

Jack Payne was a legend in the P2 Lodge, so much so that the CIA recruited him for some of its most delicate work. His name meant competence, work well done. The P2 was an arrogant organization. It would not hesitate to demand that certain forces in the CIA serve its purposes, a useful means of gaining the benefits of American technology and of charging a monthly fee on top of that, but he didn't approve, then or now, of the lending of its members to Uncle Sam's agency, especially its top performers such as Jack. At times, however, when this Masonic Lodge thought it could gain something from the practice, it simply authorized the use of some of its members, as happened with Jack on three or four operations that he completed under

Barnes's orders. Jack Payne was the kind of man a director liked to have in his ranks. Barnes had even made the proposal for his admission to the CIA.

What a huge mistake. It'll be my downfall at the agency, Barnes reflected, leaning back in his chair, exhausted by all the events of the long night. He realized that he'd be fired from the job he'd earned through so much blood, sweat, and tears. It was for good reason that Americans said, "No pain, no gain." His position at the agency was truly the result of a lot of effort, a lot of pain, a lot of hours without sleep, and without a decent meal, like today. If there was anything that this night reminded him of, it was the uncertain times of the cold war, when the world was crazy.

"You must have been crazy, Jack, when you decided to follow me," the great bulk of a man muttered resentfully to himself.

Suddenly the door opened and a weary Staughton appeared, putting an abrupt end to Geoffrey Barnes's musings.

"Sir."

"Staughton."

"They've disappeared."

38

"Now we're going to disappear," was what Rafael told Sarah, still inside the car.

They continued their visitors' tour through the British capital a while longer, while the city slowly began to awaken. They were almost out of gas. Rafael asked Sarah to turn left at the intersection with King's Cross Station and to slow down. Then the double agent moved to the backseat, under Sarah's close scrutiny.

Jack folded down the backseat to gain access to the trunk, from which he took out a green wooden box. He returned the seat to its normal position, sat up, and rolled down all the windows. Following this, he opened the wooden box, took out the small balls it contained, and began throwing them one by one to one side of the street, and then the other, almost rhythmically. The balls rolled under the automobiles parked at the curb.

"No matter what happens, don't stop until I tell you."

The car was already about a hundred yards from Euston Station.

"Now speed up and then stop in front of the station," Rafael ordered, throwing the last ball.

"What are you doing?" Sarah asked.

"We're almost there," he said.

Then, when the car was just outside Euston Station, the unexpected happened.

"Okay, shut off the engine."

Sarah obeyed, and right away all hell broke loose. A succession of small explosions moved toward them from the King's Cross intersection, approaching from both sides of Euston Road. A thick cloud of tear gas invaded the street. Shouts could be heard. People who lived in the neighborhood woke up terrified.

Shielded by the gas barrier behind them, Rafael and Sarah ran toward Euston Station.

Without exchanging a word, they ran to the taxi stop on the lower level. From there, everything became much simpler. They asked the taxi driver to take them to the Waterloo Station, where they arrived in time to catch the Eurostar headed for Paris.

They took advantage of the comfortable trip to rest a bit. Sarah slept almost the entire way, and Rafael leaned back in his seat, although only after making two inspections of the whole train. No one was following them.

Two hours and thirty-seven minutes later they arrived at the famous Gare du Nord in the center of Paris. From there they moved on to Orly. They had managed to disappear.

39

The Airbus A320 reached its cruising altitude of 36,000 at a speed of 540 miles per hour. Within approximately two hours it would land at Portela Airport, Lisbon, the destination of the 111 passengers that included Sarah Monteiro, now officially Sharon Stone, a French citizen, and Rafael, officially John Doe, a British subject. Flight TP433 had left Orly a bit more than twenty minutes before, behind schedule. Since they were both awake, Rafael had to face questions and more questions from the career reporter at his side.

Rafael had once heard someone say that "the fathers were in Jerusalem." Probably the reference was to the mythical builders of the Temple of Solomon. Those venerable architects had conveyed their knowledge to the carpenters and stonecutters of the West, the same ones who erected the cathedrals in the Middle Ages. They were the *maçons,* users of the drop hammer, chisel, square, compass, and plumb line. Those powerful guilds knew the Lord's secrets. Even now, in Notre Dame or Reims or Amiens, one could see that those men truly knew what God wanted for the world. The Lord Jesus Christ proclaimed: "Render to Caesar that which is Caesar's and to God that which is God's." The whole world knew this, including politicians, university professors, doctors, bankers, civil servants, soldiers, writers, and journalists. Even the pope knew it. "God is to be found everywhere, my child, even in arms factories and bank safe-deposit boxes."

From what Rafael had heard, the Masons had been on the scaffolds when the bloody heads of kings and nobles rolled in revolutionary France. And later they were behind the wars and violent regime changes in Europe and the Americas. The members of the P2 could take satisfaction in belonging to the same organization as many presidents of the United States and of Europe.

In Rome, Italy's Grande Oriente began to suffer from internal schisms near the turn of the twentieth century. It was then that Propaganda Due was founded. Those who held the strings of power around the world complained that Masonry was being bandied about, with members' names in the papers and their activities directed by inept, vain politicians. The number *2* would provide the anonymity they sought, ending the announcements, photos, and leaked names. The P2 did not exist. Nobody should know anything about it. The *loggia coperta* welcomed, among those privileged to know God, everybody ready to devote his life to building the Kingdom of Heaven on earth.

"Those were very bitter times for them," Rafael told Sarah, who listened eagerly. "Hitler and Mussolini fascinated them, but as they saw it, their spiritual goals were being betrayed by those men."

Licio Gelli, who headed Italian Masonry in the mid–twentieth century, was the true driving force of the P2 Lodge. "Gelli had more ideas than ability to carry out his projects," Rafael told Sarah. The Grand Master of the Grande Oriente of Italy granted him powers far beyond his talents. Gelli was a small businessman from Tuscany who venerated Der Führer, Il Duce, and El Generalísimo. In fact, he enlisted as a volunteer, fighting against the Republicans in the Spanish Civil War. He also served as a Nazi spy in the Balkans, actively collaborated with the CIA, and incited several coups d'état in South America.

"Gelli's rise in the organization is a mystery," Rafael continued. "The Lord's ways are beyond understanding. That's why it's surprising how many idiots manage to gain power, glory, or fame."

Licio Gelli was at the top of the P2 Lodge in the early seventies, and in 1971 he became one of the most powerful men in the underworld. Gelli, always with a penchant for conspiracy, founded the P1 Lodge, even more secret than the P2, exclusively to cover presidents, high dignitaries, secretaries general, and CEOs.

Some of Rafael's older comrades told him about those meetings. As many as twenty shiny black armored cars with tinted windows would gather at a luxury hotel near Lake Como or in Geneva or Baden-Baden. The cars stayed for two or three hours, then left using back roads and eventually merged onto the European highways.

It was probably Gelli who persuaded many of the Masons from the Giustizia e Libertà organization to join the ranks of the P2. There they met with all sorts of politicians, military men, and bankers. They all felt privileged, belonging to such a select group.

"Vanity is a tragic flaw, Sarah. Gelli couldn't resist having his picture taken with Juan Perón at the Casa Rosada."

When Gelli found himself under judicial attack in the mid-seventies, he sealed off his organization, severing all ties with any other Masonic Lodge. That was how the P2 became a supersecret entity and Gelli himself became Grand Master. Those times were dubbed "the Cosa Nostra era." The P2 operated exactly like mobsters or the Mafia—"the Gelli," became their moniker. Gelli's neofascist ideology prevented his lodge's advancement in the divine master plan. But seen from a different angle, his work was highly effective, because his collaborators managed to infiltrate all sectors of the Italian government, in addition to the Vatican and several foreign national security agencies.

Many politicians during this period considered the real president of the country to be Licio Gelli, who manipulated the media, investigations, voting, and electoral campaigns so that the country's top spot would be filled by his own predesignated nominee.

Rafael was watching Sarah's reaction.

"Gelli was done in by that scumbag, what's-his-name, Pecorelli. The Gellis dug their grave when they let the lodge's membership list fall into that journalist's hands.

"The judges started asking questions, and old man Gelli needed to hide out in Uruguay.

"Along came the current leadership of the lodge," Rafael went on. "They distanced themselves from Gelli and got busy trying to get the organization back on track. Those years involved a lot of work. They had to amend the Constitution, reorganize the judiciary and the university, and influence certain men, particularly Craxi, Andreotti, and Bisaglia. It didn't much matter what party they belonged to. The crucial factor was getting them to 'collaborate,' even without knowing they were doing so. Reporters, in general, were on board. They liked money," he concluded.

The lodge was now a collection of shadow figures that nobody could uncover. It was a fantasy of conspiracy addicts, an irrational urban legend, an organization that inspired terror only among solitary investigators on the Internet. They did not exist. And nonexistence was highly recommended for someone trying to carry out a plan like his.

Sarah began to realize that the organization had grown and continued to extend its networks worldwide. Even in the Vatican, where the P2 was called the Ecclesia Lodge. When Pope John Paul I died suddenly, the lodge included numerous members carrying out their duties in the palaces of the Holy See.

"In those years, Rome was the best place in the world. Archbishop Marcinkus was involved in the finances, and everything he touched turned to gold," Rafael continued. "Of course the investments were in pornography, contraceptives, and other businesses ill suited to the image of the Church. But the funds Marcinkus invested in arms factories, political subversion, bribes, blackmail, and money laundering proved much more productive in the long run."

"I don't know if you're trying to tell me the truth or terrify me," Sarah remarked, then fell silent.

Sarah was deep in thought, and Rafael retreated into his own reflections. A peaceful quiet ensued between them.

The flight attendant offered the snacks tray to both of them. They ate silently, buried in their thoughts.

"What I need now is a shower." Sarah twisted in her seat, trying to wake up her numbed arms and legs.

"We can arrange that," Rafael assured her. "When we land, we'll take care of it."

"Is that a promise?" she asked, half smiling.

"No. I never make promises. But I do keep my word."

They were silent a few moments longer. The noise of the plane's engines drowned out the other passengers' conversations. Sarah turned to him again.

"Do you think my father's all right?"

"Yes. Don't worry." His voice was so assured that she believed him.

"What I'm afraid of now is having them catch us at the airport," Sarah said.

"You can relax. That's not going to happen."

"How can you be sure?"

"It's one of the advantages of my position. We may have half the world after us, but we know how they think. We're always one step ahead. And what matters for us is to keep going like that. We have to keep the initiative."

"And how do they think?"

"The first thing they're going to do is clear the scene of the shooting and the street where I threw the tear gas."

Somehow Rafael's voice inexplicably calmed Sarah. To her it was a killer's voice, the voice of a man without scruples, but its effect was reassuring.

"What will we do after talking to my father?"

"We'll see. We've got to go step by step."

"You're always holding back information."

"That's true. But in this case I don't have much more to tell you. The objective is to have you reunite with your father. That's basic. Then we'll see what to do next."

"But isn't there a risk that when we arrive in Lisbon, they'll have photos of us in some paper? It's possible the authorities will be looking for us."

"Definitely not. It's in their interest for us to go through unnoticed. Their objective is to see us six feet under. Besides, as long as we have the list, no one's going to let us appear in the papers. If they did that, they'd lose everything."

I hope you're not wrong, Sarah thought.

"How did Firenzi get my address?" she asked herself out loud. "Of course, considering my father belonged to the organization, I can see why they knew my home address. What I can't figure out is why he wrote to me."

Rafael didn't even seem to react to her. Once more he brought his hand to the wounded arm.

"Does it hurt?"

"Yes," he answered, massaging the area softly. Hours before, he'd bandaged it in the bathroom on the train, and the pain had eased somewhat. But now it was bothering him again, badly.

"Do you need anything? Can I help you?"

"No, thanks, I'll be fine," Rafael replied.

As they circled the airport, flying over the northern part of Sarah's native land, she felt a renewed anguish suffocating her.

"Do you know the man who broke into my house?"

"Yes."

Rafael kept silent again, just staring out the small window.

"Who was it?" Sarah insisted.

"It was an American Secret Service agent. Actually he was a Czech-born naturalized American, though that's irrelevant. But other people connected with you have died recently. There was a Spanish priest named Felipe Aragón, and an Argentinian one, Pablo Rincón. Both of them received information concerning John Paul I's papers."

"Papers like mine?"

"On the night he died, the pope had various papers with him. The list that you got is only part of it." Rafael seemed to want to talk.

"And they also received papers?"

"Probably, but they had worse luck than you. Father Pablo couldn't manage to get away. And unfortunately, Father Felipe died of a heart attack at almost the same time."

"If Father Pablo received any papers, then they must be in the P2's hands now. If, on the other hand, he received only an indication, let's say, as to the whereabouts of the remaining documents, the P2 could also have obtained that information before killing him," Sarah reasoned.

"That may be, I don't know. Your father might be able to clear all of this up for us."

"How can you be acting like that, making decisions without sufficient information?"

"In my work, we're all small cogs in a big wheel. What counts is for us to know our part and perform effectively. As for the whole puzzle, only its inventor knows."

"And you aren't curious?"

"Curiosity is very dangerous."

The plane completed its approach, and moments later landed smoothly.

"We have just landed at Portela Airport in Lisbon," the flight attendant announced, and repeated the usual litany.

"At least they didn't attack us with missiles midflight," Sarah joked, trying to shake off the gripping tension.

40

S ister Vincenza had been looking for Don Albino all afternoon. Walking
the hallways of the Apostolic Palace, carrying a small tray with a glass
of water and a pill on a saucer, she stopped by a window and saw him sitting
on a bench in the gardens. The Holy Father was holding his head with both
hands and seemed engrossed in disturbing thoughts.

"Gethsemane," Sister Vincenza said, almost reflexively.

The old woman descended the stairs leading to the wonderful gardens,
and continued on one of the gravel paths toward the rotunda. Just on the
other side, Don Albino was sitting in his pure white cassock, staring down
at his shoes.

Sister Vincenza stood in front of him.

"The doctors recommended that you *take walks* through the gardens.
They didn't say you should *sit* in the gardens."

There was a hearty smile on Don Albino's lips as he looked at his loyal
nurse.

"Yes. They suggested I go for walks to get rid of this swelling in my feet.
But as it happens, with my feet so swollen I can't walk. So, what can I do?"

Sister Vincenza, well acquainted with Don Albino's unshakable logic, admitted that the doctors' prescription wasn't very practical.

Without a word, the pope took the pill and the glass offered by the nun, and after looking at the medication with a resigned sigh, he swallowed it, delighting more in the cool water than in the promised benefits of the pill.

"Did you know my father, Sister Vincenza?" Don Albino asked his nurse, still standing before him. "When I went to the seminary at eleven, my father spent two months without saying a word to my mother. She was a very devout woman, but my father—"

"Don Giovanni was a rebel," Sister Vincenza said.

"No. Don Giovanni, as you call him, was a socialist. But, considering what is going on now, I don't know if an immigrant, a laborer, or temporary worker who has always lived in misery can be anything else. In fact, when I entered the seminary, my father said, 'Finally, a sacrifice has to be made.' I'd say that, for being avidly anti-Church, he had a premonition almost like a spiritual vision. That's what I was thinking about when you came."

"God will help you carry this burden, Holy Father."

Don Albino glanced benevolently at Sister Vincenza. No good could have come from his starting a conversation about the poor conduct of the directors of the Vatican Bank. What would this innocent nun think after being told that the Mafia's money was being laundered through intermediate enterprises in the stock markets of Zurich, London, and New York? What would happen to Sister Vincenza's simple faith if she learned that, since August 6, 1966, affable Cardinal Villot's name appeared with the number 041/3 in the archives of the P2 Lodge? How could this venerable old nun sleep, knowing that her Don Albino didn't head Christ's Church, but a financial conglomerate that would end up exploding in his face if he didn't fix it? And as for himself, how could he look that good woman in the eye, knowing that his Church had been converted into a den of thieves?

"I could bear this burden, Sister Vincenza," he added finally, "but I don't know if others would be willing to put up with me."

"Put your trust in God, Don Albino," the dear old woman said, turning back on the gravel path toward the Apostolic Palace. "Trust in God."

John Paul I stayed a few minutes longer on that bench in the rotunda, engrossed in his thoughts and looking at his swollen feet. It was time to go back to his office. He had so much to do! With a resigned shrug, he got up, and a grimace revealed the pain in his ankles as he stood.

"'Finally,' as old Don Giovanni had said, 'a sacrifice has to be made.'"

And he slowly walked back to his office, hands clasped behind his back.

41

Staughton was making a supreme effort to follow his boss's orders. The fat man's bad mood was obvious, but Staughton couldn't allow himself that kind of luxury. Even though he hadn't slept all night, he had no subordinates available to relieve him. And he didn't have any family nearby to relax with. His parents were happily retired in Boston, and women could never put up with his work patterns. Anybody who worked at the agency was so committed that, little by little, duty became all-consuming, eventually disrupting family ties, even close friendships. A true secret agent had no relationship with the outside world, and that facilitated his performance.

In this regard, Staughton was no different from the rest, although he did maintain some ties with his parents and other family members. Recently he contacted his mother to tell her he was doing fine. To her, Staughton was a software specialist in the London office of an American company, a cover containing a grain of truth. His childhood friendships had been shrinking over time. Concerning women, Staughton did make an effort. Twice he came close to putting a ring on his finger, with the usual marriage commitment before the laws of God and country. He failed the first attempt on

September 11, 2001. His fiancée couldn't be faulted, because Staughton spent three months without returning to his country after the World Trade Center attack, and he limited himself to a skimpy weekly phone call, always promising he would be back the following week. The same was to happen with another woman in 2003, before the second Gulf War. The wedding was scheduled for April 9, the same day the combined forces reached Baghdad. But Staughton was, in effect, incommunicado for five months, during which he mailed an occasional letter to report his mental and physical well-being, and to say that he would be back the next month.

When he finally returned, his sweetheart had moved to another city, so utterly crushed that she wouldn't answer or return a single one of his many calls. He decided then to be done with long-term relationships, and now, at thirty-two, he lived just for work, hoping the day would come when he could have a family, with time to love and care for it. He lived in terror of becoming another Geoffrey Barnes, with no love life, no interests outside work, except to fill his stomach in any restaurant where he could eat well. To Staughton, Geoffrey Barnes was an insensitive, unscrupulous son of a bitch.

"Is it ready?" Barnes asked, leaning over the screen of the computer Staughton was using.

"Not yet, but almost."

"Do you already have something?"

"What I have is in the printer."

Barnes headed for the printer next to the window, and grabbed the handful of papers in the tray. There was a lot of information that would take hours to process. He looked toward the outer room, which was bristling with activity. Men and women moving from one side to the other. There were shouts, orders, phone calls. Three young agents were engaged in a very lively conversation.

"Hey, you three," Barnes called out. "I want you to analyze this in full detail. And when you finish, there's more."

All smiles instantly vanished, but they promptly complied with the order.

"Keep Staughton posted on whatever you find."

"Yes, sir," one of them answered.

Barnes withdrew to his office. The day was flying by and there was no news.

The young men sat at a table to carry out the work order. One, the most outgoing, went over to Staughton.

"Haven't you eaten today?"

"I haven't eaten, or drunk, or slept, or fucked," Staughton spat out, his eyes still glued to the computer screen.

"We're ready."

"Pray that we find them soon, because if we don't, you can't even imagine how ready we'll be."

The agent leaned toward Staughton, as if to share a secret. "I came in today, man. I haven't the slightest idea what we're looking for."

"For Jack Payne, a traitor, and for Sarah Monteiro, a very skillful reporter. They want them alive."

"Jack Payne? The famous Jack Payne?"

"The one and only."

"I once worked with him. He saved my life."

"Now you can be sure he wouldn't do that anymore. Go on, Thompson, there's no time to waste," Staughton said, dismissing him.

"What are you doing?"

"Searching the lists of passengers who left the country this morning. An endless job."

"Like looking for a needle in a haystack. They will have false documents."

"I'm aware of that. But for the time being, it's our only option. We've got to find that needle, by whatever means."

"Let me make a call. I'll be right back," Thompson said, moving toward a secretary whose phone was free.

Sitting in his chair, Barnes observed the outer room through the window. He needed to have all those people working on the operation, but this, unfortunately, was impossible. It was a big world, and for the United States there were other priorities, or at least that's what the president's cabinet members thought. He considered requesting additional forces from Langley. They wouldn't be denied, but it was like giving up, tantamount to admitting failure to headquarters. So, for now, he'd leave things as they were. If the fugitives hadn't shown up by the end of the day, his decision would need to be reviewed. Meanwhile, something out there caught his attention. More precisely, the lack of something. He got up, heading at a furious pace for the main room, to the table with the two men analyzing the passenger lists for flights that left the United Kingdom before the airspace was declared closed.

"Any results?"

"Nothing. Have you considered the possibility they haven't left the country?" one of the agents asked.

"They've left. I'm sure." He looked at the spot that had caught his attention. "Where's Staughton?"

"He left with Thompson."

"With Thompson? Where'd they go?"

"They didn't say."

Barnes was returning to his office when his secretary intercepted him.

"Sir—"

"Have they brought my lunch yet?"

"It's on its way."

"They're taking longer than usual."

"Twenty minutes, as always, sir."

Barnes shoved his office door. He was really on edge. "This is going to end badly for me," he repeated obsessively.

SEATED ON THE STAIRS and concentrating on the PlayStation game, the little girl paid no attention to the two men going past her, headed for another floor. If not for her concentration on the game, the girl would have heard the man walking behind, scolding the first one that this was not acceptable and that this was not what he was supposed to do. There was nobody else around.

The girl was absorbed in the meteorite shower that she had to avoid with her spaceship. The earphones kept her from hearing the tremendous racket caused by a door being kicked in on the third floor. The tenant woke up, startled by the noise. He tried to flee through the window, but the gun held by the first man stopped him cold.

"Hans, my dear Hans," Thompson greeted him gaily, closing in, with Staughton close behind, also holding a gun.

"How's business?"

42

Though it had been barely two hours since landing in the Portuguese capital, Sarah was already in the shower in a room at the Altis Hotel on Castilho Street, where the two of them managed to get something to eat as well.

Sarah still felt weird to be sharing a room with a stranger. Because he was a stranger, even after all she'd been through with him, events that she would never manage to erase from her memory, and that bonded her with Rafael in a way she hadn't ever experienced with any other man. She went around the room wrapped in a white towel, and he sat there indifferently, which did not make her any less uncomfortable.

Suddenly the television offered the latest news report. Sarah heard her name.

"We have late-breaking news, just in. The Portuguese journalist Sarah Monteiro, who was being sought by English authorities as an eyewitness to the murder that took place in her home, has been taken into custody here in London this morning."

The accompanying video showed a woman getting out of a car, her head covered with a jacket, and entering the famous Scotland Yard Building.

"That's a surprise!" Sarah exclaimed, flabbergasted.

"We're doubly clean," Rafael commented.

"Why are they making up that story?"

"To keep outside forces from interfering. They're absolutely convinced that we've left the country."

"Is that what it means?"

"Yes," Rafael answered, getting up. "I'm going to have a shower and then we'll leave."

When Rafael came out of the bathroom, a towel wrapped around his waist, he didn't find Sarah in the room. The young woman came in just as he was starting to put on his pants.

"Where were you?"

"The reception desk."

"Why?"

"Do I need to explain my every movement?"

"No. But if I don't know where you are, I can't protect you."

"I only went to the reception desk. Now I'm back, safe and sound," Sarah said sarcastically. "And now, are we leaving?" she asked, changing the subject.

"As soon as I finish getting dressed."

Sarah saw the strange tattoo on his arm, and the bullet wound he'd bandaged. "That doesn't look good."

"It's getting better."

"Let me at least clean it." Without waiting for a reply, Sarah headed for the bathroom, grabbed the soap, moistened a towel with hot water, and took another dry one. Returning to the room, she put everything on the bed.

"Sit here."

"Leave it alone. It's already better."

"Sit down."

Not wanting to argue, Rafael obeyed, sitting down on the edge of the bed. Without alcohol, the best available disinfectant was the soap. Sarah began by cleaning the wound with the wet towel. Next she used the dry one to wipe it off, and then tore the fine hand towel into strips and bandaged it. After finishing, she stood up and looked at him. Rafael's gaze had been fixed on her since the beginning of her work, so gently accomplished. Neither of them looked away for a few seconds. The situation was growing uncomfortable, at least for Sarah, but she kept her eyes steady.

"What's wrong?" Sarah finally asked.

"Nothing," Rafael answered, shifting his eyes off her as he finished putting on his shirt. "Thank you."

"Always happy to be of service," Sarah replied, standing up. "Hey, that's quite a tattoo," she commented, trying to ease the emotional tension.

"When you see one like it on somebody else, start running and don't look back."

"Why?"

"Because it's the Guard's insignia."

"The guard's? What guard?"

"The P2's Advance Guard. It's a kind of small army, trained as an overland rapid response force. Today you've trashed the reputation of that elite corps."

"Not me. You," Sarah corrected. The serpent tattoo, extending down his arm to his wrist, was now hidden again by the long shirtsleeve.

"Let's phone the desk to ask for a taxi."

"It's not necessary."

"Are we going to catch one somewhere else?"

"No. We're not going by taxi. I have a car ready."

A little while later they found themselves on the highway leaving Lisbon, headed north. Very soon Sarah was to see her father, and she could think of nothing else.

43

After a whole night without sleep, the two men remained in the same place, their eyes fixed on the lobby door through which the old man had disappeared many hours before. They maintained the same alert, watchful attitude, especially the one sitting next to the driver.

"I'm beat," the more alert one complained.

"Cars weren't designed for sleeping," the other replied.

They had some coffee and doughnuts that the first one had gone out to buy from a coffee shop no more than a block away. Given his companion's taciturn nature, he had a lot of extra time to think. He thought about stores that stayed open all night and about more important matters. Payne, for example, the famous Jack. He condemned what the man had done and yet admired him. It took a lot of courage—real balls—to make a move like that. He had to put his ass on the line to play a double role inside the Guard and, even more important, not to be exposed, until he decided the time was right. Good old Jack Payne. A fox. And speaking of old men and foxes . . .

"The target just came out," the driver said.

"I saw him, too."

"Are you going to follow him?"

"No. You are."

"And you?"

"I'm going to take a look around his place."

"Now you're talking," the driver said, satisfied. Finally, a bit of action.

"Don't let him out of your sight. When I'm finished, I'll give you a buzz to find out where you are."

The driver slid smoothly out of the car and followed the old man's steps, walking up Seventh Avenue toward Central Park. He turned toward Broadway and headed for Times Square. Taking walks delighted the old man, and it simplified the work of the one trailing him.

Why don't we just put a bullet between his eyes and be done with this whole business? the driver wondered. What makes him special? Why should we treat him any differently from everybody else?

Barely fifteen minutes later, the other man managed to get into the old man's flat. He did a professional job and was extremely careful, now that he had exceeded the limits of his assignment. His boss's clear instructions did not include entering the apartment. Moreover, they expressly prohibited any action that could jeopardize the overall plan. Why was he placing himself in such danger? He was risking all of his previous accomplishments and taking his life in his hands, knowing that the Master's hand did not tremble at the moment of exacting punishment. But he was trying to gain an edge, something that could please the old boss, whose arrival was imminent.

He'd had everything planned, waiting at a prudent distance from the residence. Less than ten minutes had gone by when a car stopped in front of it and the doorman went to open the car door for the lady and her children ready to climb in. The man wasted no time, already finding himself in the service elevator, on his way to the seventh floor. No one had seen him go in.

Now, inside the apartment, he inspected it with precision. The decor was modest, with old furniture and nothing too luxurious. Dark tones were predominant and there were many crosses, dispersed through all the rooms. The faith of the man living there was also evidenced by a humble wooden altar with enough extra space facing it to say Mass for ten or fifteen people, and by various copies of the New Testament, in different editions, sizes, and bindings.

During his hourlong inspection, the man made three phone calls to keep track of the tenant's jaunt, well into Central Park, to the despair of the driver, who was already fed up with following him around. By the time he had completed his task, he had no doubt that what he had hoped to find wasn't there. He had searched in the darkest nooks and hidden corners. Cautiously poking his head out the window, he saw the endless traffic on Sixth Avenue. He glanced at his car, still neatly parked. He tried to compose himself, for he couldn't go out in an agitated state.

With a thoughtful expression, he sighed deeply. "Nothing."

44

The Mafra National Palace, one of the most important architectural relics of Portugal, was located in the town from which it got its name. The enormous edifice was built according to the wishes of King Juan V of Portugal, who had promised to build it if the queen, Doña María of Austria, gave him an heir. The birth of Princess Doña María Bárbara made him keep his promise, and the king spared no expense in building that baroque architectural masterpiece. The luxurious royal quarters occupied the entire top floor, but the building also contained a monastery for more than 300 Franciscan priests, a basilica, and one of the most beautiful libraries in Europe, covered with marble and exotic woods. Its rococo shelves now housed more than 40,000 volumes, leather-bound with gold engraving. In addition to many other literary marvels, it held a first edition of *Os Lusíadas,* by Luíz Vaz de Camões. The building had not housed any Franciscan fathers for a long time now, since the religious orders were dissolved in 1834. In addition to its great intrinsic value, the palace also held many treasures. The basilica had two towers and a cupola, six pipe organs with an exclusive repertory, which couldn't be heard in any other place, and two carillons of ninety-two bells, considered the best in the world.

"What are we doing here?"

"We're going to meet your father."

"Here?" Sarah was in a terrible mood. "He's coming here?"

"He's already here."

They passed the enormous doors of the monastery and went into its magnificent interior. Rafael's manner suggested he knew where they were going.

The serenity of the monastery began to ease Sarah's anxieties. This environment served as a balm. A group of students was ahead of them, with a guide explaining the history of the place.

"Saramago, the Nobel Prize winner in literature—in his book *Memorial do convento*, which I recommend, by the way—describes the misfortunes and complications that occurred during the construction of this building."

Rafael and Sarah were sneaking through a restricted-access doorway. Her heart began beating much faster. "He's close."

"Did you know it's said that the height of this monastery is the same as its depth underground?" she asked nervously.

"I'm sure," Rafael answered mechanically, obviously thinking about something else.

They went into what had once been a hospital, with an adjoining chapel, from which the patients could hear the Lord's words. In one corner, Rafael skillfully opened a small wooden door.

They descended a narrow spiral staircase, illuminated by the flashlight Rafael had pulled out of his pocket.

"It's also said that the basements have been inaccessible for centuries, due to the thousands of rats living there." Sarah's voice sounded tremulous, revealing her anxious jitters. "Countless treasures were lost because of that."

They came to a very old door with rusty hinges and moldy wood. There was utter darkness. Sarah began picturing bats awakened from their sleep, infuriated by the two intruders. Rafael opened the door, which screeched sharply.

"Watch your head," he warned, stooping to go through the narrow doorway. Sarah followed him, convinced she was about to enter fifteenth-century Portugal.

"What *is* this? Where are we?"

"Take this," Rafael said, handing her the small flashlight.

Sarah grabbed the chance to survey the place, disregarding Rafael's moves. But the only thing she managed to see was dirt. Dirt and more dirt. She couldn't tell if it was a continuation of the passageway or a kind of catacomb.

"Would you mind pointing that over this way?" Rafael asked. "It has to be somewhere around here."

"What?"

Set in the rock, or dirt wall, Sarah couldn't tell, was a stick with a cloth wound around one end. A primitive torch.

Seconds later, using a lighter, Rafael ignited it. The fire spread an orange light that partly lifted the darkness. Before them was an enormous tunnel that looked endless, dug out of the rock.

"Where are we?"

"Welcome to the catacombs of the Mafra monastery," Rafael said, noticing Sarah's bewildered expression. "Shall we go?"

Sarah didn't answer for a moment, stunned into silence.

"My father's coming to meet us here?" she finally asked.

"No, your father lives here."

45

GOLF AND MONEY MATTERS
SEPTEMBER 1978

There's certainly nothing like the blue smoke of Havana cigars. It traces beautiful, unpredictable swirls, slow-moving and soulful, and their fragrance permeates rooms with an incomparable, refined elegance.

Paul Marcinkus was savoring a Havana cigar in his Rome office, while watching the television recap of a round of golf. Just at that moment, while an elegant golfer in a yellow jersey competed in the tournament against the all-powerful Jack Nicklaus, a bitter workday was coming to an end. Only the Masters at Augusta or the British Open could soothe life's troubles. Although there's nothing like Wimbledon, of course. he thought

False holiness made the Illinois archbishop sick, and he couldn't understand certain cardinals' disgust with life's pleasures. "Holy rubbish!" was his usual response when some humble priest reminded him that the Church's elaborate display wasn't exactly the best model for the world's faithful. In those cases, even if the observation came from a member of the Curia, Archbishop Marcinkus reminded them of a passage from the Gospels that always disarmed his opponents. "The Son of man, who ate and drank, came, and people said, 'This is a gluttonous drunkard, friend of sinners and carousers.' But his deeds bore witness to his wisdom." Luckily for him, the prelates reproaching him never mentioned the passage where Jesus warned that one could not serve two masters, particularly if one of them was God and the other gold.

"That's a three-iron," Marcinkus said, when the RAI commentator didn't know which club the golfer was using.

Pope Paul VI entrusted him with the directorship of the Vatican's finances in 1971, when he was only forty-seven. Marcinkus could still remember the ailing pope's admission, after Vatican Council II, that the coffers of the Holy See were full of cobwebs. It was a divine mission, Marcinkus thought, grinning ironically. The institute for religious works, the IOR, really housed distinct financial organizations that needed updating and renovation.

One of the first modern banking institutions depending on the Holy See was the Banco Ambrosiano, founded by Monsignor Tovini in 1896. That financial entity, as Marcinkus read in various old reports, was intended to "support ethical organizations, beneficial work, and religious groups devoted to charity."

"Naturally," the cardinal said out loud, remembering that one of the former Banco Ambrosiano directors had been a nephew of Pope Pius XI. "Charity matters most."

During the 1960s the Banco Ambrosiano moved its central offices to Luxembourg, a country that worshiped money. "Small countries are such delights: Luxembourg, Monaco, Andorra, the Vatican, the Bahamas." In Luxembourg, Banco Ambrosiano Holding was formed, with its beneficial work being diversified around the world.

The smile on Marcinkus's face showed he was thinking of those pleasant sixties, when Michele Sindona, incomprehensibly labeled the Mafia's banker, began to develop friendly ties with Roberto Calvi. According to the cardinal, Sindona was not a terribly clever man. He had been arrested in the United States, and found guilty of illegal financial activities in Italy. But as for Calvi, Marcinkus could only find him worthy of admiration. Based on that, strong ties developed between the IOR and the Banco Ambrosiano. Marcinkus decided, through a series of high-finance maneuvers, to absorb the Banca Cattolica del Veneto, then headed by an ignorant cleric named

Albino Luciani. Marcinkus had to make a superhuman effort to recall his brief, and acrimonious, exchanges with the Venetian patriarch at that time. And, years later, when Luciani was elected pope, Marcinkus assumed the Venetian had his mind set only on revenge. Now he had been able to prove he was right. Luciani had accused a good number in the Curia of moral corruption, and intended to make a clean sweep in the heart of the Church. Fortunately, the P2 was taking care of that at this very moment.

Because of Marcinkus's efforts, the Church was saved, thanks to his connections with big names in finance, thanks to the pious men who had advised him well. There was nothing wrong with obtaining high profits and, in addition, collaborating in various charitable works.

But Albino Luciani didn't see it that way. He didn't understand anything. In all those years, he had learned nothing. And he had threatened to destroy them all.

At that moment, on television, Nicklaus putted for a birdie, and the ball went smoothly into the hole.

"Brilliant! Brilliant!"

46

The jet cut through the air at top speed, at an altitude above 42,000 feet. The cabin on this plane was like the passengers' London office, with people going back and forth, some giving orders, others bent over computers, talking on the phone, engaged in an endless variety of tasks no different from the ones they performed on land. The only difference was that they couldn't go out for coffee, and they had to adjust to a few minutes' rest inside the aircraft. They were confined, seat belts fastened, only during takeoffs and landings.

In heaven as on earth. Geoffrey Barnes still had a separate office from the rest of his crew, with a luxurious leather chair.

Thompson proved to be a good recruit. He served himself coffee in the director's office and sat on a chair considerably less comfortable than Barnes's.

"Sharon Stone. Damned bastards," Barnes declared, brooding. "The guy wasn't joking."

"What guy?" Thompson asked.

"Somebody at the British Museum. It's not important."

Unlike Barnes's London office, this one lacked the glass windows that gave him an overview of his agents' work. Even so, he liked the change, since they couldn't see him, either, leaving him free to do as he pleased.

Outside, Staughton applied himself to his first duty—which he preferred over any field assignment—the analysis and cross-checking of facts. Whether it was in a plane or in an office made no difference. It was always better than gathering information on the street, as he recently had to do at Hans's flat. Staughton didn't have the temperament for that. His weapon was the computer. The printer next to him started to vibrate, and immediately began to spew out paper at a surprising rate.

Those guys put my nerves on edge, he thought, glancing at the four men in black sitting in the back of the cabin, completely motionless since the plane had taken off. At no point did they exchange words, looking like statues or mimes. They were identically dressed, and without a single wrinkle. Or maybe they suggested something else.

Staughton couldn't stand the dark suits, the agents' formal style. He favored casual clothes, wearing whatever he felt like. It should be enough not to have three-day-old stubble and not to have messy, uncombed hair. But the day a suit and tie was required, Staughton would be the first to resign. The printer ejected the last page, and after gathering the pile into a folder, the agent headed for his boss's office.

"I can't stand seeing those guys sitting there," he complained as soon as he went in.

"Then don't look at them," Thompson said.

"Do they belong to the Guard?" Staughton asked. "They don't look very dangerous."

"Lower your voice, Staughton. Those guys are beasts," Barnes warned. "Any news?"

"Well, something. They took the Eurostar from Waterloo to Paris, and then a plane from Orly, which landed in Lisbon two hours ago. We already have men on the ground trying to find out what they did there and where they are now."

"Sharon Stone," Barnes repeated, sighing. "Damned bastards."

"Any idea of their reason for the trip?" Thompson asked.

"Surely to talk with the girl's father," Barnes answered.

"The army man isn't at his Beja estate. We already searched the place. Now we're checking relatives."

"This is our only chance, guys," Barnes muttered. "They aren't going to use their passports again. Jack won't make that mistake."

"Everything's tougher when the target is somebody who knows how to take care of things."

"What's our estimated arrival time, Staughton?" Barnes asked.

"We'll be landing at Figo Maduro air base in two hours."

"Fine. Get the staff to search in hotels, car rental services, taxi companies, private planes. Have them show photos, but don't leave the photos with anybody. We don't want the Portuguese police getting involved, and it goes without saying, we don't want reporters, either. Be quick, but don't stand out. Make sure of that. We need good clues to follow as soon as we land."

Staughton, who had gone in with a bunch of papers, left with a bunch of tasks to do, just as he liked it. A few phone calls and he got everything going full blast, ready to gather leads as soon as possible. His only lingering hope was that Jack Payne wouldn't outsmart them all.

"What made them decide to go looking for her father in Portugal?" Thompson asked, still relaxing in Barnes's office.

"I think they're looking for answers. And trying to determine their ongoing strategy."

"But doesn't he belong to the P2?"

"In theory."

"In theory?"

"There are theoretically two tiers of people in the P2, the old and the new. Her father belongs to the old group."

"Then there are two lodges?"

"Not exactly. There's only one P2. The old members have no power at all in the present circumstances. But they exist, they are there. And they're giving us a lot of trouble."

"Is all of this caused by their maneuvering?"

"Yes. Even the Vatican is on the alert. We've got to get hold of those papers as fast as possible, to keep all the shit from hitting the fan. We're part of the shit, Thompson, and we'll be sent flying."

47

"What did you mean, my father lives here?" Sarah wanted to know as they trekked through the long passage dug out of the rock. It was high enough for both of them to go through fully upright, with space left over.

"Just that," Rafael answered, pointing the torch upward. He seemed to know the way.

"How can that be?" she asked, unable to picture anybody able to live there.

"You'll see."

"It was true," the young woman said, changing the subject. "The monastery had tunnels."

Sarah's heart was beating faster with every step. The moment of reunion with her father was fast approaching. She realized that her image of him had been incomplete, even false. She didn't know him at all. She had always trusted him for his exemplary behavior, his flawless social conduct. To her he was a good man—a model father, soldier, and man. Now, back in her native land, she went through the catacombs of the Mafra monastery—

known only to a few, and visited by even fewer—trying to convince herself to stay strong. In spite of everything, her eyes were tearing.

After a few minutes she caught sight of the huge wooden door that ended the tunnel. Something flew over their heads, making Sarah scream.

"That was a bat," Rafael reassured her.

Sarah looked at the black opening the creature had come out of, and then the one it flew into, right in front of her.

"What are those holes?"

"Passages to other places."

"What places?"

"This is a network of tunnels that lead into separate galleries, shelters, and other passages. I've never really had time to explore it fully, so I don't know exactly where they all go," Rafael explained, totally calm. "Did you know that during the period of the French invasions, the royal family thought about moving down here?" he asked. "But in the end, the royal family decided to go to Brazil. It was safer."

"And farther away."

They finally reached the door, and Sarah waited for Rafael to open it. He approached the giant wooden slab and struck three hard blows. One. Silence. Two. Silence. Three. Silence.

After waiting a few minutes, they heard the sounds of the bolts being moved. Sarah felt tremendous anxiety, which only increased as she waited for the door to open. There was a brief silence, which seemed much longer than it really was. The hinges creaked and the large door started to move. A face appeared, smiling broadly. Sarah was burning up inside but kept her nerves under control, except for a slight tremor in her arms and legs. The person greeting them was Raul Brandão Monteiro, her father.

"How are you?" Rafael asked, pulling Raul close to him in a heartfelt hug, accompanied by firm slaps on the back. It was the reunion of two friends.

"Fine. Everything's going fine here."

Once the embrace was over, Raul looked at his daughter, his eyes glassy.

"Sarah, my child," he said, getting closer to her.

Tears ran down both their faces.

"Forgive me, my dear. Forgive me," he pleaded, his voice torn with emotion.

The excitement of the greetings subsided and reality set in again.

"Let's go," Raul affectionately said to his daughter. "Come on in."

On the other side of the door, there was light at the end of a hallway lined with painted tiles representing the themes of the Portuguese discoveries. The caravels of the order of Christ in turbulent seas, the giant Adamastor, the new lands, the enemies. Each painting was separated from the next by a stanza from *Os Lusíadas.*

Rafael closed the door, locking it again and restoring the security of their refuge. He put out the torch. It was not needed anymore, since the candelabra fixed on the wall provided enough light. Marble tiles covered the floor, lending an air of splendor to the place. Sarah now understood that the coarseness of the network of tunnels meant nothing. The passages needed no display of luxury. That was reserved for the shelters. The enormous door truly separated two worlds.

At the end of the hallway a large balcony spread before them on both sides. Several columns supported the weight of the arches. At the bases were wrought-iron railings for anyone who wanted to admire the salon below, a tremendous space with all the comforts of daily life. Two stairways led down to it, one on each side of the balcony. A big hanging chandelier in the shape of a cupola illuminated the entire area, and the walls were covered with tapestries. There was a grand piano, various sofas with cushions, and a dining table suitable for at least twenty dinner guests. The decor fired Sarah's imagination, leading her to picture either a palace or a harem. Only the women were missing, and the sultan.

From the balcony, Sarah noticed three doors on each side, probably leading to private chambers.

Raul went toward the left stairway, and as soon as they descended the marble stairs, he invited them to sit on a large sofa.

"Would you like something to eat? To drink? I don't have much, but surely I can find something you might like." His voice conveyed how happy he was to see them safe and sound.

"Are you alone here?" his daughter dared to ask, ignoring the offer.

"Yes."

"And Mom?"

"She's fine, don't worry."

"Why didn't she come here with you?"

"Because she wouldn't be able to stand this solitude. There's no television, no radio, no Internet—nothing."

"Where is she?" she asked, somewhat resentfully. The relief at seeing him was already gone. Her mind was back in control, recalling all that had happened, the questions, everything that was in play.

"Your mother's in a safe place. Near Oporto," her father answered. "I filled her in on everything. Her reaction wasn't the best, as you can imagine." Nodding slightly, Sarah signaled her understanding. They both knew this woman. "She wanted to come get you in London, but once she understood the magnitude of the problem, she went along with my plan. She can't be out there alone. If they caught her, they'd be able to use her as a bargaining chip. They know how to do that. Besides, the CIA agents involved in this are very active."

"That's right," Rafael agreed. "But we are still a few hours ahead."

"Hours?" Sarah asked, not sure she'd heard right.

"Yes, hours," her father repeated. "These people are extremely well prepared. They can't reconstruct our every step, but there's always some clue left, and they are certainly going to find it."

Fear again overpowered Sarah, raising her heartbeat and giving her chills.

"Can they find us here?"

"Not here," Rafael hastened to clarify. "But they can place us in Mafra."

"How?"

"By checking with the company from which we rented the car."

"Then they can also find out what hotel we stayed in?"

"Yes, theoretically. If they check the registers of all the hotels in the area. But if they locate the taxi driver who took us from the airport to the hotel, we're not in danger, because—"

"I know," Sarah interrupted, remembering that as they left the airport

Rafael had asked the taxi driver to take them to the Hotel Le Meridien. At the end of the trip, when Sarah thought she would finally be getting some rest, Rafael started walking away from the hotel. And when she asked him where they were going, he answered that they wouldn't be staying there. They walked a half mile or so to the Altis Hotel. Now she understood his tactics. "They'd think we stayed at Le Méridien."

"Exactly."

"I see," Sarah said, thinking. A moment later she looked intently at her father. "Obviously we haven't got any time to waste, so start telling me, from the beginning, everything I don't know, don't leave anything out."

Raul sat across from them, separated by a dark, very ornate table.

"That's fair. You have the right to know everything. What has Rafael told you?"

"Nothing good. Mostly horrible things, considering that I received a list of offenders that included my father's name."

"Let's be calm, my dear," the captain asked her in a conciliatory tone.

"Calm? You're asking me to be calm? Some guys are following me, guys who killed important people, who even liquidated a pope! See if you can be calm."

"Fine. Now you're going to be quiet and listen to what I have to say. But first I'm going to serve us all some port, understood?" Finally the military tone appeared in Captain Monteiro's voice. He got up to keep his word, filled three glasses with a Ferreira Vintage port, and handed one to each of them.

Rafael remained serene, unaffected, sitting next to Sarah. Raul finally returned to his place and took a sip of his drink.

"Every man makes mistakes in the course of his life. And I'm no exception. In 1971 I was admitted into the P2 because I thought that by doing so I would be helping my country. We had a dictatorship in Portugal, and the P2 offered me the chance to try to change that situation. Or at least that's what I wanted to believe. When I discovered the true objective of its leaders, I separated very quickly from the lodge. Unfortunately, no one gets to leave the P2 of his own free will. I wasn't the only Portuguese member, as you must have seen from the list. And there were many more who had the good luck not to appear either on that list or on the one published in 1981."

"I recognize that," Sarah agreed. "Some of our most famous political figures."

The captain disregarded his daughter's remark.

"My relationship with the P2 ended in 1981. Mine and many other people's. But the organization continues to exist, as you had the chance to witness in the worst possible way. During the eleven years that I belonged to it, I never put anyone's life in danger, and I didn't kill anybody." He uttered this last statement looking straight into his daughter's eyes, so there wouldn't be the slightest doubt. "I kept an eye on many people in Portugal, people the organization wanted to keep under constant surveillance. Some were foreigners or transients. But as far as I know, only one of those people ended up dead, but not by my hands. One of them was Sá Carneiro."

"Oh, my God," Sarah said, and gasped, bringing her hand to her mouth. "The prime minister. He died in a plane crash."

"That story put an end to my involvement with the lodge."

"And when does mine begin?"

"We're getting to that. First I've got to explain what those papers are. We're talking about thirteen pages."

"Thirteen? But I only have two. I mean three. I had three but lost one, in a man's stomach." She turned to Rafael. "The one with the code."

"What code?" her father quickly asked. "No, wait, we'll talk about that afterward. Let me finish. Those thirteen pages include the list you received, four pages with information concerning high officials in the Vatican, and another list with the pontiff's future appointees, some of whom were going to be put in place the day the pope died. The papers also contain his various annotations concerning papal measures—short, medium, and long term— for a controversial papacy. And there is also the Third Secret of Fátima."

Sarah was perplexed. "The one that John Paul II revealed in 2000?"

Raul shot a surprised glance at Sarah.

"Of course not. The true third secret, which reveals the death of a man dressed in white at the hands of his peers."

Some people thought that the third part of the secret of Fátima had not been published in its entirety. What Sister Lucía had written referred to an appeal by the Blessed Virgin Mary, who had warned, "Repent, repent, repent!" She had then seen a bishop dressed in white, which she identified as the Holy Father. She also saw other bishops, priests, monks, and nuns climbing a steep mountain, at the peak of which was "a great cross of rough beams, as if they were of cork oak, still with the bark on." Before arriving at that cross, the pope, or the figure that Sister Lucía identified as the pope, went through a great city in ruins. The pontiff seemed to be "trembling, his gait unsteady, overwhelmed by pain and sorrow as he prayed for the souls of the corpses he found by the road." The vision continued, always according to what the Vatican published, describing how the man dressed in white arrived at the mountain peak, knelt at the foot of the great cross, and was murdered "by a group of soldiers who shot him several times using guns and crossbows." The prophetic vision concluded with the assurance that other bishops, priests, nuns, and monks died with him in the same way, including many men and women of different stations. Beneath the arms of the cross were two angels, according to Sister Lucía, each of them holding a large glass vessel in which they retrieved the martyrs' blood.

Sarah was still thinking about her father's story, trying to assess its consequences. Given the choice, she would prefer to keep it all hidden, never to be discovered by anybody.

"Then why did they bring that story out in 2000?"

"Because they had to think of something. And it was better to disappoint expectations than to say that the third secret predicted the murder of a pope by his own men."

"Of course," Sarah agreed, still holding on to a thoughtful attitude. "I imagine it can't be easy to handle a revelation that way."

"No, it isn't. That's why they waited so long before letting it be known. Then they prepared the 2000 event, very carefully staged. The faithful bought the goods, along with the unfaithful, and the case was wrapped up."

Sarah's wineglass was still untouched. Rafael's, in contrast, was already empty.

"Why did those papers come out now? If he was murdered by the Vatican, why did they save those papers, instead of destroying them?"

"First, let's make something clear. The Vatican, as an institution, had nothing to do with this. A group of men, even hiding beneath a habit or a red cap, do not amount to the whole Church. Today the Vatican continues to have undesirables, just as in 1978. The difference is that they aren't so influential. Even though the Roman Curia is as conservative as it was then, the P2 doesn't hold any power over it. It can't manipulate conclaves or papal decisions. Certainly there are other organizations playing that role now, but we can't be sure whether they are laundering money and producing false titles."

"Manipulate conclaves? And the cardinals? And the Holy Ghost?"

"The only Holy Ghost I know is a bank," her father wisecracked. "Clearly the conclaves are, above all, political events, subject to external influences and manipulations, like any human election. Until the beginning of the conclave, eligible cardinals carry out campaigns intended to produce the greatest possible number of votes. The Curia, supported by powerful organizations, elects its candidate, and when the cardinals enter the conclave, everything is practically decided."

"Then, it's all a farce?"

"Theoretically—the Church has various factions. The most conservative, represented by the Curia, and other, more liberal ones. Once one of these factions gains dominance, the other cardinals are pulled to it."

"They follow the locomotive."

"Yes, I suppose you could put it that way."

"And that's what happened in 1978?"

"No. The Curia didn't succeed in securing the election of Cardinal Siri, their favorite. One faction of non-Italian cardinals gave its support to Albino Luciani. And that sealed his fate."

Silence again for a moment. The captain then continued.

"In the second conclave in 1978, the 'three-pope year,' the Curia didn't take any chances, and elected someone they would be able to control. It goes without saying that they hit the nail on the head. Not only did the

Curia keep him under their control, but as pontiff he managed to establish an excellent relationship with the faithful. He was very useful to them."

"I didn't think of John Paul II that way."

"Nobody does. But it's difficult to blame him for it. First, because he received a very serious warning in 1981, when Mehmet Ali Ağca tried to assassinate him. The original plan wasn't to give him a scare, but to do away with him entirely. And later, because the Vatican, indirectly, put nearly a billion dollars into the coffers of Solidarity, the Polish labor union in Gdansk that overthrew their communist regime. They did it with funds from the Vatican and from the United States."

"But you still haven't answered my question. Why did the people who killed the pope not destroy those papers? That's what I would have done."

"Listen," her father continued, "the pope didn't die because of the papers in his hand. But someone immediately took care to remove them. That person gave them to the man in charge of the job, who took them out of the Vatican. The order was to destroy the papers, but he never fulfilled it."

"Why?"

"Good question. Maybe so he could keep them for blackmail. Or even as a kind of 'life insurance,' in case the people on top wanted to get rid of him in the future."

"I see," Sarah said, nodding. "Then the time has come to explain the murder. Why did they kill the pope?"

"Are you going to drink your port?" Rafael asked unexpectedly, his voice absent for some time. Sarah looked at him.

"No," she answered, holding out the glass. "Help yourself."

"Thanks," Rafael said, instantly taking it.

"I want to know who killed the pope and why," Sarah continued. "And who is that Firenzi? I need to know how I fit into this whole business."

"Forgive me for interrupting, Captain, but we should continue this conversation in the car."

"What car? The one we drove here in?" the young woman asked.

"No, the one I've got outside," her father explained. "How did you think we'd be leaving?"

"I don't know. With him, anything's possible," Sarah answered, looking at Rafael. "But where are we going? Aren't we safe here?"

"Yes. But very soon Mafra will be crawling with agents, and we can't run the risk of being surrounded. It's important to keep some maneuvering room, to stay always a step ahead," Rafael explained.

"Do you really think they'll manage to place us in Mafra?"

"Yes. Beyond the slightest doubt."

48

The pope died because he knew too much," Raul said, sitting in the passenger seat of the Volvo, looking back at his daughter. Sarah leaned forward in order to hear better. Rafael seemed focused on his driving. She surmised that he already knew the story her father was telling, and was absorbed in his own thoughts.

"Knew too much about what?"

"He knew that important figures in the ecclesiastical hierarchy, including his secretary of state, Cardinal Jean-Marie Villot, belonged to Masonic organizations, an offense subject to the automatic penalty of excommunication. He also came to understand that the Institute for Religious Works, the IOR—better known as the Vatican Bank—was directed by a corrupt man who, in collaboration with someone from the Banco Ambrosiano, laundered Mafia money and funds from other not-so-holy enterprises."

"Who are you talking about?"

"Paul Marcinkus, from the Vatican Bank, and Roberto Calvi of the Banco Ambrosiano. And the key figure, the one who manipulated both of these men, the brains behind the whole black-market money-laundering scheme, Licio Gelli."

"How is it possible to do something like that?"

"By means of shell companies based in South America and northern Europe, and later by purchasing foreign banks or using subsidiaries of the Banco Ambrosiano in order to bring money in or divert it. A lot of money. When the business prospered, Paul VI nicknamed Calvi 'God's banker.' At some point, they expanded the operation. That is, Gelli began to demand that they launder more money, always through the Vatican and the Ambrosiano. Naturally, it wasn't long before suspicions were aroused, and despite being brilliant bankers, Calvi and Marcinkus made mistakes. Actually, many mistakes. And it all blew up, in 'the Vatican Bank scandal,' shortly after the pope's death.

"The Banco Ambrosiano," Raul continued, "fell into the hands of Roberto Calvi, a known member of the P2 Lodge. Gelli, the Grand Master of the lodge, arranged for the Vatican Bank to take more than a twenty percent share of the Ambrosiano, involving it in irregular activities in Europe and America, with parallel, undercover societies for laundering money and other fiscal frauds."

All of this crashed when the Bank of Italy declared a depletion of billions of dollars, which the Ambrosiano would not be able to cover. In the early eighties, when the investigations started, the Holy See's tolerance of Calvi and his operatives' manipulations was discovered, and it was also understood that the Vatican was willing to participate in the Ambrosiano Bank's illicit activities. Calvi asked for help from the Vatican Bank, headed by Archbishop Marcinkus, but Marcinkus had enough trouble trying to save his own skin.

Albino Luciani was aware of these manipulations long before he became pope, because, as the patriarch of Venice, he was president of the Catholic Bank of Venice, one of the Holy See's financial institutions. Later, from the papal throne, he had even greater access to information, which only brought increased danger.

"So they killed the pope because he was about to ruin them," Sarah concluded.

"Exactly. And he was also planning to expose them publicly. They would all end up in jail. There was so much garbage piled up. For example, the

Vatican Bank was intimately linked, through the P2, to the purchase of the Exocet missiles used by Argentina in the Falkland Islands War. Can you imagine all the implications this has?"

"Oh, my God."

"They even used a Mafia type named Michele Sindona, who brought them large sums of money, serving as a link with Cosa Nostra."

"Was he part of the group, too?"

"Yes, but Sindona wasn't involved in the pope's death, although a lot of people's blood, including that of some notable magistrates, was on his hands. But at that point he was already up to his neck in other problems."

"And nobody took care of the other frauds?"

"At some point, various European enforcement agencies and the U.S. Justice Department put two and two together. Even so, it took them a long time to unravel all the threads. But John Paul I, soon after being elected pope, met privately with U.S. Justice Department officials, who updated him on the situation, so that he could take whatever measures he deemed appropriate. John Paul I knew then that there were criminals in the Vatican and that he had to get rid of them. But they overtook him."

"Were they the ones who killed him?"

"It's not known. I believe they were morally responsible for the crime, just as guilty as whoever killed him."

"Who was?"

"Licio Gelli, Roberto Calvi, and Archbishop Paul Marcinkus, along with Cardinal Jean-Marie Villot. Of course, someone inside the Vatican had to facilitate the actual killer's entry, and then destroy all the clues. His Holiness was found dead at four thirty in the morning, and by six in the afternoon his private quarters were already cleaned and sealed, with the key under Villot's control. And in a little over twelve hours, every vestige of Albino Luciani's presence in the Apostolic Palace had been erased."

"That's efficient."

"That's really being in a hurry. At five thirty in the morning the same day, forty-five minutes after the pope was declared dead, the embalmers were already in the Vatican. With all that had to be done, it was suspicious that the Signoracci brothers were there so soon. Especially if we consider that Italian law permits embalming only twenty-four hours after death."

Sarah shook her head.

"At six in the afternoon that same day, John Paul I was already embalmed. It was a flagrant violation of the law."

"But what kind of poison would fool the doctors?"

"The pope wasn't poisoned."

"He wasn't?"

"No. And no doctor was fooled."

"Then—"

"Even a moron could see there was something fishy. A simple heart attack would never have made the pope's enemies act so foolishly or hastily. When Paul VI died, barely a month earlier, the Vatican behaved in a completely different way."

"And who exactly killed him?"

"Nobody knows his name. But I think he's the man on our trail."

"Then he's got to be connected with the P2."

"Yes. The one who killed John Paul I was, and is, a member of the P2."

"And you don't know his name?"

"Only his initials: J.C."

"And where do I come into all this?" Sarah asked for the umpteenth time, hoping her father would finally make it clear.

"Where do you come into all this?" the captain repeated out loud, sighing as he tried to arrange his thoughts and make them understandable to others. "Valdemar Firenzi, who's an old member of the P2, like me, found the famous vanished papers. He spent many years pursuing leads and gathering evidence, and finally, when he had already given up, he found them in the least likely place."

"Where?"

"In the Vatican's Secret Archives."

"How would they end up there?"

"I haven't the slightest idea. You'll have to ask J.C.," Raul answered. "After the people connected with the case started to die off, I think he felt more secure. It really wouldn't have been at all wise for him to keep the papers."

"Agreed. It doesn't matter. Firenzi found the documents, and then?"

"A short time earlier, Pietro Saviotti had reopened the case of the death of John Paul I in the District of Rome, and those papers acquired a tremendous importance as evidence. Aware of their value, and of the fact that many people would rather have them disappear, Firenzi decided to take them out of the Vatican and send them to people nobody knew, intending to save them. But since the walls of the Holy See have ears, he felt threatened. So what did he do? He sent a photo of Benedict XVI to Felipe Aragón and to Pablo Rincón, with a message intended to be understood only by them. And something happened, I don't know what, that made him send the list to you."

"But why me?"

"Because you're his goddaughter. Don't you remember our talking about him when you were little? He moved to Rome a long time ago, that's why you don't know him.

"He needed someone that didn't belong to the organization, and figured that, after seeing my name on the list, you would get in touch with me and I would understand right away. The worst that could happen was that you wouldn't pay any attention. He wasn't thinking that he'd be captured. But he was, and somehow they found out about practically everything."

"And now?"

"Now he must be dead," her father said, his voice choked up.

Thinking about it, Sarah grew very serious.

"I didn't remember that I had an Italian godfather."

"Don't let the name fool you. Firenzi was of solid Portuguese stock."

"All the same, he endangered everybody."

"Don't say that."

"It's the truth. He stuck his nose into something that was just fine as it was. What did he expect to accomplish?"

"To bring the truth to light."

"That truth was fine as it was, locked away."

Rafael looked for something inside the pocket of his jacket, pulling out a sheet of paper and a photo of Benedict XVI.

"What's that?" Sarah asked.

"What Father Felipe received in Madrid."

He handed the letter to her. Although she didn't speak Spanish, the language was so similar to Portugese that she understood nearly everything.

Today, on my seventy-fourth birthday, my past mistakes have caught up with me. Divine irony doesn't pass unnoticed, and I know that He is the one behind all of this. As life unfolds, it's difficult to understand the implications and consequences of our decisions and actions. We start from the right principles, having the noblest of dreams, and in time we come up against our own monstrosity, the vile and cruel consequence of what we have done. No matter how much we may spend the rest of our days using good to atone for the bad, completely denying ourselves for the other, the stain remains, always sneaking up behind us, whispering, "You won't escape, you won't escape." Until it ends up fulfilling its promise, as happens today, on my birthday. Before saying good-bye, I want to present you with this letter and the photo of my beloved pope, to whom you'll know how to apply the tender light of prayer. As for myself, I bid farewell with a confession. Because of my cowardice I let a pope die, and I did nothing to prevent it.

"The Spanish authorities gave this to me when I went to arrange for Felipe's funeral. My good friend Felipe."

"And they didn't find the content strange?"

"They didn't put two and two together. And luckily, I arrived before anybody from the organization could get hold of the letter. In Buenos Aires that wasn't possible, and not only did they kill Pablo, but they also took the photo."

"What's special about the photo?"

Raul took out a small pocket flashlight with ultraviolet light.

"Come closer."

Hesitant at first, Sarah moved closer to her father, driven by curiosity. Rafael took an occasional glance, without neglecting his driving. They saw, under the application of the black light, how the face of Benedict XVI disappeared, and there was instead the face of an old man, skillfully traced with thousands of fluorescent filaments.

"Who is it?" Sarah asked.

"I don't know," her father answered.

"A double portrait," Rafael said.

Raul removed the magical light, and immediately the image of Benedict XVI reappeared.

"I'm confused."

"I don't know who it is, but they must know already. I suppose," Raul added, "right now it's the man who has the papers."

"And that brings us to the two other elements that Sarah received," Rafael said.

"Which?" Raul asked.

"A code—"

"That your friend swallowed, for better or worse," Sarah noted.

"And the key."

"That's right, the key." Sarah had completely forgotten about this. She retrieved it from her pants pocket and showed it to her father. A very small key to a padlock.

"Where could it be from?" Raul asked, studying it. "What would it open?"

They were silent for a few seconds, each analyzing possible theories about the key, the photo, and Raul's most recent revelations.

"You mentioned a code."

"Yes, but it's gone," Sarah pointed out.

"The original disappeared, but I have a copy," Rafael announced, holding a piece of paper he'd removed from his pocket. It was the paper on which he'd copied the code, before having Margulies try to decipher it.

Raul looked at it, paying close attention to the code.

18, 15–34, H, 2, 23, V, 11
Dio bisogno e IO fare lo. Suo augurio Y mio comando
GCT (15)–9, 30–31, 15, 16, 2, 21, 6–14, 11, 16, 16, 2, 20

"Did your friend manage to decipher it?" he finally asked.

"He didn't have time," the young woman explained. "They killed him first."

"Then it's going to take us a few hours."

"Wait," Rafael said, thinking, trying to remember something. "He looked at me before he died."

"Who?" Sarah asked, wondering.

"Margulies. He looked at me before he died, and told me to count the letters."

Raul stopped listening. He set the paper in his lap, meanwhile scribbling with his mechanical pencil, and counting on his fingers. In a very short time, he straightened up.

"Now I've got it."

L, A—C, H, I, A, V, E
Dio bisogno e IO fare lo. Suo augurio Y mio comando
GCT (DI)—N, Y—M, A, R, I, U, S—F, E, R, R, I, S

"*La chiave*—the key?" Sarah exclaimed. "Marius Ferris? Who is Marius Ferris?"

"It must be the man in the double photo," her father guessed.

"If you'll permit me, Captain, I think we can interpret it two ways. Either the key is Marius Ferris, or else the key opens something in New York."

"New York?" Sarah wondered why he referred to New York.

"Yes. NY must be New York."

"And GCT?" Raúl asked.

"GCT," Rafael repeated, thinking, but nothing came to him. "And the two letters in parentheses? It's not so simple."

"Is it correctly decoded?" Sarah asked.

"I think so," her father affirmed. "Notice the first words: *la chiave*. They leave no doubt. Marius Ferris could be the man we need to find. We just have to decipher GCT and the letters in parentheses."

"Let's look at that during the trip, Captain."

"You're right."

"You're exactly sure where we're going?" Sarah asked, noticing the lights of Lisbon in the distance. "And what if we go to a hotel, for a decent night's sleep?"

"Don't even think about it. We've got a lot of miles to go to get to Madrid."

"Madrid?"

"What's your itinerary, my friend?" Raul asked, trying to reassure his daughter.

"By car to Madrid and then by plane to New York."

"New York?" Sarah was intrigued. "And we're not even sure the code is sending us there."

"Yes," Rafael declared, totally confident. "Burn the code, Captain. I already know what it says."

49

Finally the long-awaited moment came. The one he had anticipated for many years. Including, if he really thought about it, even going back to the times when he held his father's hand in the streets of old Gdansk.

His father, a metallurgist by profession and an active member of Solidarity, cherished the deeply rooted ideal of a free Poland. He hated the dictatorship in his country, but was blind to the one that he imposed on the boy's mother, who never lost her cheerfulness, despite the physical and psychological hardships she had to face. It touched her to see how the boy managed to keep in his mind a fixed, happy image of his father and mother together, on the bank of the Motława, when his father's most noteworthy traits were violence and prolonged absences from his family, as a result of his unequal battle against a totalitarian government. In that area, at least, one had to give him credit for his steadfast commitment to his cause. It was too bad that he failed to establish those same hard-won freedoms in his home. For instance, he very easily could have granted the boy's mother freedom of expression. The image of the river could well be the happy picture taken by a happy mother. But no. That in no way represented reality. That photo never existed, was never taken. What did exist was fear, the everyday terror of hearing the key turn in the lock to make way for the devil. After a long absence, it was the end of peace. Once again there was the black suitcase full of dollars for the cause. "It's from the Americans," he said, wolfing down the dinner prepared by his wife, so pure-hearted that she never once thought to season it with rat poison. That's what he would have done. "It's from the Vatican," his father continued. "This time we will finish them." And he laughed like a child on the verge of seeing his dreams come true. He said they couldn't talk to anybody about the source of the money. Should its existence become known, they would all deny it. Besides, it was dirty money, obtained at other people's expense—from drugs, from trafficking in poorly guarded secrets. Dirty money to finance noble ideals, of equality, justice, and liberty. Foreigners, prying eyes, and naturally enemies couldn't learn the source of the money. It was from the Americans and the Vatican, his father said, without specifying the twists and turns those bills had taken, the hands through which they had passed, the shadow enterprises, the administrators of corrupt banks. No one would ever know.

The younger man remembered, as if it were yesterday, the day he came home and saw her. Her eyes open, glassy, inert, their vision gone. The blood that ran down her neck into a puddle on the floor. One could barely discern that the original color of her blouse was white. His father was seated on the floor, leaning against the wall, drunk, cursing, trying to explain how she had failed to respect him. Before he knew it, the damage was done. "Now there's just the two of us, son," his father said, inebriated and maudlin. "Come here, boy. Give your father a hug." It wasn't a plea but an order, obeyed by the boy, who hugged his father with his body, and his mother with his mind. The knife went deep into his body, up to the handle, while the boy kept hugging his father tightly, with great love, eyes closed. When he finally died, his son drew away from him, and looked for the last time at his mother's body.

"Now I'm alone."

Finally, the moment he'd anticipated for so many years had come. At last he was to meet the Grand Master, who must have already landed on American soil, on one of the runways here, at New York's La Guardia

Airport. This servant of his was waiting for him on the secluded tarmac, at the space assigned for the plane to stop. He brought a car befitting a dignitary of such stature. His smile concealed the nervousness eating him up. The Master was like a father to him. Though he didn't know him personally, the man had given him all the benefits a real father provides for his children. A roof over his head, education, work, and encouragement. Although it had all been done long distance, maybe that was exactly why he had developed such great love and respect for the Master.

The plane was already on the runway. Once the engines were shut down and the door opened, the first person to appear was the man in an Armani suit whom he had met in Gdansk. This one waited to help the gentleman of advanced age coming behind him, leaning on a cane topped with a golden lion. He gripped the cane with one hand, and the assistant's arm with the other. At last, all three of them were face-to-face. Father, Son, and Holy Spirit. The master, the servant, and the assistant.

In a scene worthy of bygone centuries, the Polish servant knelt before the Master and reverently bowed his head.

"Sir, I want you to know what an honor it is for me to finally meet you," he said, eyes closed.

The old man placed his trembling hand on the servant's head.

"Stand up, my son."

The servant quickly complied. He wouldn't dare look his master directly in the eye. The old man got into the car, and he shut the door.

"You have served me well. Always with great efficiency and dedication."

"You can truly count on my total, absolute devotion," he said with sincere reverence.

"I know it."

"Where's the target?" the assistant asked.

"Visiting a museum, right now."

"He likes to cultivate his mind," the man in black sneered.

"Where would you like to go, sir?" the Pole asked shyly.

"Let's be tourists for a while," the old man answered. "Take us for a drive."

His words were orders.

A hushed exchange, not intended for the servant's ears, was under way in the backseat.

Once this was over, the Master made a call and had to wait a few seconds for a response.

"At what point are we going to meet?" he asked directly, without any prior greeting. He listened to the response, and spoke in a curt tone. "Mr. Barnes, pay close attention to my orders."

50

For a while now, the three occupants of the Volvo had remained silent, speeding along at nearly ninety miles an hour on the Lisbon access routes. Only at this hour was such speed possible on one of Europe's most congested highways.

Sarah looked out, distracted. They went past farms, stadiums, business districts, cars, trucks, but she didn't really see any of it. What schemes were being plotted right at this moment, she wondered, so that some people would control others, or certain countries would dominate weaker ones? She felt there were two types of politics, the kind offered for public consumption, a pure facade, and the other hidden, the truly decisive one.

"Are you all right, dear?" her father asked, turning his head.

"As well as you might expect." Her response was distant, still absorbed in her thoughts. "I was thinking. The P2 killed the pope, and surely many other people. Who else have they disappeared?" She emphasized the last words, staring at Rafael, who sensed it, in spite of keeping his eyes on the road.

"It's hard to know for sure. But you would probably find Olof Palme, the Swedish prime minister who was assassinated, among their victims."

"Yes, it's easy to see they don't have any trouble doing away with whoever interferes with their plans."

"That you can be sure of."

"And why did they kill him?"

"Because he was impeding some of their major operations. Probably arms sales."

"And what does the CIA have to do with all of this?"

"A lot. Those deaths occurred because they seemed convenient at the time."

"Did the death of John Paul I interest them?"

"As allies of the P2, the CIA was interested, but it's an unusual case, because the U.S. Justice Department had John Paul I as a collaborator. And his death did a lot of damage to the progress of their investigations."

"So much confusion."

Her father turned to Rafael.

"Which way from here?"

"South. We'll cross the Twenty-fifth of April Bridge and then go straight to Madrid."

"Sounds good to me," Raul agreed.

"I just want to make sure they're not following us."

Sarah immediately became agitated. "How can we know?"

"By taking a narrow or a dead-end street. That way, if anyone's behind us, he'll give himself away."

"But then we wouldn't have any escape, either," Sarah objected.

"True, but we would know whether they were following us. It's a tactic drug traffickers use. That way they don't risk getting caught in the act. If nobody is following them, they go on. Every so many miles they repeat the maneuver. If anybody's watching them, they abort the operation. They get into a shooting match with the police, are trapped, and the drug kingpins are left untouched in their mansions, comfortably planning the next deal."

Dazed, Sarah listened.

"I don't have the slightest intention of getting into a shoot-out. The one yesterday was more than enough."

"I said that's what usually happens in these situations, not that we're going to do it. There are other solutions."

"Such as?"

Rafael stopped sharply in the middle of the road. There was a clamor of honks protesting his grossly irresponsible move.

"Are you nuts?" Sarah yelled.

"Calm down, Sarah," her father said reassuringly. "He knows what he's doing."

Rafael looked back, but she was right behind him, her eyes blazing.

"Would you mind moving to one side?" he asked her.

Sarah glared at him. Rafael saw three cars at the edge of the highway, about sixty yards back. There was a continuing chorus of honks from those that barely avoided ramming the Volvo.

"Three cars," Rafael announced.

"Maybe there was an accident," Sarah suggested nervously.

Rafael turned around and put his seat belt back on.

"Please check to make sure you have your seat belts securely fastened."

Sarah quickly obeyed, getting more and more alarmed. "My God, I don't like this one bit."

"Me neither, Sarah, but listen closely." Rafael looked at her in the rearview mirror. "So you won't tell me later that I didn't warn you, we're going into an urban zone at high speed. Try not to worry. Please hang on tight."

The Volvo's tires burned the asphalt and the motor roared menacingly. The brutal acceleration threw Sarah back into her seat. She looked behind and saw the three cars following them. The Volvo got off the highway and ran a red light. Weaving in and out, they dodged traffic at seventy, eighty miles an hour.

Rafael maneuvered the car with professional skill, Sarah noted. Looking at her father, she observed his apparent calm, reflecting on how little she knew him. Two strangers and, at the same time, so close to her. The captain gave precise feedback to Rafael concerning their pursuers, now openly chasing them. Like Rafael, they were speeding through central Lisbon, racing along the Avenue of the Republic.

Upon reaching Duke of Saldanha Square, they followed a long avenue toward the huge Marquis of Pombal Square. Red lights meant nothing to the four cars involved in the chase. Dozens of shouted insults and honking horns accompanied them. Rafael, ignoring all of this, continued at full speed.

"Hang on," he warned. "Hang on tight."

He had barely finished speaking when suddenly he braked, so that the pursuer on his tail almost rammed them. The two on both sides overtook them, and before they could reposition themselves next to the Volvo, Rafael made a fast left, crossing into oncoming traffic.

Her nerves frazzled, Sarah looked around her. They were moving against traffic on a one-way street. The approaching cars honked and, as best they could, dodged the Volvo and its pursuer.

"I think I'm going to throw up," Sarah moaned.

After a crazed run, they came out on Commerce Square, still closely tailed by the other car. When they reached the east side of the plaza, the car got close to the Volvo. There was no option but an all-out race. Rafael accelerated to a suicidal speed as they entered 24th of July Avenue. The street was long and wide, but winding, forcing him to slow down and then speed up, over and over again.

The car behind them moved with equal dexterity, but the Volvo began gaining. Gaining too much.

"This doesn't look good. They're lagging too far behind."

"Maybe they're having some mechanical trouble."

"Let's hope that's it."

On Avenida da India an intense light from above encircled them. A helicopter beamed its spotlight onto the car.

"Now what?" Sarah asked, struggling to control her rising panic. "What are we going to do?"

"We can't run anymore," Rafael explained matter-of-factly.

"It's over?"

Rafael gave her a very sober look.

"It's over."

"They're going to kill us," Sarah said, deathly pale.

"Not yet. If they wanted to kill us, they would have already." He turned to Raúl.

"What now, Captain?"

"Let them capture us."

Still moving on the avenue, they now passed the majestic Belém Palace, official residence of the president of the republic. A bit farther on, Rafael glimpsed the lights of a vehicle barricade cutting off the street near the Jerónimos Monastery. There was no escape. The barricade was getting closer and closer.

Six hundred yards.

"Captain, I beg your forgiveness for having let you down."

"Nothing to apologize for."

Five hundred yards.

Four hundred.

"Stop the car," said a voice coming from the helicopter. "Halt the vehicle immediately."

"Captain, I need your decision," Rafael repeated more forcefully.

Civilian vehicles, police cars, and vans were lined up to form the barricade, blocking the street. Various men were shielded behind the opened doors of the cars, guns in hand.

Two hundred yards.

Without prior warning, Rafael stopped the car in the middle of the street.

"This is it, Captain."

Raul looked at his daughter.

"Give me the papers," he said.

"What are you going to do with them?" Rafael asked. "They mustn't end up in their hands."

"Don't worry. The glove compartment has a secret hiding place. They won't find it easily, and that will earn us a little time. Give me the papers," Raul repeated to his daughter.

It depends on the cards we get to play at a given moment, Sarah thought, now less tense.

"The papers?" Raul said again.

"I don't have them. I only have copies," Sarah answered, holding out two white sheets with a copy of the list.

"Where are they?"

"Stored in a safe place."

Rafael cracked a half smile.

"Right. That being so, what do we do?" he asked Raul.

"Well, this changes things a bit."

"It's our trump card," Sarah said.

"Without a doubt," her father admitted.

A man left one of the vehicles and was walking, alone, toward the Volvo. His firm, decisive steps held up a mountain of flesh.

"Okay, the games are about to begin," Rafael said, pointing at the man who was getting close.

The man reached the Volvo, approaching the driver's window.

"Well, if it isn't the famous Jack."

"Geoffrey Barnes. We meet again."

"Look around you, Jack," Barnes ordered. "Everybody look. Look at all the work you made us do."

Other agents came up to the car, opened the doors, and pulled Raul and Sarah out.

"Do you need help getting out of the car, Jack?" Barnes asked sarcastically.

Barnes's men kept to their auxiliary roles, leaving the initiative to their boss.

Rafael opened the door and got out of the car, collected, never taking his eyes off the big man.

"Take the woman and her father away. Follow your orders."

Several agents moved off with them, two staying with Barnes. Sarah was still looking back.

"Is that fat man going to kill Rafael?" It was strange how she worried more about him than about herself. The agents put the young woman and her father in separate vehicles.

Meanwhile, Barnes turned to Rafael.

"Jack, Jack, Jack," he said caustically. "What a disappointment, what a tremendous disappointment."

Without warning, the huge man punched Rafael in the stomach. He doubled over. A few seconds later, he straightened up, but Barnes punched him again, this time knocking him down.

"How could you do this to me? To the agency. You've betrayed all the values they instilled in us."

Rafael tried to get up, but another kick in the stomach kept him down.

"You're a bastard," Barnes continued. "And an ungrateful wretch."

Another kick.

"Take him away," he ordered his agents. "We're going for a walk. A long walk."

51

This man, a true lover of the arts in all their forms, basked in a delicious afternoon at New York's Museum of Modern Art. As he had so many other times, he loved contemplating the masterpieces on display there.

Usually a dedicated walker, he was now in a taxi on his way home. His age, combined with the extended tour of the museum, had left him over-tired. Through the car window, he peacefully watched city life.

For nineteen years he had partaken of the Big Apple's pleasures. Museums, movies, restaurants, conferences, religious meetings. Despite all this, he still felt like an outsider. The city was so big, so expansive, and so bountiful in its attractions that one life was insufficient to take it all in. He considered himself privileged; first, to be serving God, and second, to be doing it in this center of the civilized world. His job was to spread the word of God, almost as the old-time missionaries had done. In this case he was doing it in a great city, one evidently very much in need of the Savior's teachings. The preceding pope had congratulated him for his work on two occasions, for his devotion, his commitment, and his dedication. One of his fondest memories was of the day he visited the

Vatican and had the opportunity, honor, and privilege to kiss the ring of John Paul II.

That was in 1990, but it felt like yesterday. Now there was a different pope, a German who had succeeded the Pole. He hoped he would live to enjoy the same opportunity, the same honor and privilege to kiss the ring of the new pope, and have a few minutes of private conversation with His Holiness.

There was no reason to think that such an event could happen, not only because of his relentlessly advancing age, but also because these were exceptionally dark times, too hard to analyze and understand. His beloved Church was threatened by unfathomable dangers. Impure forces attacked the very heart of the holy institution, aided by weak-willed members ruled by the temptations of money and power, members who accepted no limitations on their actions.

Quite recently he received a package from his beloved brother in Christ, Monsignor Firenzi. It contained information of such importance that it stunned him. There were papers of John Paul I with astounding revelations, written in His Holiness's own hand. People who up to now had enjoyed positions of high standing and respect turned out to be false men of God who used their influence for personal gain. Sinners, even murderers, concealed themselves beneath a habit.

Monsignor Firenzi's instructions were clear: for him to zealously guard the contents of the package, and to transmit its location using extremely secure channels. He had done that, even sending him the key to the hiding place where the papers were stored.

Firenzi had called him a few days ago. He was very worried. He said he didn't have much time left and asked him for details concerning where the package was hidden, and the man now heading home in a yellow cab had explained everything to him. Firenzi had spoken as if that would be his last conversation. His farewell message was "Keep your eyes wide open and be very careful." He had heard nothing about Firenzi since then, and he knew that Firenzi was no longer among the living. He could feel it. It was like a priest's implicit sixth sense. For him, being a priest meant not only delivering the word of God but also perceiving the messages being sent from above. He always knew how to decipher those messages. He could interpret the warning of a plate breaking, a dog howling, the unexpected stopping of a car. And he was sure he knew the moment that Firenzi died. He was saying his morning prayers, kneeling at the small altar he had installed in his apartment, to say Mass for friends and neighbors and the faithful who would visit him. The candle went out. The flame of the large candle, in the candelabrum he always kept lit on the left side of the altar, went out at the exact moment that he was praying for his friend the monsignor. He concentrated even harder, praying for God to rectify the situation and give Firenzi another chance, but all in vain. He couldn't manage to relight the candle that day. It sputtered and died, as if someone were constantly blowing on it. The next day, having accepted divine will, he asked the Lord to care for his dear friend's soul. "Thy will be done." And the candle readily allowed him to relight it.

Though he knew that Firenzi died because of the papers, he still couldn't know whether his own involvement in the matter would be discovered by whoever was trying to get them. They would probably end up locating him, but God's designs were unfathomable, and he would readily accept what was to come, for good or ill, with equanimity. He was ready to accept his fate, whatever it might be.

It wasn't humanly possible to speak with Felipe, from Madrid, or with Pablo Rincón, from Buenos Aires. Both of them received letters from Firenzi, telling them what they should do. But it was too late. Two days after his last prayer for Firenzi, he heard about the death of one and the murder of the other. Still, he remained convinced that God would try to reward those who served his purpose. If it was His will for the papers to remain in his hands, that would come to pass, just as the opposite would occur if that was His intent.

"Keep your eyes wide open," Firenzi told him the last time they spoke. "Keep your eyes wide open." But his age no longer allowed him to get involved in adventures or quick escapes. He would continue to conduct his life as before, routinely, normally, saying Masses, attending museums and exhibits, going to the theater. If somebody was looking for him, or already stalking him, then he needed patience. The stalker knew nothing about the location of the papers, nor would he.

The cab had just turned onto Sixth Avenue, and traveled the short distance to the corner of Thirty-eighth Street. The old man paid the driver and got out. When he entered his building, the uniformed doorman wasn't there to open the door or press the elevator call button.

Where's Alfred? he wondered. It wasn't normal to find the front desk empty, nor was it safe for the building to be unguarded. In spite of the doorman's fancy garb, he wasn't there just to provide comfort and appearances for the tenants. He also served as a security guard, one who ensured that no one entered uninvited or without authorization. The old priest looked at the front desk again, and tried to open the doormen's office, but it was locked.

Being a meticulous man, he locked the front door of the building with his key, to prevent any intruder from taking advantage of the doorman's temporary absence. Tenants who wanted to enter or leave could use their own keys.

Finally, he went into the elevator. He got out on the seventh floor and, going down the hall, reached for the key to his apartment.

He turned the key in the lock, but it wasn't necessary. He only needed to turn the doorknob.

"Strange," he said to himself. "I could swear I had turned the key twice."

Inside, he headed for the telephone and picked up the handset. But he noticed that something was out of order. His copies of the New Testament were out of place, strewn on the floor, in a row, as if marking a path. A path leading into the next room. He put down the phone and followed the trail of books. He was about to enter the room with the altar, but the light was off, and the candles out. He could see nothing. He felt for the switch on the inner wall and turned on the ceiling lamp. On the floor in front of him he saw the doorman, leaning back against the wall, his hands and feet tied, and his head covered with a bag. Then he noticed three individuals, sitting comfortably beside the altar: the Master, the servant, and the assistant.

"Marius Ferris," the Master said firmly, his cane across his lap.

"Who are you? How did you get in here?" the old man asked the Master, who had called him by name.

"I've descended from the heavens to pay you a visit," he answered jokingly.

"Who, who are you?"

"You can call me J.C."

52

VILLOT
SEPTEMBER 28, 1978

Villot couldn't manage to remain calm in his office chair. He got up and started pacing back and forth, cigarette in hand. Once more he would exceed his self-imposed limit. He had vowed to himself countless times that under no circumstances should he smoke more than two packs a day. This poison was killing him slowly. But he couldn't escape it. The smoke toned down his nervous anxiety. Unfortunately for him, it also helped bring him closer to his eternal reward.

Smoke was billowing from his mouth, but the cardinal was also puffing with rage. He looked for the umpteenth time at the papers on top of the impressive wooden desk. Over the centuries, thousands of documents had moved across this invaluable piece of furniture. Behind this antiquarian's piece, dozens and dozens of secretaries of state had presided over the destiny of the holy institution. If the desk had the gift of speech, it could reveal secrets, intrigues, plots, and machinations that could chill the spine of even the most stouthearted. In addition, his desk had also accumulated desires, dreams, ambitions, and utopias. There, above all, a perceptive eye would discover badly disguised ambitions to occupy the papal throne. Indeed, what else could one aspire to, after attaining the second-highest spot in the Church hierarchy?

But at that moment, ambition was not the source of Villot's anguish. For years, he had been resigned to his failure to receive the glory of being a successor to the prince of the apostles. What he wished for with all his heart was to have a different man in charge, one who didn't cause all the headaches of the current pontiff.

It wasn't even an hour since he received certain papers from the office of Albino Luciani. They contained orders, decisions, and replacements. Some of those imminent changes would be confirmed within hours or the next day. Villot took the papers from the top of the desk, and reread what he already knew by heart.

Benelli in my position? he said to himself. Can you think of a greater outrage?

"This is overly risky, Holy Father," Villot had said when he received the papers and was able to take a glance at the first papal decisions. "What will be left of the Church if we do this?"

"The Church will survive in its purity, humbleness, and humanity," was Albino Luciani's only comment.

Villot held the papers with one hand and stroked his cap with the other, as he read the absurdities written by the man who was supposedly the supreme voice of Christianity. His desire to make the Church's position concerning birth control more flexible was only one of the pontiff's misdirected notions.

"But Holy Father, this goes against Church doctrine. It opposes the dictates of other popes." The secretary of state was visibly disturbed.

"Infallibility," was the answer.

"Sacred infallibility," Villot emphasized.

"Sacred? We both know that it's a mistake," the pope declared with his usual serenity.

"How can you say such a thing?" the cardinal asked, hypocritically crossing himself.

"I can say it because I am the pope and know that I err like any human being."

"A pope is infallible. And these dictates put in question decisions made with the assurance of papal infallibility."

Villot's combative nature wouldn't allow him to address his superior with submission and obedience. He argued with John Paul I as if he were talking to an assistant or secretary. Albino Luciani seemed to ignore Villot's lack of respect, although he felt uneasy. He would never have thought Villot capable of such behavior.

"A Church that calls itself infallible can't cure its own ills," Luciani declared. "You and I know how the idea of infallibility was made official only in 1870."

On July 18 of that year, Pope Pius IX issued the constitution for dogma *Pastor aeternus,* in which it was specified that the supreme pontiff was infallible when he spoke ex cathedra, that is, by virtue of his high representation and position as spiritual heir to Saint Peter. Whatever contradicted the pope's words could and ought to be considered anathema.

"Are you criticizing the acts of Pius IX?" Villot asked.

"Can one who doesn't criticize his own ever improve?"

The cardinal sat down on one of the many chairs facing his desk, and covered his eyes.

"I can't believe what I'm hearing."

"Stop acting like a naive parish priest, Cardinal Villot. You know as well as I do that infallibility only serves to keep us in shackles."

Villot withdrew his hands from his face. "What are you saying?"

"I think I have said exactly what I meant to say. A pope is infallible in his directives concerning the doctrines of faith and morality. Isn't that right? Doesn't it seem to you that this is an exceptional way of ensuring that certain customs, perhaps pernicious ones, will never change?"

"Anathema, sacrilege!" Villot sputtered, despairing before this enigma, a hurricane acting like a pleasant summer breeze.

"Sacrilege?" Albino Luciani repeated with a faint smile. "The time has come for me to tell you that you would do well to show some respect for the person you're talking to. After all, I'm infallible."

The cardinal bowed his head.

"I won't be using my position or the supposed divine faculties you attribute to me, because that would indicate my acceptance of what they represent. I only want to remind you that, in holding your post, you ought to behave differently. Respect for others isn't something that depends on you, Cardinal Villot. And I repeat that infallibility is an error and an unwarranted pretense. And that is why it's going to be terminated."

Villot understood that it would be fruitless to keep beating his head against the wall. In fact, those papers from Pope Luciani contained even more outrageous proposals than his heresy concerning infallibility.

"And as to the replacements, Holy Father, do you have any idea of the trouble they would cause in the heart of the Curia?"

"I think I have a pretty good idea, Cardinal Villot," the pope replied naturally.

"But, but, what about the cardinals? And the moderate prelates who voted for you?"

"I didn't ask anybody to put me in this place. And I don't think the decisions I have made could be considered belligerent in any sense. I'm only concerning myself with what I believe should concern me, Cardinal. Don't forget that my obligations are to the faithful and to God."

Villot had used most of his arguments. No matter how he pressed his reasoning, so skillful and wise on many occasions, Luciani responded nobly and forcefully, and with unassailable firmness. There was no way to convince him, at least not with words.

"Holy Father, let me study the situation more thoroughly. I will review the names carefully, and give you some alternatives, particularly concerning my own replacement and for the leadership of the IOR." If the Holy Father agreed to this delay, perhaps there was still some hope.

"It won't be necessary to go to that trouble, Cardinal Villot. That is my final word. Don't burden yourself with looking for alternatives. I'm sure that your candidates will be good, capable people, but I won't accept them. My decision is irrevocable. It should start with Archbishop Marcinkus's immediate replacement with Monsignor Giovanni Abbo, and the dismissal of De Bonis, Mennini, and Del Strobel. De Bonis is to be replaced with Monsignor Antonetti, and I will try to fill the two other vacancies after I talk with Monsignor Abbo."

"But—"

"Good afternoon, Cardinal Villot," the pope concluded, heading for the door.

Villot didn't even have a chance to respond. Never had he imagined that Luciani could be so resolute. His own position was getting progressively more complex and tougher to handle. Gelli was right. They had miscalculated. This man meant nothing but trouble for them.

"I am counting on you to make a quick transfer of power of the secretary of state to Cardinal Benelli," the supreme pontiff said, at the door.

"Your Holiness," Villot stammered. "Shouldn't you think this over at greater leisure? After all, you haven't been in your position for very long."

Pope Luciani gave his secretary of state a long look. Fixing his gaze on the cardinal, he answered with a solid calmness.

"Thank you for your concern, Cardinal Villot. But my decision is irrevocable."

And he went out, leaving Villot entangled in tortured reflections. He meditated, pondered, prayed, but couldn't find a solution to the problem. He looked at the telephone next to the papers that had caused the disagreement. He found it at once tempting and threatening. Several times he pressed the first digits of a number he had memorized several days ago. Suddenly he put the phone down, in hopes that some other idea would come to him. How he wished that this weren't necessary! He decided to risk everything on his last card. If he alone couldn't manage to persuade the pope, he would hold a meeting of the monsignors who also felt their future was threatened. Together they would make one final effort to convince the pontiff to reconsider.

53

It's just the two of us, Jack," Barnes said to Rafael. "You and me." He sat down, facing him. "I'm sure we're going to have a very productive conversation." The place was shadowy, like a scene in a movie. Two chairs; a square, dark wooden table, old and worn; and a hanging ceiling lamp casting light over the two seated men.

"Where are we?" Rafael asked.

"Jack, Jack, Jack, it seems you haven't quite understood your place." Barnes didn't let up on his sarcasm when he got up from the table and walked around. "I'm the one asking the questions here."

"Go to hell, Barnes. I'm no fucking idiot. Don't give me your usual treatment. I'm not going to pee my pants just because you're here. You don't scare me."

The answer was a punch in the face that sent him crashing to the floor.

"Get up," the fat man ordered. "Get up," he yelled again, seeing that he wasn't being obeyed.

Rafael got up at his own pace, not saying a word or showing the slightest sign of pain. Then he straightened the chair and sat down, putting his hands in full view on the table.

"Don't think you can fool me, Barnes. I know we're in the United States. I just want to know where exactly," Rafael continued, calmly. In spite of his difficult situation, he was attempting, as much as possible, to control the chain of events. Nonetheless, he knew he was at a clear disadvantage.

"What makes you think you're in America? You could be anywhere."

"That many hours on the plane tell me we're in the United States. London was only two and a half hours away. So we're either in Washington or New York, right?"

"We're smack in the middle of hell, Jack. What difference does it make? Or were you planning to go sightseeing?"

"Not a bad idea."

Another punch, not so hard this time, hit him squarely in the face, splitting his lip.

"Do you have any idea of what she's going through right now, Jack? Can you picture it?" Barnes changed tactics. "Such a pretty, sweet face, spoiled by a brute like me."

Rafael, of course, could imagine it. The two punches he had received were nothing, compared to what could be on the way.

"Are you going to tell me where the papers are?" Barnes asked in a more condescending tone.

"You know very well I'm not. First, because I don't know. And, second, because if I did, I wouldn't tell you."

Staughton's sudden appearance interrupted the interrogation.

"Mr. Barnes," he called from the doorway.

"Come in, Staughton."

He approached, and whispered something in his ear.

"Are you sure?" Barnes asked in his usual loud voice, not liking the news. He thought silently for a moment.

"Right, give me a few minutes," he said finally, dismissing Staughton. On his way out, the agent closed the door, once again leaving Rafael at Barnes's mercy.

"I'll give you one more chance, Jack, for old times' sake." Barnes returned to the chair facing him. "Where are the papers?"

"The last time I saw them," Rafael said, thoughtfully, "they were stuck in your mother's ass."

Barnes froze, his face turning red. Rafael was crossing the line. Barnes got up again and headed for the detainee. Standing close, he whispered in his ear.

"Why are you wasting my time, Jack?" As he spoke, his saliva spattered Jack's face. "Don't you get it, that I've got the woman and don't need you? Maybe you won't talk, but she'll cackle like a parrot. So can you please explain to me, what could it possibly be that keeps me from killing you?"

"What I know, that she doesn't know," Rafael declared firmly.

"And what do you know that she doesn't?"

"I know that she only received two pages out of a total of thirteen."

"Go on."

"I know where the other pages are," he said, arrogantly, casting a line and hoping Barnes would take the bait.

Barnes observed him for a few seconds, weighing his words and trying to read his mind.

"You're lying," he said finally.

"You wanna risk killing me? What if I'm not lying?"

"I've got the daughter and the father, Jack. I can do quite well without you."

"You'd be making sense if you weren't wrong."

Barnes could barely contain his wrath. He wanted to crush this bastard. He shook him, grabbing his lapels.

"Don't tempt me, Jack. I can finish you off in a second."

Bound up as he was, Rafael still defied him with his look.

"It's not in your hands, Barnes."

The latter tightened his grip even more.

"What do you mean?"

"I mean that the great Geoffrey Barnes could have bashed in my brains long ago. You haven't done it because it's not up to you. Not that you don't want to—I can see it in your eyes—but there's a motherfucker above you who won't let you pull the trigger."

"Shut up," the big man yelled, shoving him against the wall. Infuriated, he punched him in the stomach. Rafael collapsed to the floor, but Barnes didn't let up, and started kicking him amid an avalanche of insults. Suddenly a strong pair of hands pulled him back.

"Hold it. Right now," an elegantly dressed man ordered, grasping the still-raving Barnes. "What are you doing?"

"I'm gonna kill this son of a bitch," Barnes roared, glaring at Rafael, who was struggling to stand up.

"Get a grip," the man shouted.

Staughton and Thompson poked their heads in, to see what was happening.

"Take him out of here," the man ordered Staughton and Thompson. Obeying quickly, they started dragging Rafael between them.

"Not that one, this one," the newcomer corrected, keeping a firm hold on Barnes.

The fat man simmered down, taking several deep breaths and recovering his composure.

"Okay, I'm fine," he said. "I'm fine."

"I'm taking over as of now," the other man announced. "Go have something to drink and settle your nerves." Then he turned to Staughton and Thompson. "Take this gentleman over with the others. The Grand Master's already here."

His orders were immediately followed. Barnes went through the door without looking back. "Fucking bastards," he mumbled. The other two were supporting Rafael, who couldn't stay on his feet.

The man who'd restored order in the room readjusted his Armani suit. The time had come.

54

The four men were walking through a long, dimly lit hallway, with closed doors dotting both sides. The place was cold, dilapidated, but not abandoned. There was no dirt or cobwebs. These quarters seemed to be used only sporadically.

Rafael walked with Staughton's and Thompson's help. The man behind them in the Armani suit didn't allow any threats or punches. There was an intense light coming out of an open door. Voices could be heard. The pair walked the last few feet almost dragging Rafael.

"This fucker keeps getting heavier," Thompson complained.

"He's doing it on purpose," Staughton remarked.

Staughton wasn't far from the truth. Rafael pretended that his condition was getting worse, just to make their task more difficult. He wanted to irritate them, and didn't expect to gain anything. Even so, he felt a slight ache in his chest. Could be a broken rib, making it harder to breathe. But he would have to worry about his health later, after this nightmare ended, if ever. This hallway could well be his death walk.

While being dragged along, he thought of Sarah. Was she having to endure the same abuse? Rafael had been trained for it. Barnes's wrath, his uncontrolled punches, were minor disturbances for him. It was a different story for Sarah, though she had demonstrated her courage in their brief amount of time together. Despite the tension, she held herself together again and again. And what she did with the papers, knowing they were their only bargaining chip, the only card they could play, spoke volumes about her character.

When they entered the room, Rafael saw, backed against a wall but attached by the wrists to ceiling chains, Captain Raul Monteiro, Sarah, and an older man he didn't know, though his face looked familiar.

Next to the group, dressed in black like most of the agents, was an individual Rafael instantly recognized. It was the Pole. Staughton and Thompson dragged Rafael over to the others, and locked both his wrists to a metal ring linked with the ceiling chains. Barnes's two agents left the room. Now the detainees were at the mercy of the assistant and the Pole.

Rafael looked at Sarah, searching for signs of torture. Nothing—they hadn't even touched her yet. He was afraid they'd taken her somewhere else. They'd been separated during the flight, and from then on, he didn't know what had happened to her or her father.

The captain showed no sign of mistreatment, either, nor did the man next to him, whom he still could not identify. The assistant was the first to speak.

"Finally we're all here."

"Isn't there anything to eat?" Rafael asked.

The assistant ignored the provocation.

"My deepest apologies for the treatment you have received, but I assure you it will all be over very soon."

"Who are you?" Rafael asked the older man.

"I'm Marius Ferris. And you?"

"Marius Ferris. The one in the photo," Rafael said, finally recognizing him. "My name's Rafael."

"We all know why we're here, so let's get straight to the point. Where are the papers?" the assistant asked.

On the only table in the room was a black suitcase, which the servant opened at that moment, handling the various cutting tools inside. They were torture devices capable of producing a confession from even the most stalwart. In some cases, simply displaying these terrible instruments was enough to make the detainees crumble.

"The papers are in a safe place," Rafael asserted.

"They'll be much safer with us," the assistant countered. "Be reasonable. Isn't it better to end this as soon as possible and avoid more suffering?"

Silence was their only answer. The assistant waited a few more minutes. Someone might give up. After all, it was unlikely that all four of them would be prepared to be tortured for something that didn't directly concern them. But nobody said a word.

All right. He would start with Sarah's father, since perhaps this could put psychological pressure on his daughter, forcing her to talk.

"Take care of the military man," he ordered the servant.

Sarah's startled eyes revealed her dread, her greatest fear. They were going to be tortured and would end up having the truth forced out of them, if not right away, then later, when they couldn't stand it anymore.

The servant wielded an instrument like a lathe, its blade about a half inch wide and eight inches long, meant to pierce the skin and cause pain but not to harm any vital organ except by special intent. He slashed the captain's shirt, exposing his torso. He aimed directly at the right side of his stomach, resting the sharp point on the skin.

A heartrending scream of agony announced the metal's piercing of the flesh and cutting in a revolving path inside the body, producing acute, excruciating pain. The relentless point came out through his ribs. Very slowly, the torturer's extremely steady hand withdrew the instrument. The damage was done, to the captain's body and to the mental states of both Sarah and Marius Ferris, who watched, horror stricken. The suffering showed on the captain's sweat-drenched face, contorted with pain.

"And now? Would someone like to say something?" the assistant asked. "Isn't it starting to seem better to have us take care of the papers?"

"What would seem better to me is a nice hamburger," Rafael suggested.

The assistant approached him, stone-faced, eyeing him directly.

"Is there something else you'd like to share with us?"

"With cheese, extra cheese. And smothered with ketchup."

The assistant held his stare, inches away from Rafael's face.

"I think Jack needs an appetizer. Something to remind him of what he shouldn't do to his mates." He signaled the servant. "Like betray them, for instance. That's a no-no." He stepped back to make way for the servant, who still held the terrible torture instrument he'd used on Raul.

Rafael didn't change his sarcastic tone. He was well aware that the two men knew he was no ordinary person. They could tear him to shreds if they wanted, and he would let them kill him without saying a word. But that couldn't save him from torture.

"Aren't you going to clean the blood off that gadget?" he asked the Pole. "I could get an infection." He turned to Raul. "No offense, Captain."

"You can't imagine the pleasure it'll give me to cut you up, piece by piece, and watch you bleed like a pig until your last breath," the torturer said, his face very close to Rafael's, making sure he caught every word.

"At your disposal," Rafael responded, "whatever you want."

The servant answered the provocation, spitting in his face. There were many things he wanted to say, but it was better to concentrate his rage on the tool he was holding in his hand. The Pole savagely tore Rafael's shirt, scattering most of the buttons on the floor.

"Stop that. Nobody here is going to gut anybody."

The female voice filled the room, by surprise, catching everyone's attention. All heads turned to look at the one who had spoken with such unqualified firmness.

"It's a pleasure to see there's one sensible person in the room, and that she has decided to be merciful to her companions," the assistant said, facing Sarah, the one who expressed herself so unexpectedly.

"It's hard to find anyone with any sense in this room," she answered convincingly. "Tell your friend to back off."

The assistant hesitated a few seconds, but finally ordered the servant to step back.

"Start talking," he ordered.

"No, not yet. I'll tell you everything you want to know, but—"

"Shut up," Rafael interrupted her.

"You can't do it, Sarah," her father pleaded in a weak voice.

The servant hit Rafael with a well-aimed, painful smack.

"Shut up. Let her talk."

"Please continue," the assistant asked Sarah, regaining control of the situation.

"I'll tell you everything you want to know," Sarah repeated, "but only to the one in charge."

"What?" The assistant seemed startled. "I'm the one in charge here."

"No, you aren't. You're only an employee," Sarah staunchly contradicted him. "What I know, I'll tell J.C., and no one else."

The Pole was astonished.

"Who do you think you are, giving orders here?"

A look from the assistant made him stop. Sarah was playing her card. She had earned that right.

"J.C. won't speak with you. It's better for you to say whatever you have to say now."

"You want something that we have. I'm ready to give it to you, but that's my condition and it's not negotiable. I'll only talk to J.C. Otherwise, you can continue with your torture until you kill us all. Nobody will say anything."

The assistant walked over to Sarah, took out a gun with a silencer, and balanced it on her forehead.

"Who do you think you are, making demands on me?" His voice had a chilling tone, a mix of anger and impatience. "Haven't you realized your situation? You're in no position to demand anything. Tell me what you know."

"If there's anybody here who can demand anything, it's me. I may be in chains, but if that's the case, it's because I've got what you want," Sarah said defiantly. "Take the gun off my forehead and do what I say. Call J.C."

"Don't abuse my patience," the man threatened, switching off the safety on the gun. "Nobody's calling J.C. Talk."

Sarah was determined not to submit, not to give up. She wanted to close her eyes, but even that could be interpreted as a sign of weakness, just when the man in the Armani suit pointed his gun and prepared to shoot.

"Your stubbornness only makes it worse," Sarah said, in a final attempt to convince him. It could all be over in seconds, her life and that of the others, but if she could manage to open a tiny crack in the assistant's resolve, there was a chance to save everyone. Perhaps she could find it, risking a bit more. "Surely your boss won't be pleased to have you waste our lives without any tangible results."

"Don't underestimate my intelligence. For the last time, spill it, or your father will be without a daughter."

"You're risking too much," Sarah challenged in desperation. "If you think killing me will solve the problem, you're very mistaken. You'll create another, bigger problem."

"Shut up." The man was incensed. "One of you is going to talk. There's always someone who ends up talking."

"Stop," said a voice behind them, catching everybody's attention. The assistant turned toward the doorway, where the Master had called out the order. He leaned on his usual cane and was carrying a black briefcase.

"Sir," the assistant began, removing the weapon from Sarah's head.

"Silence," the Master answered. "Would you like to talk with me?" he asked Sarah.

"If you're J.C., then yes," the young woman answered, her eyes wide, as though she were confused by the turn of events.

The old man turned around and walked away.

"Bring her along."

"But, sir," the assistant mumbled.

"Bring her over here," the old man repeated, now from the hallway. His tone allowed no rebuttal. "And leave the others alone until further notice."

55

For Geoffrey Barnes, one of New York's greatest advantages was the food. For the first time in several days, he enjoyed a first-rate lunch in a good restaurant. He was now much calmer, and understood that the whole business with Jack was part of the job. A game, which Jack had played masterfully, making him lose his head. It was apparent that if Barnes had been able to dispose of Jack at will, he would have handled the matter differently. That bastard, that sly fox, realized this, and knew how and when to take advantage of him.

To hell with the Italian, or whatever he might be. The fact that he spoke the language didn't necessarily mean he was from that country. The man had said categorically, "Nobody dies without my authorization." And when the boss spoke, everybody bowed their heads and obeyed. In that moment of confusion, he lost track of his orders. He got caught in the trap Jack set for him. It wasn't easy to avoid. It was a mistake to have lost his temper.

But it was better not to think about it anymore. He devoted himself to enjoying the rest of his meal, his eyes already set on the dessert. And then his cell phone rang, the damned cell phone that robbed him of marvelous moments like this. He fished it out of his pocket without paying attention to who was calling.

"Barnes."

During the next moments, Geoffrey Barnes confined himself to listening and answering with a few monosyllables. "Yes." "No." "Done." One could readily infer he wasn't talking to a subordinate, since whatever he was hearing made him shift restlessly in his chair. A few more monosyllables followed, and then a good-bye.

When he hung up, his expression was changed. Small beads of sweat trickled down his forehead. He put down the fork, still in his hand. The shit had just hit the fan, and if he didn't act immediately, it wouldn't take long to splatter everything. He left his money on top of the check on the table, and quickly headed for the door. He pressed some numbers on the cell phone and, now out on the street, brought it to his ear. His pace was fast and steady.

"Staughton, it's Barnes. Don't let them do anything till I get there." The exertion affected the sound of his voice. He was walking very fast as he talked, but even so, his was a firm, emphatic voice. "Nothing about anything. Don't explain why, just say I'll clear everything up when I get there." Barnes listened for a few seconds and then spoke again. "Not even Payne or anybody. They shouldn't touch anything, or even move. And tell the rest to do the same, or else this is going to blow up." He crossed the street without looking. Cars grazed past him, but he kept talking. "The reason? I'll tell you, and you only, understood? But you can't talk to anyone, Staughton." The subordinate assented, on an office phone in the heart of Manhattan. "I've just received a call from the top levels of the Vatican." He sighed. "The girl has tricked us."

56

"How did you kill John Paul I?" Sarah asked without preamble as she sat on the chair, in the same room where Rafael had been with Barnes. She rested her hands on the table to appear relaxed.

The Master stayed on his feet, his back to her, in a thoughtful pose. On hearing the question, he turned to Sarah and smiled.

"You're not here to ask questions, Miss Sarah Monteiro. You demanded my assistant allow you to tell me personally all that you know. That's why you're here." It was an old man's voice, hoarse and cracked, but also definitive.

"It will be a small exchange of information. You'll tell me what I asked you, and I'll give you what you want so much. You know I wouldn't be able to use anything against you that you tell me."

"Don't underestimate me, miss. I'm no cheap-movie villain. I'm flesh and blood, very real."

"I don't understand why you're telling me this." The old man's answer had confused her.

"Forget it. It's a digression," J.C. explained, taking his seat in the chair across the table. "Actually, it wasn't meant for you."

"How did the pope die?"

There was a silence that Sarah found disturbing.

"The official version is that he died of a myocardial infarction," the old man finally answered.

"We both know that's not what happened."

"We do?" J.C. said. "Do we really know that? Are you trying to contradict an official truth?"

"An official truth doesn't have to be true. In the past few days I've learned that we're all victims of deceit," Sarah answered, with an insolence she never would have thought herself capable of.

J.C. let out a throaty but real guffaw.

"What does a girl know about all this?"

"Do you admit that the official truth is false?"

"False or not, it's the only one we have." His tone of voice still seemed normal. The old man never lost his cool, never said anything he would later regret.

Then he looked for something in his suitcase, which he had left by the table and was now rummaging inside. He finally found what he was looking for, an old piece of paper that he handed to Sarah.

"Read it."

"What's this?" She looked at its printed heading: DEATH CERTIFICATE.

"Read it," J.C. repeated.

It was the death certificate of Albino Luciani, John Paul I. CAUSE OF DEATH: myocardial infarction. PROBABLE TIME: 23:30, September 28, 1978. An illegible signature, possibly of the Vatican doctor on duty.

"That's the official truth of the pope's death," J.C. declared with a satisfied smile.

Sarah examined the document. How did the Master have this with him? she wondered.

"Let's move on to what matters," the old man insisted.

Sarah returned the certificate and looked into his eyes.

"No, not yet. I want to hear your truth."

"What truth do you have in mind?"

"That certificate was made without any examination of the pope's body,"

Sarah said, remembering the conversation with her father at the Mafra monastery. "Tell me the truth. You know, a simple exchange of facts."

"I've got other means of obtaining what I want from you."

"I don't doubt it. But that could take hours, or days, and there's no guarantee you'll get it. What I'm proposing is a fair exchange."

"Why do you want to know?"

"No reason in particular. Just anybody's normal curiosity after seeing so many long-held beliefs come tumbling down."

There was a momentary pause in the conversation. The Master was lost in thought. For Sarah it wasn't just curiosity, though it might have seemed so, but also a way of buying time. Beyond that, she had no idea where she wanted to go.

"Come on. Tell me what happened the night of September 28, 1978."

The old man took some time before he spoke.

"Before even starting, I'd like to clear up one historical error. Albino Luciani died in the hour after midnight, very early on September 29. No need to ask how I know. I was the last man to see him alive and the first one to see him dead. Surely you already know why he died. He had become an unwanted pope, a dangerous enemy, and he had to be eliminated."

"I'm not talking about religion. There was a mistaken evaluation of his character. If we had a sliver of hope after the conclave, we quickly learned it was misplaced. His fragile appearance was just that, an appearance. He intended to clean house right away.

"Archbishop Marcinkus and Cardinal Jean-Marie Villot were going to be the first to fall. The most valuable cards in the deck. And, believe me, many others were going to be running the same risk. With Marcinkus and Villot out, it wouldn't have taken long to get to Calvi and Gelli, and after that, the collapse would be total. John Paul I was actually digging his own grave. He wasn't like Paul VI, who stayed focused on religion and faith, and delegated the rest to the Curia and other competent people. John Paul I stuck out. He was going to end the Church as we knew it."

"How?" Sarah was paying close attention to the Italian's words.

"Do you think the Church could have survived the housecleaning he intended to do? Of course not. The faithful would have been scandalized by even a hint of the Church's financial excesses. Even though Paul VI wasn't to blame for any of it, he would have been seen as a crook ordering his people to launder black market money, and to invest it in enterprises forbidden by the Church, such as the manufacture of condoms, birth-control pills, and weapons. All of this in the attempt to make a lot of money, and to siphon off as much as possible into personal accounts."

"But this was all found out later, and nothing happened."

"Exactly. By that time we no longer controlled the information and couldn't avoid it. Even then, it was done so as to minimize the damages."

"How can you be so indifferent about the murder of the pope?" Sarah asked.

"The end justified the means, young lady. There was a lot at risk. And I don't mean just the court trials. Many people, and countries, would have been damaged because of the actions planned by the pontiff."

"Who was only trying to restore justice."

"Justice is a very subjective ideal. By now, surely you understood that. Licio Gelli felt obliged to devise a plan that could be executed in a matter of hours, a drastic plan. That's how I came on the scene as Albino Luciani's executioner. My job was to stay by the phone and wait. Villot tried to postpone the plan as long as possible. He tried to dissuade the pope, arguing, offering reasonable alternatives. But the pope showed his inflexibility. He sealed his fate on September 28, when he told Villot and the other monsignors about the replacements to be made over the next few days, starting with Marcinkus, effective immediately. When we got wind of the papal decision, we had no choice but to act."

"The final solution," Sarah threw in with enraged sarcasm. "The solution to all problems. If he doesn't serve our purposes, we kill him, and the sooner the better. There are numerous victims of that attitude."

"You can't imagine how many. Anyway, the night of the twenty-eighth, twenty-ninth, I showed up at the Apostolic Palace. One of the monsignors had arranged to keep the entrances open and for me not to be intercepted. And that's how it happened. He did his job perfectly."

"Do you mean you were wandering around the Apostolic Palace at midnight?"

"No. I entered the pope's private quarters directly, by one of the out-of-service stairways. The doors to the lower and third floors were generally locked. As you can imagine, that night was an exception. The Swiss Guard hasn't been guarding the papal quarters since the times of Pope John XXIII. I didn't cross paths with anybody on my way in. I had no trouble at all getting into the pope's private rooms. He was still awake and we exchanged a few words. When I left, I had completed my assignment. The cardinals would have to bury the new pope and elect another one."

"You talked with the pope? I hope you haven't forgotten that conversation."

"That's irrelevant," J.C. retorted, now starting to show his impatience. "The next day, the same monsignor who helped me get in also asked me to go see him in the Vatican. So I went. He wanted to give me the papers, the ones we're now trying to recover, for safekeeping, and that's what I did"— the old man smiled sneakily—"putting them in the safest place in the world. Besides, the idea amused me. How could I have imagined that Firenzi, the idiot, would finally find them and end up taking them out?"

"But weren't you asked to destroy them?"

"No, not at all. Except for the list and the secret of Fátima, the rest is harmless. There were only papal orders concerning Church reorganization. Some of them more controversial than others, but nothing explosive, at least for anybody who follows religious matters.

"But the list is another story. As you surely know, it's not about the list of P2 names that everybody knows, but a much more sensitive version. It includes the names of great personalities and, specifically, of one prime minister. Any third-rate judge would have a clear basis to prosecute them for the death of a pope. Nobody could have imagined that any such thing was going to happen. That damned prosecutor of the District of Rome . . .

"Nobody would have suspected any irregularity in the pope's death, except that Villot, in his excessive zeal, made a series of mistakes after the body was found by Sister Vincenza. He demanded an absolutely unnecessary vow of silence from all the residents of the palace, and he then invented an official story, later proved false by the Vatican itself."

"I don't understand."

"The first official version said that John Magee, the pope's secretary, found him dead at five thirty in the morning, when actually he was found forty-five minutes earlier by Sister Vincenza, his personal assistant."

"Why did he do that?"

"It didn't seem appropriate for a woman, even though she was a nun, to be freely entering the pope's private quarters. Image issues. Then Villot got too personally involved. He issued a series of mistaken declarations and made outlandish decisions. He said that the pope had his bedside book, *The Imitation of Christ,* by Kempis, in his hands. This special edition was actually in Venice. He hastily summoned the embalmers. Soon it was learned that the nun had discovered the body. If one added the rushed cleaning of the papal private quarters to all these incongruities, it became easy to understand why everybody would think this reflected the personal behavior of somebody who had something to hide.

"On the other hand, the doctors would collaborate with us only if they didn't have to face another doctor's opinion. Luciani's physician was Dr. Giuseppe de Rós, who always attended him in Venice, and during his month in the Vatican. It was important that he corroborate the diagnosis of his colleagues when he arrived in Rome. Villot would not, however, authorize an autopsy, also prohibited under canon law. Villot was the cardinal camerlengo and, as such, the head of the Church until the end of the next conclave. He was very busy, and very nervous about all that had occurred."

"Understandable," Sarah remarked.

"Dr. Giuseppe de Rós approved the diagnosis of the other doctors, but he actually had little chance to do anything else, because he could only conduct a superficial examination. Since an autopsy was out of the question, if Villot had not acted so precipitously, it would have been a perfect crime. A new pope was elected and life went on. But the death of John Paul I had already aroused too many suspicions, and everything began to fall apart, and in a way particularly damaging to the P2, which disbanded in 1981. Since then, we've been more in the shadows than ever."

"And how did they manage to bury the P2?"

"The details are complicated. Let's just say that, for years, judges, journalists, and some police organizations followed clues that led to the IOR, the Banco Ambrosiano, the P2, and businesses that connected them."

"And what happened with Villot, Marcinkus, and the manager of the Banco Ambrosiano?"

"Villot was very sick at the time of Luciani's assassination. He himself had asked to be relieved, but he wouldn't allow Benelli to serve as his replacement. Villot wanted to choose his own successor. Benelli was a man too much like John Paul I. He, too, would have caused irreparable damage. After Luciani's death, Villot relaxed a little, and he died in peace in March 1979, very well attended.

"Marcinkus continued with his shenanigans in the IOR for a long time, until he was taken away, and he returned to Chicago. Later he retreated to a parish on the outskirts of Phoenix, Arizona."

In old J.C.'s opinion, Marcinkus was a villain. He had no friends, no associates, no allies. He was only a friend to himself and served his own interests. Because of that, he could continue his businesses for a long time, after both John Paul I and Villot had left this world. There he was, at the head of the IOR until 1989, under the aegis of Pope John Paul II himself.

"As for the others," J.C. went on, "Calvi was found dead in 1982, strangled beneath the Blackfriars Bridge in London. The embezzlement of the Banco Ambrosiano finally amounted to some two billion dollars. That money was lost, but it was very profitable for Gelli and Marcinkus."

"Would you like to know where Gelli is?" the old man asked, making a dramatic pause. He knew he was nearing the end of his story. "He's fulfilling a residential imprisonment in Arezzo, Italy. And as for me, well, I'm not anywhere."

Again he fell silent. Then Sarah threw out a question that still hadn't been answered, perhaps the one she was most interested in.

"How did you kill the pope?"

"Come on, Miss Sarah Monteiro, you can't expect to be told everything in exchange for nothing, right? One thing for another, isn't that what you said? I more than fulfilled my part. Now it's your turn." He smiled, satisfied, like someone who knew he had reason on his side.

"It's my last question. I need to know how you did it."

"And I need to know where you stored the papers."

"You yourself said that they don't contain anything explosive."

"I guarantee you they don't. And if they had appeared on the night of the murder, except for the list and the secret of Fátima, there would have been no dire results. But if they reappeared now, after all these years, they would be looked on differently."

Sarah couldn't avoid agreeing with the old man. The Holy See would be revealed as an institution entirely at odds with the scruples and morality that it pretended to defend. Those documents, among other things, would confirm that someone made them disappear. They would point the finger at the top figures in the Curia, and the Church might never recover.

"What does all of this matter to you? It's hard to believe you pay much attention to the Church."

"There are secrets that ought to remain in the shadows, truths that should never be uncovered."

"Sooner or later, somebody will bump into them again and the truth will come to light."

"Then let that happen as late as possible. When I'm dead, it will hardly matter to me what anybody does with those papers. But until then, it's better for me to have them."

"Don't you want to destroy them?"

"No. I might need them at some point. Now, cooperate with me and keep your word."

"I'll keep it. I only want you to answer my last question," Sarah replied, in a final attempt to buy time.

The old man was wrapped in a disturbing silence for some time. Sarah became anxious. Though it might not have seemed so, she needed to know how J.C. killed the pontiff. She didn't know why, but she felt a compulsion to know.

"We'll do the following. You'll tell me what I want to know and then I'll tell you."

"But—" The young woman was hesitating.

"I always keep my promises," the old man added.

Sarah didn't doubt it. Hers was a different problem. As soon as she spoke, J.C. would forget about her, or kill her.

"I'm waiting," J.C. pressed.

"Very well. The papers are kept in a safe place."

Sarah paused.

"I know that very well. Please finish." His dry voice announced it would no longer tolerate any more detours.

"Then you'll understand that they're so secure that I've no control over them."

"What do you mean?" He raised his voice, threatening. "Explain yourself."

"The papers are in the Vatican," Sarah answered, very sure of herself. "That's where they came from, and that's where they needed to return. A pope's papers belong in the Vatican."

"Surely you're joking."

"No. I'm serious."

The somber expression on J.C.'s face left no room for doubt. His sudden pallor accentuated the deep wrinkles of his face. Suddenly he was gasping like an asthmatic. For the first time Sarah was aware of his humanity. Rather than an automaton who arbitrarily disposed of people, he was a fragile old man at the end of the road.

"Do you have any idea what you've done?"

"Do *I* have any idea?" she spat back, both indignant and frightened.

"Your father and your friends are dead men, thanks to you."

"So be it." Her eyes welled with tears that she tried to contain. "I did what I had to do. You won't have your way."

"Do you really believe I won't recover those papers just because they're in the Vatican? What makes you think I don't have people working there, as in 1978?"

"Times have changed."

"Don't kid yourself."

Sarah wanted to believe that, yes, things had changed. It was true that conservatives had progressively gained more and more power in the heart of the Church. Now it was much less modern and liberal than Albino

Luciani would have wanted, but there were also different people at its center now. There were no Villots or Marcinkuses in the new Vatican.

"If they haven't changed, you have no reason to worry. Tomorrow, or at most in a couple days, you'll have the papers under your control."

The old man's look indicated he thought that would not be the case. "And where are the others?"

"The others?"

"Don't play the fool. Only you had the list. Where are the rest of the papers?"

For a moment she thought of making up something, but then rejected the idea. It was better not to tighten the rope too much. She may have already gone too far.

"I can only talk about the list. I know nothing about the rest."

The old man waited a few minutes. When he was done, he struck the floor three times with his cane. The assistant immediately came in.

"Take her away. Eliminate the father, the daughter, and the double agent—the three of them. Then bring me Marius Ferris. We've got a lot to talk about. But first have him watch them die."

"That would help loosen anyone's tongue," the assistant responded, smirking.

"Where are you taking her?" someone who had just come in asked.

"To the gallows," the assistant answered sarcastically.

Barnes grabbed Sarah by her other arm and, without further ado, yanked her out of the assistant's hands.

"What are you doing?" J.C. asked.

"Sit down," Barnes ordered Sarah before he turned to the old man. "She sent the papers to the Vatican."

"I know. She'll pay for that."

"I got a call, precisely from the Vatican, just minutes ago."

The old man shuddered. Disbelief darkened his eyes.

"And what do they want?"

"It's not what they want, but what they ordered."

57

H ans had survived a hectic day, but he had the sense that the next few
hours would lead to an endless, sleepless night.

The chief of security for the Swiss Guard had spent the whole afternoon
receiving contradictory instructions. While many had come from the secretary of state, there were others from the head of the Vatican Archives,
from the secretary of the synod, and from the Congregation for the Doctrine
of the Faith.

That same afternoon, Cardinal Jean-Marie Villot's secretary asked to
have the Leo XIII passageway, usually kept closed, opened. Later, none other
than the prefect of the Doctrine of the Faith told him that this was an unnecessary measure. Archbishop Paul Marcinkus's office had recommended
that he open all points of access to Pope John Paul's private quarters. Other
assistants to different cardinals stopped by the Swiss Guard's offices to give
him notes with even more unusual security details.

Hans finally guessed that a critical meeting was going to take place in the
pope's office, which was next to his private quarters, in the Apostolic Palace.
Naturally, in the security chief's judgment, this was a highly important political gathering, though informal, since there was no communication from

the Vatican public-address system. All he could conclude from that bundle of faxes, phone calls, and loose notes was that those attending would include Secretary of State Jean-Marie Villot, Archbishop Paul Marcinkus, and the Archbishop Vicar of Rome, Ugo Poletti.

Hans headed for the Apostolic Palace and reinforced the Swiss Guard at the main entrance. Then he called an assistant to deploy guards at the back of the building. Each of the various attending groups was instructed to lead the cardinals through a discreet doorway. From there they would climb a side staircase and gain access to the palace corridor without interference. The Swiss Guard took care to seal off all the entrances and prevent any possible intrusion. This way, the cardinals, whoever they might be, would avoid meeting anyone en route and would arrive at the pope's office within four minutes and fifty seconds. Hans also arranged for a pair of non-uniformed guards stationed at eighty-foot intervals, and at the entrance to the office, two of his best men in full regalia, according to custom.

The office anteroom had a reception desk, usually occupied by a former assistant to John XXIII whom no one wanted to dismiss, and who was given tasks better suited to an office boy than to a pontifical door guard.

In the middle of the afternoon the pontiff's two secretaries left their offices, and Hans knew that the meeting was about to take place. The names of the attendees were going to be relayed to him through his walkie-talkie.

"Cardinal Villot is coming up, sir."

Exactly half a minute later, there was a new walkie-talkie announcement.

"Cardinal Ugo Poletti and Cardinal Agostino Casaroli are coming up, sir."

Cardinal Casaroli served as counselor for Church Public Affairs, a kind of foreign minister for the Vatican.

A couple of minutes later, the sergeant's speaker crackled again as the agent stationed at the entrance identified the next guests.

"Archbishop Marcinkus and Monsignor De Bonis, sir."

Paul Marcinkus and Donato de Bonis both belonged to the management of the Vatican Bank.

Exactly four minutes and fifty seconds later, the first to arrive appeared at the end of the corridor and waited at the top of the stairs for their colleagues.

Hans observed the guards. Everything was in order.

When the five cardinals gathered, they exchanged a few words and almost immediately moved toward the pontiff's office. It was a strange retinue. In the Vatican it was said that "the friends" of Villot, those who familiarly called him Jeanni, were angry about the supposed innovations being introduced by Pope John Paul I. Given all their precautions, it was obvious that Villot, Marcinkus, De Bonis, Casaroli, and Poletti did not wish to be seen together.

Hans felt a cold shiver watching those five men advance down the corridor. Their friendly, pious mannerisms suddenly seemed menacing, and their billowing black robes produced a somber, sinister effect.

Without a word to him, they went inside and shut the door behind them.

HIS HOLINESS didn't see the five prelates come in. He was looking at the rooftops of Rome from his office window. By then he had almost grown used to these untimely visits. Since that unlucky conclave in which they had named him supreme pontiff, the members of the Curia hadn't let up on their intrigues for one moment. He knew too well that he was surrounded by wolves. Without turning around, Albino Luciani spoke softly.

"It's taken you a long time."

Villot observed his companions out of the corner of his eye and, with a slight wave of his hand, asked them not to respond, to let the pope speak.

John Paul I turned around and observed them with his typical roguish smile. It only served to compound his enemies' intense mistrust.

"Yes. You've taken a long time and, besides, I expected a few more cardinals. It would have pleased me greatly to see all of you together. Since you've got certain activities in common, I imagined that you'd try to mount your defenses."

"They are lies, Holy Father," De Bonis pleaded, hidden behind Marcinkus.

"Of course, Cardinal. Otherwise, you couldn't be here," the pope responded, then going over to his desk and sitting down. The five cardinals remained standing. The pontiff opened one of the folders on his desk and observed the prelates over the top of his glasses. Then he looked back at the papers. "Several days ago, as you surely must know, I received a commission from the Secret Service of the United States."

Villot sighed audibly. Finally the Americans were doing something useful. Surely the CIA had informed the pope of certain politicized factions in the Curia that were attacking the secretary of state and Marcinkus. Hopefully the Americans would try to convince John Paul I of the nonexistence of the P2 Lodge.

"That's great news, Holy Father. Maintaining friendly relations with the United States of America is a wise decision. The CIA has always been very helpful for the Church, and its directors are godly men."

"You may not be aware, Cardinal Villot, that the CIA is not the only American investigative agency. And, luckily, not all the American politicians and judges are as 'godly' as you would like. For instance, these friends who visited me were not exactly godly concerning you."

"These are crosses the Lord gives us to bear," Cardinal Casaroli mused. "We resign ourselves to having to stand up to the devil's temptations, Holy Father."

"Yes. I hope you're able to stand up to them."

Albino Luciani got up with the folder in his hand and waved it in front of the cardinals. His eyes showed more sadness than anger, but he could not tolerate the contents of this report.

"What have you been doing all this time?"

"Our life is devoted to the benefit of the Church, Holy Father," Villot answered firmly.

"To the benefit of the Church?" Luciani asked angrily. "What Church needs to have its servants making clandestine plots and holding secret meetings, Cardinal Villot? Since when did the Church require its priests to get involved with the Masons, Cardinal Poletti? What Church needs to be defended by making filthy money in the Bahamas, Archbishop Marcinkus? Since when has it been Rome's wish to invest in pornography, Monsignor

De Bonis? And are we being godly, Cardinal Casaroli, when we get into schemes that could put countries on the brink of war?"

"These are most grievous accusations, Holy Father!" Villot replied.

"This is outrageous!" Poletti blurted out.

"Who has been spreading this slander?" Casaroli asked.

Pope John Paul I looked askance at them.

"Somebody who doubtlessly knows you very well."

Marcinkus dared to step forward and vent his anger.

"If the Holy Father is incapable of recognizing when an action is beneficial to the Church, perhaps he should make a resolution in this regard!"

As the one responsible for Vatican finances, Marcinkus was among those who had been investigating a possible cause for dismissal based on the pontiff's mental deficiency.

"Certainly Archbishop Marcinkus ought to distinguish between 'acting for the benefit of the Church' and 'acting well in the Church'!" Albino Luciani declared.

De Bonis scooted around the wall of Jean-Marie Villot's cassock, trying to get closer in order to plead for mercy.

"Holy Father, perhaps we acted badly, but we meant well—"

"Get away from me!" the pontiff shouted. "If you erred maliciously, God will exact his due. If it was out of ignorance, that's because of my predecessors' blindness. In either case, you shall not keep your positions."

Villot glared at the Holy Father.

"You can't do that!"

"Tomorrow I'll submit your dismissal papers together with those corresponding to other positions of authority in the Curia, Cardinal Villot," Luciani announced.

The pope left the office, visibly changed. He leaned against the door after it closed. His enemies were on the other side. He begged God's forgiveness for unleashing his anger.

HANS, THE CHIEF of security for the Vatican, witnessed the departure of the five most powerful cardinals in the Curia. There was Jean-Marie Villot, violently shaking his black cape edged in red, and spouting curses until he turned to descend the staircase. De Bonis left directly behind Paul Marcinkus, from whom he was humbly seeking an explanation. "Is the Grand Master not planning to act, Cardinal?" "Leave me alone," God's banker replied. Casaroli and Poletti left in a hurry, taking short steps and waving their hands. "I already said so, already said that this pope would give us grief."

Hans had overheard the shouts, but wasn't able to determine the cause of the upset. He ran his hand through his hair, from his forehead to the back of his neck, and turned abruptly to the two Swiss Guards stationed at the entrance to the office.

"What did you hear?" he asked.

"Nothing, sir," the senior member of the team replied.

"Very well."

58

It's not about what they want, but what they demand," Barnes repeated in the interrogation room in the heart of Manhattan.

"Demand?" J.C. exclaimed. "Don't be ridiculous."

"They have the list."

"W-w-what?" the assistant stammered.

"It's true," Barnes assured him. "Do you swear it?" he asked, turning to Sarah.

The young woman nodded.

"All right," the old man said. "What are they demanding?"

"To end this here and now, and they won't take any action. No more dead, no more wounded. Otherwise they'll use all available means against us, putting the papers in the hands of public opinion."

The old man's breathing was getting more and more labored.

"There's something here that doesn't jibe."

"What do you mean, sir?" the assistant asked.

"If the Vatican has the papers, why are they demanding that everyone be freed? That should be a matter of no importance."

His reasoning was logical, but as the practical man that he was, he didn't engage in speculation. The woman had deceived him. He wouldn't have thought her capable of it. The Master decided to follow Sarah's game, to see where it would lead. Perhaps this would prove more effective than torture.

"And if we go along?" the old man asked unenthusiastically.

"Everything will stay as it is. Nobody will lose anything. But they are insisting that the woman confirm to a Vatican messenger that they have been freed."

"We shouldn't accept, sir," the assistant declared. "We can still recover the other papers."

Sarah could see that they were undecided, and thought she had to do something to squash their doubts.

"The other papers are also on their way to the Vatican," she lied.

"What did you say?" The Master's frown grew even more intense, his suspicions more acute.

"I also sent the other papers to the Vatican," Sarah repeated.

"But you said you couldn't answer for them."

The wretched old man's got a good memory, Sarah thought.

"Of course. They're not in my hands, nor have they gotten to the Vatican yet. Someone totally reliable was charged with taking them."

"She's lying," the assistant said.

"We can't take the risk," Barnes warned.

"We run a much greater risk by not having the papers in our hands," the assistant pointed out.

"The Vatican's position is clear. If this ends here, the papers will remain stored in a safe place. Nobody will learn of their existence and, even more important, there will be no unfortunate consequences for any of the participants in this ill-fated operation."

"Sir, give me two more hours and I'll force the truth out of the older man," the assistant said.

"Unfortunately we don't have two hours," Barnes retorted. "The woman has to meet the Vatican messenger at the Waldorf-Astoria in less than an hour."

J.C. listened to all this without interrupting. It seemed that the best cards were in the opponent's hand. There was only one thing left to do.

"May I have a few words with you in private?" Barnes asked the Master, interrupting his reflections.

"What did you say?" The Master was disconcerted. "Yes," he finally answered, getting up with the help of his cane. "Let's go out in the hall."

Barnes followed the old man, who was still deep in thought.

"Did you confirm the source of the call?" he asked suddenly.

"I ordered it but don't have an answer yet," Barnes replied.

"Do you think it was credible?" A CIA man's opinion counted, especially coming from a veteran like Barnes.

"It's all quite strange. The Holy See doesn't act that way, but it still could be true. It's a bomb threat and we can't risk having it explode."

"While we wait for your men to confirm the authenticity of the call, we're faced with an ultimatum from the Vatican."

"Yes. I'm afraid we're in a precarious situation."

"Sure." The old man returned to his thoughts. "It could be our salvation," he said after a few moments of reflection.

"You think so?" The American didn't seem very convinced.

"They have to meet the messenger at the Waldorf within an hour, right?"

"Yes."

"Fine and good. We'll try to regain the initiative. Take them where they need to go."

"Are you sure?"

An icy stare showed the futility of the question. "Take them. I'll take care of the rest."

"Will you disregard the ultimatum?"

"Of course not." The old man's mind was running at full tilt. "But it's the only means of recovering the papers."

"Are you thinking she didn't send them to Rome?"

"Maybe the list, but not the rest."

"What makes you think that?"

"All the evidence points to Marius Ferris, in New York. And here we are. We can confirm with total certainty that they haven't put their hands on those papers since they got here. So they must still be here."

Barnes thought it over for a few moments.

"And if you're wrong?"

"If I'm mistaken, they'll meet the messenger at the Waldorf, just a little behind schedule. Right now, it's essential to get the documents. If she sent out the list, the only way to get it back is for us to get the rest of the papers in our hands."

"What do you have in mind?"

As the two men talked, the assistant approached Sarah.

"You think you're so clever, bitch?" he muttered, his mouth almost pressed against her ear. "If you manage to get out of here alive, remember that I'll always be watching you. I won't give you a moment's peace."

Sarah shuddered, but she knew that nothing depended on the man threatening her. The old man was the one in charge, at least up to now, because luckily the Vatican had entered the picture. The following minutes would be decisive. Nevertheless, she didn't want to kid herself.

"And one day," the assistant continued, "when you least expect it, I'll get into your house, go straight to your bed, and wake you up."

Shut up, asshole, Sarah said to herself, wishing she could say it out loud. But it was still best not to step on his toes. He could lose his temper and forget the Master's orders.

Barnes and the old man reappeared with the same sullen look as when they left.

"Let them go," the boss ordered.

"But sir—" the assistant tried to object.

"Quiet," the old man cut him off, his voice showing renewed strength. "Let them go. And make sure she meets the messenger on time."

The resigned assistant grabbed her roughly and dragged her toward the doorway.

Barnes kept looking down the hall, failing to notice the half smile on the old man's face.

"Are you sure about this?" the CIA man asked.

"Completely. Relax. I'll have control of the documents. It's a matter of time."

"But we have very little," Barnes warned apprehensively. "And after that?"

"Once you have the papers, kill them all."

Immediately he made a call on his cell phone.

"Francesco, Your Excellency, I need to ask you a favor."

59

And that seemed to bring to an end the persecution of Sarah Monteiro and her companions, the ones whom, with some help from on high and a bit of luck, she had managed to save from J.C. She wouldn't go down in history for this, though, because historically speaking, neither J.C. nor Sarah Monteiro existed, and John Paul I died of natural causes.

That seemed to be the case when the group went out to the street. Rafael was in pretty bad shape, but even so, he helped Sarah support the captain, who could not walk on his own. Close behind them was Marius Ferris, who still couldn't believe their good luck. All the others—Geoffrey Barnes, Staughton, Thompson, the servant, the assistant, the Master—helplessly witnessed their exit. In the end, Barnes would not have the pleasure of erasing Jack, after all.

"Take the van," Barnes ordered. "Someone will come to get it later."

Rafael was the one who drove the vehicle to the meeting with the Vatican messenger, who in turn was to lead them, safe and sound, out of the country, and they were to recover the valuable documents that Sarah declared she had asked someone to send to the Holy See. Raul Brandão Monteiro touched his wound, lying in the backseat with his head resting on his daughter's lap.

"Does anybody know what's going on?" The question came from the shy Marius Ferris, whose melodious voice still showed some anxiety.

"That's exactly what I was going to ask you," Rafael said to him as he drove. "Do you understand what happened, Captain?"

Sarah answered for her father.

"It's very simple. While we were at the Altis Hotel in Lisbon, I called the Vatican embassy and explained our situation. The man who answered was very friendly but didn't promise anything. He insisted that I send him some proof of what I was saying, which I did immediately."

"What did you say?" Rafael asked, astonished by the explanation. Sarah had acted behind his back, surely while he was taking a shower.

"I faxed the documents."

"And then?"

Sarah didn't appreciate Rafael's grilling. He didn't seem to like the idea that she had solved the problem and saved everyone's life.

"Then the man asked me to send the originals to the Vatican Library in Rome, and I asked the receptionist to take care of it."

"Go on."

"The nuncio's secretary emphasized that he couldn't promise anything, but he assured me that the matter would be presented to the appropriate authorities."

"And that explains our here and now," Rafael concluded.

"Exactly."

Rafael looked at Sarah's father through the rearview mirror.

"What do you think, Captain?"

The officer attempted to utter a few words but could only manage to produce an incomprehensible sound.

"Speak slowly, don't force it," his daughter recommended, gently.

"Am— am—"

"An ambush?" Rafael guessed. The officer nodded.

"An ambush? Why?" Sarah was confused by the two men's conviction. "Didn't I solve the problem?"

"Of course not," Rafael declared emphatically.

Raul squeezed his daughter's arm, as if asking her to listen to Rafael.

"Look. The Vatican doesn't act that way. It uses much more subtle tactics. It would never give an ultimatum of that type, much less to save our lives. J.C. knows that."

"Maybe," Sarah said mysteriously, "but I've still got an ace up my sleeve."

"Do you think they're following us?" Ferris asked nervously.

"That's easy enough to find out," Rafael said. "The Waldorf is north of us, and we'll change our route. Captain, what do you think about stopping by a hospital to have them take a look at that wound?"

Rafael turned right at the first street and sped up, heading into the tumultuous heart of Manhattan. In less than a half minute there were three patrol cars from the New York City Police Department with lights flashing. Rather than block the way to force the van to stop, they did just the opposite: two patrol cars followed behind them, while the other led the way in front, through the dense traffic in the area.

The New York City police escorted them to their destination, for security reasons. "Please follow us," sounded the loudspeaker from one of the patrol cars.

"How nice!" Rafael exclaimed ironically, at once following the new route marked by the police vehicles. "Now, tell me, did the Vatican also send us this escort?"

"Supposing that you're right," Sarah said, "why stage this farce if we were already in their power? They're giving us a chance to escape. What are they gaining?"

"No matter how hard we tried, we couldn't throw them off our track. Surely there are several satellites watching us. Besides, the van is theirs. It's equipped with all the detection devices you ever dreamed of," Rafael pointed out. "As for the *dramatics*, I think the old man, deep down, knows exactly what he's doing. In spite of everything, our situation hasn't improved."

"Yeah, we were better off chained up in that room," Sarah agreed sarcastically.

"You don't have . . . don't have all the pieces to . . . to put the puzzle together, Sarah," her father said.

The young woman turned to Rafael.

"All right, then, mister puzzle man, tell me what we're going to do."

"Nothing."

"What do you mean, nothing?" Sarah and Marius Ferris asked in unison.

Rafael disregarded the priest and looked directly at Sarah. "I do sincerely appreciate your having granted me another half hour of life."

"Hail Mary, Mother of God . . ." Marius Ferris prayed, crossing himself, in an effort to overcome his fear.

"Does this mean that they don't believe the papers are in the Vatican?"

"Exactly. They know they're not there. You aren't the only one with contacts in the Holy See," Rafael answered.

"But they seem to have believed it. It's all very confusing. Who do you think called to give them the ultimatum?"

"Nobody," Rafael answered decisively. He quickly changed his authoritative voice to a softer, more reflective tone, to avoid hurting Sarah's feelings. "Even assuming there really was an ultimatum, they would disregard it. And I can't imagine the Vatican worrying about us. Think—why are we getting this escort?"

"That's something I can't explain," Sarah said to herself. But she was still annoyed. Of course there was an ultimatum. "I'm sorry to inform you that the ultimatum is no figment of my imagination."

"How can you be so sure?"

"Do you have all the pieces of the puzzle?" she asked defiantly. "Are you sure we're not going to meet a messenger?"

"The messenger will be there."

"Well, I played my cards, I did what I could," Sarah said. "Whatever will be will be."

They exchanged looks for a few seconds. Each could see the other's worries, for themselves and for the others.

Minutes later they turned onto Park Avenue, with all the pomp conferred by their escort. They stopped in front of 301, the celebrated Waldorf-

Astoria Hotel, the lodging place of innumerable celebrities for more than a century.

After a struggle, Raul managed to sit up on the seat. Marius Ferris was the first to open the door, but before he could step out, someone slammed the door shut from the outside. It was a man dressed in black whom he'd never seen before.

"My apologies. His Excellency prefers not to meet with the whole group. Only with the young lady," the man said, peeking into the window by Marius Ferris's seat.

Rafael took the opportunity to glance at Sarah, silently asking her whether her pieces of the puzzle now fit together. Sarah didn't understand the glance at first, so Rafael signaled her to come closer, and whispered his question. Sarah said nothing, but she didn't hide her uncertainty and anxiety.

"Only the woman can come with me," the man in black insisted.

The daughter tenderly grasped her father's hand.

"Everything will be fine. Don't worry."

The man in black opened the door and Sarah stepped out of the van. He escorted her inside the hotel. Rafael also got out of the vehicle but was immediately intercepted by another thug.

"Didn't you hear my partner?" he asked menacingly.

"Yes, I heard him."

"Then you'd better get back in."

"Unfortunately that's not possible. I must go with the woman," he insisted impassively.

"Get back in the van right now," the guy ordered. "I won't ask you again."

"I can't. Do you know why?"

"Do I look like I've got any interest in knowing?"

"If you don't, you ought to." He paused for a moment to let the words sink in. "I'm the only one who knows where the papers are." Another brief silence before the crowning touch. "The woman doesn't know anything."

60

"Are you going to tell me or not?"

"Tell you what?"

"What you left out."

"What I left out?"

"Do you want me to be more direct? What else did you do behind my back?"

"Why do you think I'm hiding something?"

"The piece of the puzzle, remember?"

"If you tell me what piece is missing from your puzzle, maybe I can tell you which one I've got, assuming it exists."

"I'm not missing anything."

"You aren't?" She thought for a moment. "Then I'm not, either."

Sarah Monteiro and Rafael were sitting in a black Range Rover en route to the supposed hiding place for the papers.

The thug had reported Rafael's words to his superiors, and received the order to bring him before His Excellency, who awaited him in the lobby of the hotel. Rafael was suddenly next to the bishop, who seemed authentic.

His name was Francesco Cossega. As strange as it might seem, Rafael instinctively made the gesture to kiss his hand.

"God bless you, my son," the prelate said, the way real bishops respond.

"Is Your Excellency the messenger from His Holiness?"

The beating must have really gotten to him, Sarah thought. Or else he's up to something.

"You're safe with me, my children," he said, then looking directly at Rafael. "Are you going to take me to where the documents are?"

"Of course, Your Excellency," Rafael responded rapidly. "I'd like to ask you to release the two men outside in the van. One of them needs medical attention."

"And I need emergency psychological attention," Sarah said to herself, stunned. She was consumed with anguish, not knowing how her father was going to be after that terrible torture. All she wanted was to be done with this farce and to rush to his side.

"Of course." The prelate signaled by hand to one of his assistants, who immediately went outside.

That explained how the two of them came to be sitting in the backseat of the Range Rover, with a driver whose inevitable black suit would not clash with those of the other agents. The bishop followed them in a late-model Mercedes, armor-plated and with tinted glass.

The caravan's destination was 460 Madison Avenue. That was the address Rafael had given Cossega in the lobby of the Waldorf. Upon leaving, they didn't see the van where the captain and Ferris were sitting.

"How do you know the papers are at that address?" Sarah asked in a low voice. She didn't want the thugs to hear her.

"You'll soon see."

"Do you know this bishop? You seemed very devout in his presence."

Rafael delayed in answering.

"I've never seen him. But a bishop is a bishop. We have to show respect."

"Do you think he's actually under J.C.'s orders?"

"I think Cossega organized all of this."

"How?"

"I still don't know. I'm guessing."

They kept quiet for a short while, until they were a few blocks from their destination.

"Listen," Rafael said in a low voice after gently touching her arm to get her attention. "I need you to stay calm until I tell you. If you don't do that, I won't be able to protect you."

"What are you planning?"

"I still don't know."

"How can you still not know? Are you going to try to negotiate our freedom in exchange for the papers?"

"I'll know very soon."

"What else will you know?" Sarah asked, annoyed. "Leave the negotiations to me."

Rafael was astonished, but there was no time to ask her anything because they'd reached their stop. Everyone was getting out and going into the enormous building that rose before them, Saint Patrick's Cathedral, with its gigantic towers more than three hundred feet tall. James Renwick, the architect, had imitated the French Gothic style in 1879 to make this the site of the most imposing Catholic cathedral in the United States.

The church was empty. Only the imposing columns and vaults of the sacred place would be witnesseses.

"Guide us," Bishop Francesco Cossega said.

If there was any remaining doubt about him, it dissolved with the appearance of his driver and the man riding shotgun in the late-model Mercedes that had followed the Range Rover. They were none other than the familiar agents Staughton and Thompson.

"You can stop worrying. You're doing the right thing. I guarantee that nobody will bother you again," the bishop assured them.

Something in his voice made Sarah feel safe. She would have liked for him to be a good man, a truly pious man of the Church. It was a shame that he was on the wrong team. Sarah finally realized that all of this could only be a plan orchestrated by J.C. One had to admit it was a good plan, and probably would have succeeded if she, again, weren't a step ahead.

Rafael led the group through the wide nave. He advanced with authority, seemingly very sure of what he was doing.

"Is it much farther?" the bishop asked, looking a bit weary.

Rafael said nothing but kept walking.

"Do you have any idea what you're doing?" Sarah asked in a low voice, staying right beside him.

"Not yet. Keep going. We'll think of something."

"Things could get ugly if they discover we're not going anywhere," she warned. Then she asked what she most wanted to know. "What makes you think that this bishop is fake?"

Rafael smiled.

"This bishop isn't fake."

"Really?"

"No. He's Francesco Cossega. He's a real bishop. But he's not a messenger from the Holy See."

The young woman thought for a few moments.

"What makes you think he's not a messenger from Rome?"

Rafael hesitated before answering.

"Because I'm the messenger from Rome."

"What?" Sarah could barely hold back a scream.

"And you?" he quickly responded.

"Me what?"

"Why do you think the bishop can't be a messenger from the Vatican?"

"Who says I think any such thing?" She didn't like to admit defeat. Rafael the savior, the feared Jack Payne from the files of the CIA and of the P2— was he the messenger from Rome?

Soon they reached the transept. The vault rose above their heads, and Sarah couldn't avoid gazing at the high arches of the cathedral. The first assistant followed the prelate. But Agent Thompson, the next in line, was knocked unconscious by a violent blow from Rafael, who, without missing a step, threw a strong punch at Staughton that left him inert on the floor. Poor Staughton.

The bishop and the assistant looked back. Too late, because Rafael had seized control of the situation. Though Thompson tried to get up, a kick from Sarah put him back on the sacred floor. She was surprised by her own bravery—I'm not in the habit of kicking anybody, she thought, but he deserved it.

"Take away his guns," Rafael ordered.

Sarah handed one gun to Rafael, tucking the other into her waistband.

"You were going to tell me why you think he's not a messenger from Rome," Rafael said, as they doubled back in order to hide next to a column.

"Can't you wait?"

"Of course," he assented. "Hide back there."

He was pointing to a vacant confessional.

Behind one column they could see a gun barely sticking out, ready to be fired. As if Saint Patrick himself planned it, a sudden, heavy blow landed on the gun-wielding arm, and Rafael neutralized the gunman with a well-aimed punch. Only one bishop was left.

"I'm waiting for you," Rafael said cheerfully.

Sarah left her hiding place, searching for guns, and patted down the newly fallen agent.

Rafael admired her courage. One would think she'd been doing this all her life. She found another pistol, added it to her arsenal, and looked at Rafael.

"It's very simple. He couldn't be a messenger because I never called the Vatican embassy."

61

"Explain yourself," Rafael demanded, walking with Sarah among the rows of pews. The bishop was in front of them, prodded along by Rafael. The majestic grandeur of the cathedral was silent and empty, in shadows.

"What do I have to explain?" she asked calmly.

"What was it you didn't do that you said you did?" Rafael put it obliquely to keep the bishop from catching on.

"I didn't do it, and that's that," she replied, visibly annoyed.

"Do you really believe you're going to come out of this alive?" the bishop butted in, unusually arrogant for someone who was moving at gunpoint.

"We're all going to try, don't you think, Your Excellency?"

"You'll end up like Firenzi and all the others."

"Tell me something, Francesco. I have the feeling this all started because of you. Am I wrong?"

"What are you talking about?" The bishop turned around, confronting Rafael.

"Everything. The killings. Our presence here now. Everything."

The man in the purple robes continued walking, but Rafael kept talking.

"Look, Firenzi found the documents. Nothing serious, because no one would have noticed their disappearance. They'd been in the archives for almost thirty years. They would come to light only by chance, as actually happened. The mere fact of finding them wouldn't have put Monsignor Firenzi's life in danger."

"Shut up. You have no idea what you're talking about." The bishop objected.

"Keep going," Sarah urged Rafael.

"Firenzi could only put his life in danger by telling somebody who then exposed him. A bishop, for instance."

"Is that the way it was, Your *Excellency*?" Sarah asked sarcastically.

"Nonsense. I didn't know Firenzi well enough to be his confidant."

Right then, the conversation was interrupted. A very pious soul would have said that the voice of God descended upon them.

"Don't you think it's too early to leave the game?" The public-address system was broadcasting the very familiar voice of Geoffrey Barnes, who was standing in the pulpit.

Rafael pushed the bishop. "Keep moving."

They quickened their pace down the rows of pews, approaching the main altar.

"Don't make a move!" Barnes's voice demanded through the loudspeaker. "Where do you think you're going?"

Three men appeared through one of the side doors of the transept. The old man went first, leaning on his carved cane. The assistant and the Pole followed.

"Little Sarah behaved very badly," the old man scolded, approaching slowly. His cane clacked against the church tiles with every step. "Maybe we could have a more sensible conversation if you knew the conditions in which Raul Monteiro and Marius Ferris now find themselves. Anyway, I don't think you would be able to recognize their faces, and don't think they'd be able to recognize yours. Now, I want all the papers," the old man demanded. "Did you think you'd beaten me? You need more than good luck to go up against me."

Sarah knew there was nothing more she could do. Rafael would have to say where the papers were. She couldn't stand any more suffering. Valdemar Firenzi, Father Felipe, Father Pablo, the "collateral damage." Very soon they'd be added to the list of victims, without causing those vile people to lose even a minute's sleep. She was immersed in a torrent of thoughts when she felt somebody grab her by the waist. It was Rafael, pulling her tight against his body.

"You know perfectly well that we'll die before we tell you where the papers are!" Rafael shouted.

"That could be," the old man admitted, "but if you die, I won't have to worry anymore, right? If no one knows about their existence, there'll be nothing to fear," he added.

"I don't think you want to test your luck," Rafael countered.

Sarah felt a hand on her rear. The hand moved up until it found one of the guns she was hiding in her waistband. Immediately, she felt a cold object between her side and arm. It was the gun she had given Rafael when they had overcome the other agents.

Then the shooting started, brief but intense, ending as suddenly as it had begun. One of the bullets caught the Pole in the chest. He fell backward. with an expression of terror on his face. The final score was one dead and one wounded, and a shift in power. The ones in control became the controlled.

The old man braced the fallen assistant and shouted, "I've never witnessed so much incompetence."

Then an echoing shot hit Bishop Francesco in the heart. His face registered total surprise.

"Why? I brought Firenzi to you," he stammered, tumbling down the few steps.

"I hate incompetence," the old man snapped, now aiming his gun at Rafael, who in turn pointed two guns at him. "Do you think, my boy, that you've got any chance of survival?" he murmured with malice.

"I have my chances."

"You've got nothing," the Master answered. "Now you have nothing. With or without the papers, talking or shutting up, you're going to die."

Geoffrey Barnes's dry cough—he'd remained hidden behind the pulpit—now filled every corner of the cathedral.

"There's a call for you," Barnes said to the old man.

"For whom?" J.C. asked, keeping his eyes still fixed on Rafael.

"For you," Barnes confirmed.

"Who is it?"

"A woman."

"A woman?" The old man seemed horrified at the thought. "Are you nuts? Can't she wait?"

"I think you'd better answer."

"She can tell me from here, you idiot! Through the loudspeaker!"

Moments later, Barnes managed to activate the speakerphone on his cell phone, and the church loudspeakers projected a female voice. Everything echoed, as if even angels were filling the cathedral's domes.

"Are you there?" the voice asked.

"Who's speaking?" the old man demanded unceremoniously.

"Shut up, you bastard. You'll have to wait as long as necessary," the voice responded.

Rafael seemed as shocked as the old man. Only Sarah smiled slyly. "Are you all right, Sarah?" the voice asked.

"Yes, I'm all right."

"Who is it?" Rafael inquired softly.

"A friend," she declared triumphantly. "The same one who issued the ultimatum from the Vatican."

The old man heard her.

"Oh, so it's the young lady responsible for the fake ultimatum."

"I already told you to shut up. Sarah, are you really all right, Sarah?"

"Yes, Natalie, I promise."

"Natalie?" Rafael wanted to know. "Who's Natalie?"

The question went unanswered.

"Let's get to the point. Who's the son of a bitch that got you in all this trouble?" Natalie continued.

"His name's J.C.," Sarah answered, looking him straight in the eye.

"J.C.? What a fucking bastard. Well, then, listen J.C., I am holding a list with various names of public personalities that belonged to the P2. There's even a bloody prime minister on it."

"What are you driving at?" the old man asked, staring into space.

"To start with, I want you to free my friend and everybody who's with her."

"And what do I get for that?"

"Relax, darling. Are you in a rush?"

Sarah couldn't hide a smile of satisfaction. Natalie was something else.

"Let's see. If you do, I won't send my report to the BBC and I won't give the *Daily Mirror* the article I have here, ready to be published immediately, with a copy of the list. How's that?"

The old man's face showed his total irritation.

"If I accept, what guarantee do I have that this wouldn't come out?"

"Just think," Natalie continued, "if the list is made public, that would surely be your death sentence. That's why you'll do what you should, and free them all. We'll keep our part of the bargain. If you misbehave someday, you already know what will happen."

The old man bowed his head and walked away a few steps, thinking.

"This is a reasonable enough pact for all concerned," he announced, his voice resounding through the nave like a voice from the great beyond. "So, shall we seal the agreement?"

62

The Night

The years of Christ will be my days.
Today is the twenty-fifth day of my papacy,
the years of Christ were thirty-three.

—From the diary of John Paul I, September 20, 1978

Fortunately his contact had secured a safe entry for him.

No Swiss Guard intercepted the man with the cruel, icy expression. He couldn't have explained his presence there even if anybody had asked him. For the plan to be carried out with assured success, everyone knew it was crucial to have no person and no thing cross this man's path before he reached the third floor of the Apostolic Palace.

The person for whom all paths were opened knew every nook and cranny of Vatican City. After all, the Status Civitatis Vaticanae was no larger than a village, with scarcely a thousand inhabitants.

Everything in the Vatican appeared modest, but at the same time, very ostentatious. That was the opinion of the man crossing the streets and turning the corners that night. The desire to make the capital of the pontifical state into a representation of heaven on earth had forced the Renaissance popes to devote all their money and effort to this objective. This explained why the best artists of all times had to go to Rome, to prove to God their skills and the quality of their work.

This same man had enjoyed the privilege of visiting Vatican City on numerous occasions. He knew the exact location of every palace, office, corner, and plaza, and he knew how to hide his presence that night. He knew the schedule and the routes of the Vatican guards, and the places they were usually posted.

By the time he arrived, half an hour after midnight, nobody—with the exception of members of the guard—would be in that part of the city. He needed only the assurance that the routine night rounds would not be altered and, of course, that the doors would be open.

Everything worked according to plan, so it was easy for him to get to the third floor of the Apostolic Palace, right next to the door to the pope's private quarters.

The corridor was dimly lit, giving the place a sinister feeling. A thin sliver of light shone from beneath the door to the papal quarters, indicating that the pope was still awake. He was probably working on the changes that so many prelates, and perhaps other important people, feared. The fact that he was awake somewhat altered the execution of his plan. If the pope had been asleep, it would have been total surprise. He considered waiting until the pope fell asleep, but after ten minutes he realized that any delay would be pointless. He had a job to do anyway, and it didn't matter whether the pope was awake or asleep. He would go in and quickly overcome any reaction. The rest would be easy.

He moved up to the door. With his gloved hand, he held the door knocker and waited a few seconds, struggling to be calm. This wasn't his first murder and it wouldn't be his last, but this one was particularly repugnant to him. His job was to end the life of a pontiff. It was like a direct blow to the hearts of the faithful. Nevertheless, there was some benefit. This murder would make similar ones unnecessary. And it would take only a few seconds to end the papacy of John Paul I.

He opened the door brusquely and went in. But the intruder was in for an immediate surprise. Albino Luciani was leaning back on the headboard, writing something on a piece of paper, and didn't even raise his eyes to see who'd come in, without permission, at this hour of the night.

"Shut the door," he said, and continued writing.

The intruder was a vigorous man, still youthful in 1978. He didn't need a cane then. He radiated strength and efficiency. Anyway, Albino

Luciani's attitude surprised him, his total indifference to the unexplained presence.

Complying with the Holy Father's request, he slowly closed the door. An awkward silence filled the room, while the pope continued to ignore him. That wasn't at all the scene he'd pictured a few days before when planning the murder. He had always seen himself in total control. Go in, kill, and leave. This stupid situation was a complete departure from the way he'd imagined things. The words they exchanged convinced the executioner then that he was facing no ordinary man.

"Do you know man's most important qualities?" Albino Luciani asked, still engrossed in his papers.

"Dignity and honor?" the intruder replied with a question, like a student hoping he had the right answer for the teacher.

"Dignity and honor are incidental," the pope explained. "The most important qualities must be the capacity to love and to forgive."

"Sir, you strive for these two qualities?"

"Constantly. But still, I am the pope, not God. My infallibility is institutional, not personal. This means I sometimes forget about these important qualities." And for the first time, raising his eyes above his lenses, he looked at his executioner.

"Why are you telling me this?" the man asked.

"So you'll know that I don't blame you. I love you as my fellow man, and as such, I forgive you."

Only then did the intruder realize that Pope John Paul I had been waiting for him and already knew what he had come to do. That understanding provoked a strange, disturbing reaction in his mind and attitude, but not serious enough to make him desist. He put a pillow over Albino Luciani's face, and pressed. Those were the longest moments of his life. He was killing a man that death itself couldn't fool. That murderer knew that beneath the pillow was a human being who neither begged for mercy nor tried to flee. He could have avoided the whole thing, retreating just a little from his eagerness for reform, but he didn't. He stayed true to the end, and that fact earned him the executioner's respect. When the last breath left the body of His Holiness, the assassin got up. Without his realizing it, tears were streaming down his face. Then, in a move he couldn't account for, he placed the dead body in the same position the pope was when he came in, leaning him against the headboard. Even his eyes stayed open, with his head turned to the right.

Later, the man learned that among the papers the pope had in his hands was a copy of one of the secrets of Fátima. It announced the death of a man dressed in white, by the hands of his peers. The prophecy couldn't have been more precise.

The murderer made sure that everything remained exactly as it was before he entered the bedroom, and then left without making any noise at all. He didn't even turn off the light. Others would have to clean the scene of the crime.

63

This room on the seventh floor of the Waldorf-Astoria was well suited for the body to recover from the hardships and anguish of the past few days. Sarah had just come out of the shower, wrapped in a towel. Rafael was lying down, his eyes half-closed.

Before going to the hotel, they went to GCT (DI)–NY. Or more exactly, GCT (15)–NY—Grand Central Terminal, New York, one of the city's main train stations, located on Forty-second Street. Number 15 referred to the locker that contained the papers. The code that took so much trouble to decipher was that simple.

The papers were there, yellowed from the passing of time. In beautiful, firm handwriting that, as it turned out, was totally useless, they contained the ideas of a modern man limited by evil interests.

The emissary from Rome, that is, Rafael, had obtained them.

"Are you sure nobody followed us?" Sarah asked him.

"No. That's the least of our worries now. We have a big advantage over our enemies, and they aren't going to do anything, at least not for now."

"At least not for now?"

"Yes. These people never forget. When we least expect it, they'll attack us again."

"That's not very reassuring."

"It's the price we have to pay. We're safe for now. The future belongs to God."

As soon as they got to the seventh floor of the Waldorf, Sarah called the hospital to find out how her father was doing. His wound was not serious, despite its dramatic impact. These people knew how to torture their victims without jeopardizing their lives.

"If I'd known it was so easy to get hold of them, I'd have sent the documents to the newspaper much sooner."

"Then we would have missed all this fun," Rafael joked. "Why did you say you'd spoken with the Vatican?"

"You're not the only one with secrets."

Rafael gave her an inquiring look, but she kept talking.

"It wasn't clear to me how deeply the Vatican was involved. I also knew it wouldn't be easy to make them take me seriously. That's why I came up with my own plan. I called Natalie and sent her the documents express mail from the hotel in Portugal, before we went to Mafra."

"Was it you who planned the whole scene in the cathedral?"

"No, I didn't get that far, nor did I know what would happen to us there. I just asked Natalie to help us any way she could. She's got a lot of contacts, so I thought she would be the best one to help us. And I wasn't wrong. She even managed to find Barnes's phone number. But she didn't know how to make the Vatican take us seriously, so she made up her own plan." Sarah laughed, recalling her conversation with the Master. "She's a first-rate actress, and we were incredibly lucky."

"I thought it was brilliant. I must get to know this Natalie."

"When you come to London, I'll be very glad to introduce you to her," Sarah replied. "Do you think the CIA will keep acting independently, without the old man?"

"I don't know. But I don't think so. They've got nothing to gain and they're involved in too many other scandals. I think we're safe."

"I'm glad to hear it."

Rafael got up from the bed. "Do you mind if I take a shower, too?"

"Of course not. Do you mind if I take a look at the papers?"

"Go ahead. You've earned it."

Sarah saw that the first documents referred to the replacements and to some reports from Vatican officials. The most interesting part began on the sixth page. It was an extensive reflection on the state of the Church, which she read avidly. Despite the fact that she wasn't proficient in Italian, she found some passages very moving.

In order to spread the teachings of our Lord Jesus Christ, it makes no sense to cover ourselves with a dark mantle that overshadows our spirit in front of others. It also makes no sense to voice our own words as if they were His, obscuring a doctrine that presents itself openly to all, so that, through faith, Jesus Christ may truly commune with us.

There is no way to understand why the Holy Mother Church has covered itself with a mantle of secrecy that is at odds with the inherent joy of our Lord's teachings. Because our faith is also joy and fellowship, and not the benevolent but judgmental attitude that our faces reflect. There is joy in our commitment to propagate His doctrine, bound to the sacrifice and suffering He endured in our name. Any seminarist is heavily trained to carry on his shoulders the burden of a sinful mankind, to convert himself into one more laborer working painfully hard, instead of doing it with the very joy of the Savior's message.

The solution depends on us, because in the heart of our Church we revere old dogmas that I don't even dare ascribe to the Creator. Over the centuries, many men have occupied the throne of Saint Peter. The power and wealth accumulated during all this time are incalculable. I venture to say that we are the richest state in the world. How is this possible, if our main duty is to be close to the people? Our duty to help others became something strategically selective. Our tremendous legacy is being managed like a large corporation, and

we are talking about the legacy from Jesus to Peter the Fisherman, a patri-
mony that has endured through history to reach me.

We must reflect on a series of fundamental questions, but first we have to show
the way. And the only possible way is that of our Lord Jesus Christ, our Father.
What questions can be clarified by going to the Father? All questions. By simply listening to His teachings and recommendations, because He answered all
possible questions a long time ago, and He keeps on answering them. I daresay
all questions have been answered, even the new questions. But in these difficult modern times there is a formula that always guides us toward the ways of
love and good deeds, the ways of the Lord. We should ask ourselves: What
would Jesus do? This simple question is the answer to all our questions.
What would Jesus do?

Birth control? Life is joy and a child, too, when it is wanted. Why should we
convert a divine gift into a burden?

Homosexual relations? Thou shall not judge.

Priest celibacy? Where is this discussed in the Gospels?

Female priests? We are all equal in the eyes of the Lord.

It is the duty of the Church to devote itself to the faithful and share with them
the Word of God, helping the most needy, without regard to race or belief. To
gain a closeness to other religions without judging their values or beliefs, but
with fellowship and sharing wisdom and love. It will not be a dream created
in Heaven that a Christian could pray to his God in a mosque, and a Muslim
could pray to his in a church. Without censure or confrontation. Because
Heaven can, and should, begin on earth.

How would the world be today if this pope hadn't died? Sarah asked
herself after reading this. She felt at once moved and elated. No doubt he
would have revolutionized the Church. Finally she found a paper written in

her native tongue. She immediately recognized the Third Secret of Fátima, as announced by Sister Lucía:

> *I write as an act of obedience to you, my Lord, since you ordered me to, through His Excellency the Bishop of Lereira and Your Holy Mother.*
>
> *After the two parts already revealed, we saw to the left of Our Lady, a little higher up, an angel with a flaming sword in his left hand. Flames came off the sword that seemed about to set the world on fire, but the flames would die when they came in contact with the rays of light coming out of the right hand of Our Lady, who was moving to meet him. The angel, pointing toward the earth with his right hand, insisted in a firm, strong voice: "Repent, repent, repent!" And we saw a big, big light that was God Himself, and as if reflected in a mirror, we saw a bishop all dressed in white. We had a premonition that it was the Holy Father. Several other bishops, priests, monks, and nuns were climbing a rugged mountain. At its peak was a large cross made of rough logs that looked like cork oak. The Holy Father had to go across a great city in ruins before getting there. Almost trembling and with faltering gait, overwhelmed by sorrow and pain, the Holy Father was praying for the souls of the dead he met on his way. Once he reached the peak, while kneeling before the great cross, he was killed by a group of soldiers and some bishops and priests who were shooting bullets and arrows at him, but who were also dying in the same way. One by one, they all died: the bishops and priests, monks and nuns, and various laypeople, gentlemen and ladies from different social classes and economic positions. Two angels were on the arms of the cross, each one with a glass water sprinkler in his hand. In it they were collecting the blood of the martyrs and with it they sprinkled the souls of those approaching God.*

"'Killed by a group of soldiers and several bishops and priests who were shooting bullets and arrows at him,'" Sarah repeated to herself. "What other secrets was the Church hiding, replaced by lies proclaimed as absolute truths?" she mumbled.

"Are you okay?"

Rafael's question pulled her out of her ruminations. He'd just come out of the bathroom, dressed after his shower.

"Yes, fine. Are you going somewhere?"

"I'm leaving. My mission is finished."

The comment struck Sarah like a splash of cold water.

"You're going?"

"I'm sorry for all I put you through. You should know I did it all for your benefit."

"You're going . . . where?" Her surprise and disappointment were quite evident.

"To save more souls in difficult situations," he said jokingly.

Sarah got up and went to him.

"What about us?"

"Us?" Rafael was confused by her question. Sarah's face got closer and closer to his. Her soft perfume started to reach him.

"Us . . . what about us? When are we going to see each other again?" she asked, gazing intently into his eyes. "Why don't you stay a few more days?"

Rafael was visibly nervous, something that didn't square with his usual self-assurance.

"I already told you that none of this ever happened, Sarah. Understand?"

She got a bit closer, without fear, without any shyness.

"Aren't you going to stay with me?" she whispered to him. "You could rest, I'd keep you company."

Their lips almost touched, but he stepped back at the last moment.

"No. I can't. I really must leave now. I have to take these papers and return them to the Vatican. They will decide there what they want to do with them."

Sarah got the impression he wanted to leave as soon as possible, as if he were fleeing from the devil, not from her.

"If this is because of my father—"

"No," Rafael said. "It has nothing to do with your father."

"Then?"

Rafael took the papers and walked to the door.

"It's a life choice." And he opened the door to leave.

"Wait," Sarah held him back. "At least, tell me your real name."

He looked at her for the last time.

"But, Sarah, what did I tell you when we met? My name is Rafael."

Those were the last words they exchanged.

64

Death of a Priest
February 19, 2006

Time was running out. Lying on his deathbed, Archbishop Marcinkus knew that his real problems were about to begin when the time came to render accounts to the God he now feared so much, the one he had so often disregarded. "God's banker" pictured himself showing the Almighty the account books of income and expenses, debits and deposits, the details of specific frauds committed, in an attempt to convince Him of the need to diversify investments and launder the money received from organized crime. His feverish state and the anguish of dying made him see God as the president of a board of directors, a CEO incapable of recognizing that everything his servant had done throughout his eighty-four years had been for the good of the enterprise.

Many thought that Paul Marcinkus, the old archbishop of Chicago, had been too isolated from the world in a remote parish in Illinois, and though he in fact had stepped aside, he had never intended to give up his power, and still remained in the service of the Catholic Church, in the diocese of Phoenix.

But the Sun City was very far from the center of the world, very far from Rome, and very far from God. Ever since the Italian judges charged him with the Banco Ambrosiano embezzlement, he couldn't shed the anguish this had caused him, and that, in turn, had weakened his heart. He was afraid his old friends suspected him of having ratted them out to the police and the court, because vengeance could be extreme.

With his gaze fixed on the whiteness of the ceiling, Marcinkus could see himself as one of the Four Horsemen of the Apocalypse: Calvi, Sindona, Gelli, and himself, sent by God to put the world in order.

Marcinkus remembered Roberto Calvi's horrible fate. He himself had barely managed to stay solvent after the bankruptcy of Banco Ambrosiano. And this depended on bribes and blackmail.

"What was that woman's name?" Marcinkus asked himself out loud.

Graziella Corrocher was her name, and she was the one who had informed on Calvi before jumping out the window of her office and smashing herself on the pavement.

When the Milan judges sent him to the Lodi jail, he told them more than he should have: "The Banco Ambrosiano isn't mine. I'm only in someone else's service. I can't tell you any more." Friends don't forgive indiscretions, and if Calvi was able to gain conditional freedom, it was only by betraying family and friends.

Hounded and desperate, Calvi fled from Italy and hid in various locations until he was found. Unfortunately the Mafia got to him before the police did. It was probably Gelli's men or Sindona's. On June 18, 1982, they put some bricks and $15,000 for services rendered in his pockets. Then they tied a rope around his neck and dropped him under the Blackfriars Bridge in London. The police reported that poor Roberto had committed suicide.

Morons! You don't understand anything! Marcinkus thought. Poor Roberto.

In contrast, Michele Sindona got what he deserved. The old man used to be proud of his deals, but he was incapable of keeping a bank going. The Franklin Bank collapsed, and he lost his project with the Banca Privata Italiana to the Genovese family. He said he had studied law, but his beginnings were rooted in the fruit business, hence his nickname, the Lemon Man. At the time, he asked the Sicilians for help, and thanks to them he prospered. He went around—oh, so stupidly—bragging that he controlled the Milan stock market. In the United States he made an alliance with the Inzerillos and the Gambinos, who were even bigger scoundrels than the Genovese. With their help, he managed to get rich and to make deals with the Holy See, that is, with Marcinkus and Calvi. "Only an idiot could have people call him Master of the Universe," Marcinkus had once said. In the midsixties, when his finances and those of the Vatican collapsed, Sindona asked Calvi for help, but by then Sindona couldn't do much. Sindona felt besieged both in the United States and in Italy, where the charges and accusations against him were endless. So he put pressure on Calvi to save his empire with Banco Ambrosiano funds, but this Catholic bank and its holding company were already under the scrutiny of the judicial authorities. Marcinkus and Calvi claimed they didn't know the Sicilian, and abandoned him to his own luck. In a desperate attempt to avoid jail, Sindona ordered the murder of a Milanese judge who presided over the cases connected with their dirty dealings, but this last stupidity only served to add one more crime to his long list. He was arrested in the United States, and the Italian government asked for his extradition. Sindona had made few friends but incurred many debts along the way, and he paid for them all on March 23, 1986.

"Would you like hemlock with your coffee, Michele?" Marcinkus asked sarcastically in the solitude of his bedroom, attempting to smile for the last time.

Jail isn't a good refuge for those with a lot of outstanding debt. So Michele Sindona ended his days with the taste of hemlock in his throat.

As for the boss of the P2, Marcinkus couldn't help but feel pity. Licio Gelli had more fantasies than brains, and as much taste for conspiracies as for money. Only a poor devil could think of making a list of the names and professions of all his sympathizers, Marcinkus thought. In 1981 the list of Masons came to light. The old archbishop of Chicago smiled, thinking of Silvio Berlusconi as prime minister of Italy. When the house of cards collapsed, the Masons threw Gelli out, and the Italian judges accused him of acquiring and revealing state secrets, of slander against the judges writing the summary of his charges of conspiracy, and of fraudulent bankruptcy. Gelli spent the last years of his life between courts and jails. The old politician served his home detention at his villa in Arezzo, waiting for death. The poor devil had hundreds of gold ingots hidden in flowerpots, and they were discovered. How many months of life still lay ahead for him?

"Time runs out for everyone, old Gelli." Marcinkus sighed.

There was no more time to reveal secrets or give explanations.

Everything had come to an end.

65

Sarah often thought she would never again lead a normal life. But it hadn't turned out that way. Now she stood in Saint Peter's Square, on a day like any other, attending Sunday Mass said by Pope Benedict XVI. Her parents, Raul and Elizabeth, accompanied her. Three months had gone by since she had gotten rid of J.C. and his agents. Her father had totally recovered from the wounds inflicted on him in New York.

Sarah had gone through so much in order to get to this peaceful Sunday morning. She couldn't stop her thoughts from wandering to the chain of events leading to that day. She still had some doubts. Why was Valdemar Firenzi searching for those documents? Had he been hunting for a long time, or was it the opening of the trial that drove him to start the search? The eventual discovery of his body in the Tiber River in Rome only confirmed her worst fears, leaving those questions unanswered.

Sarah had a much clearer picture of other parts of the story. The night that poor John Paul I had been killed, the accomplices of his executioner hid the documents the pontiff was holding in his hands, and later gave them to the man she knew as J.C. After the conclave that elected John

Paul II, he managed to introduce the documents into the Vatican Secret Archives. Monsignor Firenzi found the new papal dispositions and the third secret, and, aware of their tremendous value, he entrusted them to his friend Father Marius Ferris.

The orders were quite clear: save them and wait. Ferris sent him the key to the locker where he had hidden the papers, but things got even more complicated. Firenzi, who was beginning to sense that someone was following him, ordered two double portraits with the fixed image of Benedict XVI, and behind it, that of Marius Ferris, which would appear when black light was aimed at the photo. And he sent them to his most trusted men, Felipe Aragón in Madrid and Pablo Rincón in Buenos Aires.

To the average person, they would look like the images of the pope and of an unknown old man, but those two men knew Marius Ferris. Firenzi knew that he needed to say no more. They could contact his friend in New York, who was authorized to reveal the secret location of the documents. There were three men in on the secret. Firenzi's plan was a good one, because when the men from the P2 started chasing the papers, there was a vital time lapse before they could gather all the necessary clues.

Firenzi, however, had made a mistake entrusting the finding of the papers to his intimate friend, Bishop Francesco Cossega, unaware that Cossega was also a member of the organization. And since Firenzi had continued his search in the Secret Archives, the truth about Cossega was revealed the night he discovered the list and saw the name of his friend in the second column of the first page.

Firenzi was astonished that his friend had never said anything about being a member of the P2, so he began a series of moves in order to protect the documents; he knew that when the investigation into the death of John Paul I was reopened, the importance of these papers would be decisive.

He put the key in an envelope together with the list and a simple code, and he sent it all to Sarah, hoping that her father would understand it. He could not possibly have guessed that she was then vacationing in Portugal, and that it would be some time before she opened the envelope. When she finally did, Firenzi was already dead. She was quite lucky to have avoided the same fate in London.

It was hard for Sarah to understand why Firenzi felt such an urgent need to keep the papers hidden. Basically, he was doing the same as J.C., hiding the evidence instead of destroying it. In fact, the location and custody of the documents were the only changes. But Marius Ferris had explained to her how everything had happened that fateful day in New York, on the night when they'd all been so close to death.

"At first your godfather didn't want to do anything. Just keep the papers in a safe place. He wanted to guard them himself, or give them to someone he could really trust."

"Just that?"

"Yes, at first. Later, whatever was needed would be done. Don't forget that Firenzi was a prince of the Church and his priorities were clear. He wanted the truth, of course, but he also wanted to protect the Vatican's reputation from any further damage. His Holiness would find the most appropriate solution. Most likely, the Church would opt for the classic Vatican reaction."

"Which is . . ."

"No reaction at all. Silence is the Vatican's policy. But simply recognizing the existence of the documents, just knowing that someone in the heart of the Church had been dishonest, was enough of a reason for our brother Firenzi to take some action. And I must confess it was enough for me as well. That's why you did the right thing, Sarah, and I'm grateful to you for that."

NOW, THREE MONTHS LATER, everything had ended well, and only one thing still worried Sarah. She had received no news from Rafael, or Jack Payne, or whatever his name was. She didn't know how to find him, no matter how much she wanted to see him again. She thought of asking her father for help, but finally decided against it.

The Sunday Mass had ended, and the Monteiro family was walking around Saint Peter's Basilica, like many other tourists and faithful. Later they'd dine at a restaurant and make a tour of Rome.

While mother and daughter were admiring the magnificent dome, Raul went to greet a friend he had noticed among the crowd.

"Girls, I'd like you to meet a very dear friend of mine." Raul said, as he approached them. Sarah, still absorbed in reading a tourist's leaflet about the basilica, didn't look up right away.

"Let me introduce you to Father Rafael Santini."

Sarah lost interest in the leaflet the moment she heard the name of Rafael. She looked up and down at the man wearing a black cassock.

"It's a pleasure to meet you," he said quietly

Sarah couldn't believe her eyes. Rafael, a priest!

"Father Rafael is in charge of a parish north of Rome, isn't it?" Raul explained.

"That's right. It's not far from here."

I tried to seduce a priest! Sarah couldn't get the idea out of her head. How was it possible for a man like him to be a priest, to be dedicated to Christ? Now she understood his rejection when they were in that New York hotel room. He had made a different choice, he was a man of God, and, besides, his role in life was to protect the interests of the Church. Nothing was what it seemed.

"Would you like to have dinner with us?" Raul suggested.

"I'd love to, but I can't. I brought some children from my parish to visit the Vatican. Another time."

"I hope so," Sarah's father said.

"The documents have been saved," Rafael told Sarah. "Safely kept where they always were, but with the knowledge of His Holiness."

No one had ever mentioned to Sarah the existence of the Holy Alliance, the organization that seemed to include all the Vatican Secret Services. Numerous legends, stories, and fictions were told about this institution, none of them easy to verify. Some people thought that the Holy Alliance was made up of unscrupulous spy priests, prepared to sacrifice their lives for Rome and for the pontiff.

There was no official address for the Vatican secret services. The names of its agents didn't appear on any payroll, nor could they possibly be identified. Nevertheless, the CIA and the Mossad, the CNI and the MI6, all readily believed not only that they existed, but also that they constituted one of the most powerful and most skilled spy and counterspy organizations in the world. Naturally, the Vatican agents were carefully selected from among the most capable, and they were probably trained in institutions unrelated to the Vatican.

Rafael Santini had received training very early with an objective in mind: to infiltrate the P2 and the CIA, and to come to light only when it became absolutely necessary. For almost two decades he had been a "sleeper," watching institutions and organizations that needed to be controlled, until he received an order related to the Holy See, and then he did what he'd been trained for. There were not hundreds, but thousands of priests in the world who said Mass, taught in schools, and comforted the sick, who were just waiting for orders to act according to serious Vatican directives.

"SOMETIMES I WONDER how much we lost with the death of that pope," Sarah commented thoughtfully, strolling around the outskirts of the Vatican after saying farewell to Rafael Santini.

"John Paul I?" her father asked.

"Yes. I even think, after all that happened, that nobody else would ever deserve to take his place."

Her father tenderly put his arm around her shoulders.

"I know exactly how you feel. But you must realize that life goes on for the rest of us. One day Albino Luciani will receive his just consideration."

"I hope so."

"Don't worry, Sarah," her mother interrupted. "God never rests."

Sarah wanted to believe that to be true. The secret would be well kept, this time by honorable men, in the same place where the murder was committed, as a kind of divine, mischievous wink. Where evil was king, good now reigned.

"Firenzi's plan didn't seem adequate to me."

"He did what he could," her father countered. "If you hadn't been on vacation, or if he'd possessed another means of communicating with me, things would have turned out better."

"Even so, they already had Marius Ferris."

"The fact that they had Marius Ferris didn't necessarily mean they could have forced him to reveal the location of the documents. And yet that was something we knew."

"Do you think he would have died, rather than reveal anything?"

"Let me answer you with another question. Do you think Rafael would have given away the secret?"

"Of course not. What does one man have to do with the other? They have nothing in common."

"Yes, they do. If your godfather sent the papers to Ferris, it was because he trusted him in the same way."

Rafael. Just the name still sent chills down her spine, particularly now that she knew much more than before. Her rescuer, a man capable of doing what he did in London, was an Italian priest! Was he more of the devil than of God?

"Even so, I'm still not convinced," she insisted, going back to Firenzi's plan, ready to forget the man who saved her. "What was the purpose of those double portraits? I never understood that."

"So that the two priests would recognize Marius Ferris. They knew he was the only one to be trusted. Unfortunately, Father Pablo didn't think ahead enough to store his in a safe place."

"How did you ever know it was a double portrait?"

Her father smiled.

"For someone who was very much into all of this, the letter was very explicit. A soft light had to be focused on the portrait."

"Very clever. Why didn't J.C. take the risk? He could have reached the last steps."

"Because of fear."

"Fear?"

"Yes. Fear. Those people are used to acting when they are sure they're going to win. The mere possibility of losing stops them, and keeps them quietly in the shadows, waiting for a better opportunity."

"Do you mean that someone may still try to recover the documents?"

"I don't think so. J.C. won't live forever. And this served his interests perfectly."

"Will he try to do something against us in the future?"

"I doubt that, too. Bringing this matter up again could only hurt him. We can rest assured."

CLOSE TO SIX that evening, Sarah's parents decided to go back to their hotel and rest awhile before dinner. Their leisurely tour of Rome had been wonderful. It was a pity that Sarah couldn't get the meeting with Rafael out of her head. At least, he'd never hidden his real name from her. She wandered through the streets and alleys of Rome until it was past seven.

On her ambling return to the Grand Hotel Palatino, on Via Cavour, not far from the Coliseum, she was planning to have a good bath and dinner. After such a long day that had started so early, she felt very tired, but still had the former Rafael on her mind.

Immersed in these thoughts, she entered the hotel lobby, totally unaware of the figure in black who had been following her for hours.

"Miss Sarah Monteiro," the receptionist called her, but she was so lost in thought that she didn't hear him. He had to call her again.

"Yes?" she finally answered.

"There's a message here for you," the clerk said, handing her a small envelope.

"Who gave it to you?"

"Sorry, I don't know who brought it. I wasn't on at the time."

"Fine. No problem. Thanks."

Sarah went to the elevator while opening the envelope, which was unsealed. She pulled out a small black object that resembled a button. Filled with curiosity, she got in the elevator, and realized there was also a note, which she read on her way up to the seventh floor. Seconds later she looked up, flabbergasted and nervous, thinking to herself, No, not this again. It can't be.

The note was very brief.

Sarah hesitated, but she knew she couldn't run away from destiny. She put the little object into her ear and waited. Perhaps it was just a practical joke. Even so, she couldn't imagine her parents engaging in such a charade.

"Good evening, Miss Monteiro," she heard a voice saying into her right ear.

"Who is it?" Her voice, though firm, betrayed her anxiety.

"Hello, my dear. I'm sure you haven't forgotten me that fast." There was sarcasm in the voice. "I'd be personally offended."

"What do you want?" Sarah's tone was even firmer now, trying to mask the fear that overcame her when she recognized the speaker.

"I just want to recover what rightfully belongs to me." There was no doubt that it was the old man, the one who murdered John Paul I.

"I have nothing to do with that," Sarah answered coldly. "Go to the Vatican."

A loud, guttural guffaw was the annoying answer, hurting her ears. Sarah went to her room with some hesitation, still listening.

"That's what I'm going to do, but I want you to be my messenger. Since you were the one responsible for the final destination of those papers, I think it's only fair that you should be the one to recover them for me."

Now it was Sarah's turn to laugh.

"You think so?"

"Definitely."

Sarah had the strange sensation that the old man was hiding something. She unlocked the door to her room.

"Tell me exactly what is it that you want. I've got other things to do."

"Do you see the package on your bed?"

Seeing it terrified her.

"Yes," she said in a muted voice.

"Open it."

Sarah obeyed. It was a bundle of papers.

"What's this?"

"Read those documents carefully. We'll talk later."

"Do you think this could be enough to convince the Vatican to surrender those papers?"

"Without a doubt. We all have our weak points. Wait for my instructions."

The earpiece stopped. She took it out and threw it on the bed. She sat on the edge, still with the bundle of papers in her hand, and read the heading. There was a name in all capital letters.

MEHMET ALI AĞCA

EPILOGUE

When I first contacted the author to write this book, the most important requirement was that he had to mix fact and fiction. Why? The answer was simple. I knew from my own experience that that's the way real life happens. Many historical truths that we consider authentic are no more than mere fictions. The set of circumstances surrounding the death of John Paul I is an example and, believe me, not the only one.

I must confess that the result surprised me very positively. Fact and fiction did mix adequately. With this artifice, it wasn't my intention to ask readers to use their own means to distinguish fact from fiction. I just wanted them to know that not everything that has been said with an open smile, or with a look of deep despair, is the truth.

In these pages the author has created a character who represents me and honors me. I am grateful to him for the skill he showed in developing the plot, using me for his own purpose, as well as mine.

With all the conspiracy theories about the death of John Paul I that have been generated over the past thirty years, I've enjoyed staying in the shadows, particularly with all those experts commenting on it as if they were sole proprietors of the truth.

The institutions were not to blame, but rather the people who constituted them or worked for them.

I was a member of the P2 Loggia, and as a human being I am not, nor do I pretend to be, immune to sin or to making mistakes.

However, don't fool yourselves. Only God will be my judge.

—J.C.

CHARACTERS

CARMINE "MINO" PECORELLI. Born in Sessano del Molise, Isernia province, September 14, 1928. Founder of the weekly *Osservatorio Politico*, specializing in political and financial scandals. He gained power not only through his knowledge of the ins and outs of Italian politics, but also because he was a man of vision. He joined Licio Gelli's P2. After the assassination of Aldo Moro, he began printing unpublished documents, including three letters that the former prime minister had written to his family. The articles published in his weekly enraged many people, including cabinet members, representatives, ministers, and also Licio Gelli, because Pecorelli made a list of the members of the P2 and sent it to the Vatican. He intended to publish it. He was assassinated on March 20, 1979, with Gelli's knowledge and consent. The instigator was a noted Italian politician.

ALDO MORO. Italian statesman, born September 23, 1916, in Maglie, in Lecce province. He was prime minister of Italy five times, as well as one of the two most distinguished leaders of the Christian Democracy. Kidnapped by the Red Brigades in the center of Rome, on March 16, 1978, he was held captive until his death, on May 9 of the same year. Disregarding the requests for help that Moro wrote to his party and to his family, the government adopted a tough stance and refused to negotiate with the terrorists. Moro even appealed to Pope Paul VI, a personal friend of his, but to no avail. Officially, Aldo Moro was shot to death by the Red Brigades and placed in the trunk of a car because of the Giulio Andreotti administration's intransigence, its unwillingness to negotiate. But this is only the official story.

LICIO GELLI. "Venerable Master" of the P2 Masonic Lodge. Born in Pistoia on April 21, 1919, he was involved in practically all the great Italian scandals of the past thirty-five years. He fought on Franco's side, among the forces sent to Spain by Mussolini, and he was an informant for the Gestapo during the Second World War, even maintaining direct contact with Hermann Göring. Once the war was over, he joined the CIA, and together with NATO, he provided cover for Operation Gladio, which amounted to the creation of a kind of secret rapid-response force, established in Italy and other European countries, including Portugal, with the objective of eliminating Communist threats. He was responsible for innumerable terrorist acts. The murder of John Paul I was one of many that he ordered. His involvement in the deaths of Aldo Moro, Carmine "Mino" Pecorelli, Roberto Calvi, the Portuguese prime minister Francisco Sá Carneiro, and others is well known. His illicit alliance with Archbishop Paul Marcinkus, Roberto Calvi, and Michele Sindona was responsible for the embezzlement of $1.4 billion in the Istituto per le Opere di Religione (IOR). He currently lives in house detention in his villa in Tuscany.

PAUL MARCINKUS. American archbishop. He was born in the outskirts of Chicago, January 15, 1922. From 1971 to 1990, he served as director of the Istituto per le Opere di Religione, better known as the Vatican Bank. He was directly involved in countless financial scandals with Licio Gelli of the P2 and Roberto Calvi of the Banco Ambrosiano (whose primary shareholder was the Vatican Bank), and Michele Sindona, Italian banker and mafioso, named papal financial adviser by Paul VI. Together they laundered illicit money and hid the profits made by the bank controlled by Marcinkus, supposedly to be invested in charitable works. His name was involved in many little-known stories, particularly the disappearance in 1983 of Emanuela Orlandi, a fifteen-year-old girl, in an attempt by Mehmet Ali Ağca to hold her for ransom. Marcinkus always enjoyed the trust of Pope Paul VI. Later, John Paul II had no other recourse but to keep him in his post, allowing him to become the third most powerful man in the Vatican. What John Paul I intended to do with Marcinkus is well known. He was one of the main suspects in the death of Albino Luciani. In 1990, Marcinkus returned to Chicago, after leaving the directorship of the Istituto per le Opere di Religione, and later withdrew to a parish in Arizona. He was found dead in his home on February 20, 2006.

ROBERTO CALVI. Milanese banker, born April 13, 1920, known in the press as "God's banker" for his connections to the Vatican and to Archbishop Paul Marcinkus. As president of the Banco Ambrosiano, he was threatened and manipulated by Gelli and Marcinkus, which resulted in a tremendous financial fraud. He had been opposed to the elimination of John Paul I, and that death did not benefit him much. Calvi fled to London with a fake passport, and a few days later, on June 17, 1982, his body was found hanging under Blackfriars Bridge. The British police treated the case as a suicide, despite all the indications to the contrary. His pants pockets were full of stones, along with $15,000. The case has been reopened recently in Italy and in the United Kingdom, but it is highly unlikely that the true culprit will ever be found.

JEAN-MARIE VILLOT. French cardinal, born October 11, 1905. Named secretary of state of the Vatican in 1969, during the papacy of Paul VI, a post he kept until the death of that pope and the start of the very brief papacy of John Paul I. He was to be replaced on September 29, 1978. The death of the pontiff allowed him to keep his post during the first year of the papacy of John Paul II, until his own death on March 9, 1979. He was a member of Licio Gelli's P2, and is considered by some investigators one of the suspects in the murder of Albino Luciani.

LUCÍA DE JESÚS DOS SANTOS. Born March 22, 1907, in Aljustrel, Portugal. She was one of the seers of Fátima, the one who announced the three secrets that the Blessed Virgin Mary revealed to the world and that the Church has controlled with an iron fist, spreading falsehoods in their place. She met with Albino Luciani on July 11, 1977, in the Convent of Santa Teresa, in Coimbra. Their conversation lasted more than two hours, during which she fell into a trance and alerted the future pope as to what was in store for him. She died on February 13, 2005.

MARIO MORETTI. Founder of the Second Red Brigades. He kidnapped Aldo Moro and was the only one in contact with Moro throughout his captivity. He was also the sole killer of the statesman. The circumstances of the case were never determined. However, it is known that the P2 participated very actively in that case, in addition to an organization from another continent. He was condemned to six consecutive life sentences but surprisingly was freed in 1994.

J.C. Born . . . in . . . He was the actual instigator and perpetrator of countless macabre actions. He joined the P2 in . . . Now retired from politics and financial affairs, he still maintains great influence in the world of crime. He lives in . . . He killed John Paul I on the night of September 29, 1978.

THE REMAINING CHARACTERS presented in this book belong to the world of fiction.

NOTE 1. Assumptions will be replaced by confirmed facts in a future edition.

NOTE 2. The P2 still exists, more secretive than ever.

A CONVERSATION WITH LUIS MIGUEL ROCHA, AUTHOR OF *THE LAST POPE*

Q: Does the P2 Lodge truly exist? And if so, what facts do we know about it, and what did you create as a novelist for the sake of this story?

A: P2 existed and still exists. All details in the novel before and through 1978 are true, including the names of the members and leaders of the lodge. Everything that happens with Sarah Monteiro and Rafael, as well as the idea of JC's being part of P2 in the current day, is fictional.

Q: Several nonfiction books have addressed the matter of whether Pope John Paul I was murdered. Do you believe they raise valid questions? Did you draw on conspiracy theories just to create a good thriller, or do you indeed believe there was a plot to murder the pope in 1978?

A: John Paul I was killed on September 29, 1978, at 1:00 a.m. Not at 11:00 or 11:30 p.m. on September 28, as officially stated. I'm sure of it.

There's a very good piece (published and sold together with this novel in Spain) by a Spanish journalist, a correspondent in Rome, that recounts everything that happened that night. It was because of this journalist that the story became cloudy. He managed to speak with Sister Vincenza, the nun who said she was the one who found John Paul I's body, but the official Vatican version was that Father John Magee, the pope's assistant, found him. And that version lasted through the 1980s, when the Vatican confirmed that it wasn't Magee who had discovered the body. The Vatican ordered everyone involved to a vow of silence. Why would they do that if there was nothing to hide? Because it was all a setup. John Paul I was in fact killed. How do I know? The person who killed him told me, and proved it to me.

The character JC in the book is based on a real figure, John Paul I's assassin, whom I knew as an Italian ministerial assistant. In truth, apparently, he wasn't. He told me specifically that I should write a novel about the affair, because we live in a fictional reality and we don't know anything, even the things we think we know. *The Last Pope* is that book.

Q: You were a child when Pope John Paul I died, so it's presumably not an experience you remember from direct media reports at the time. Was there anything in particular about John Paul I's life and death that inspired the novel?

A: I knew about John Paul II and a little Vatican history—not much, I must confess—but I didn't know anything about John Paul I until April 2005. It was then that an acquaintance of mine, an Italian, told me how everything had happened. Who Albino Luciani was, what he did that would lead someone to kill him, why, when, how. Later I saw documents proving what this acquaintance had told me (among these documents were the papers that John Paul I had had with him on the night of his death, which disappeared that same night). Sister Vincenza saw them, as did John Paul's close collaborator Don Diego Lorenzi, but they were never found. Now, knowing a little more about Albino Luciani and other facts of Vatican history, I'm glad I got in touch with that world.

Q: An especially haunting character in the novel is the mystic Sister Lucia de Jesus, one of the three children said to have encountered the Virgin Mary at Fátima. She was Portuguese, as you are, so was it a risk for you to write about someone who is so revered in your culture? Do you think that the secrets of Fátima are somehow linked to current events and disasters, as the novel suggests?

A: There was more a sense of curiosity here. A certain ambivalence surrounds the events of Fátima. We believe in them, but we also know that Sister Lucia was totally controlled by the Church. So some things are true and others aren't. Take, for example, the secrets. Some people believe that the secrets were all invented by the Church to control the population. And the revelation of the third secret by John Paul II in 2000 left many disappointed. Most people don't know that the secrets were really written in 1941. I know for a fact that Sister Lucia was a psychic and saw the Virgin many more times than people think. It wasn't just from May 13 until October 1917. The Virgin appeared regularly throughout Sister Lucia's life. What secrets did she tell her? Only Sister Lucia and the Church, and a few others, know. Perhaps I'll write a book about this.

Q: The CIA and the Italian Mafia both play roles in the intrigue around your protagonists, Rafael and Sarah. Are these entities as central to Vatican politics today as this novel suggests they were in 1978?

A: No. Now it's completely different. You need a unique confluence of factors for a nonreligious entity to control the Holy See. That happened from 1971 until 1981, more or less. And only in the financial department, not the religious. Today it wouldn't be possible. However, nowadays in the Vatican there are religious organizations with more power than the P2 had.

Q: What has been the reaction to this novel since its publication? Do people accept your narrative as fact—as some have done with Dan Brown's *The Da Vinci Code*—or do they recognize it mainly as a work of fiction?

A: I receive e-mail from all over the world. I have yet to get a bad review from a reader. Readers love the story, the characters; they ask if the book will be made into a movie, and they think it would make a great one. They want to know more about the case, especially Italian readers. For the most part readers accept everything as fact, even the adventure of Sarah and Rafael. That's a little odd.

I had a curious request last year for two copies of the book in Portuguese, from a journalist who works in the Vatican. It seems the copies were for someone important who sees the pope every day. That person confided to the journalist, off the record, that everything in the book is true. It's good to know. Though I do have my suspicions, I can't say who this person was—perhaps a cardinal or a bishop. There aren't a lot of Portuguese people in the Vatican. But it's overwhelming to know that they respect the work, and that's the main reason the Church hasn't reacted or reacts with silence.

TRANSLATOR'S NOTE

I wish to thank the author, Luís Miguel Rocha, for his gracious and quick answers to my questions, and to Lee Paradise, who always reads my works, for his wise comments and suggestions, which this time were so many that I should hereby give him credit as my co-translator.

—Dolores M. Koch